Caffeine Nig

Consequences

RC Bridgestock

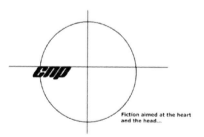

Fiction aimed at the heart
and the head...

Published by Caffeine Nights Publishing 2012

Published in Great Britain by Caffeine Nights Publishing

www. caffeine-nights com

British Library Cataloguing in Publication Data.
A CIP catalogue record for this book is available from the British Library

ISBN: 978-1-907565-16-8

Cover design by
Mark (Wills) Williams

Everything else by
Default, Luck and Accident

Aknowledgements

Thank you to Margaret Emsley, Gemma Beckwith and Ray Jordan for the reading of early drafts and subsequent support and contributions.

Also to our publisher Darren Laws for his continued hard work, dedication and belief in Jack Dylan's career.

Other Books by RC Bridgestock

Deadly Focus – A 'D.I. Dylan' Thriller

For those who strive daily to bring to justice the lawbreakers.

The victims will always come first.

To Anne

Best wishes.

Carol Bx

Consequences

[signature]

Carol Bridger

Chapter One

'Enough,' Detective Inspector Jack Dylan sighed as he slid his chair away from the desk. He had spent a good few hours with his nose to the grindstone but at last he had reached the base of the paper mountain that had greeted him at the start of his day.

He studied for a moment the last letter in his pile, yet another solicitor's request for a hard copy of a police file. Why in the age of electronic messaging did they, along with the courts and *Uncle Tom Cobley and all* still demand them? It wasn't as if they didn't have computer terminals or a network set up; so it had to be down to people being afraid of change, or their lack of trust in today's technology. The prosecution file against the child murderer of Daisy Charlotte Hind and Christopher Spencer he'd recently dealt with would fill two transit vans; yet another rain forest turned to dust. He'd already received copious letters from the defence solicitors Perfect & Best who had a reputation for being ruthless. Their business had recently moved to the larger premises of the old Co-Op buildings in Harrowfield as their popularity increased amongst the criminal fraternity. They condemned police action at every opportunity and ensured the press were there to report it. Nonetheless, their clients still got sent down, but not without a courtroom drama. Dylan knew they would have a team ready to spend hours, days, weeks scrutinizing the case, searching for that weak link, a break of continuity in the line of evidence or a failure to disclose something to the defence; anything to drive a stake right through the heart of the prosecution case. The defence had it easy in his eyes everything was delivered to their door on a platter. The main evidence was received by them a matter of days after an arrest and once they knew what the police evidence was they could then put forward a defence. Dylan smirked to himself as he packed documents into his briefcase, a case for the *three monkeys* perhaps for the defence could *see everything, hear everything and say nowt*. There were only four defences to murder: diminished responsibility, insanity, provocation or a suicide pact. Who knows, Perfect & Best might advise their client to plead guilty on this one - Nah, that wouldn't be a money-maker for them now would it?

Dylan jumped as his leg cramped and he frantically rubbed it. It was time to go home. He was looking forward to a weekend away on the Isle of Wight with his partner Jen, far from the madding crowd.

'On my way love, just crossing the yard to the car,' Dylan spoke into his mobile.

'Brilliant. We're all ready and waiting...aren't we?' she said, as he heard Max their golden retriever start barking loudly in the background.

'Let's set straight off to miss the teatime traffic, eh? We can grab a sandwich on the way. I'll drive.' she shouted over the noise.

'Sounds good to me,' he said, smiling. 'I'll see you in about fifteen minutes.' He put his briefcase in the boot of the car. He knew a couple of hours start on the rush hour traffic would make such a difference to the lengthy journey. Throwing his suit jacket on the back seat of car he pulled off his tie and opened his shirt collar. Dropping his shoulders, he sighed dramatically and could instantly feel himself relaxing as he relished the thought of time off after the pressure he'd been under, recently. The radio bellowed out an Abba song and he found himself singing along, badly. He chuckled; thank goodness no one could hear. A mile from home he joined a queue of slow moving traffic. At the approach to Stan Bridge the traffic came to a standstill. Dylan drummed his fingers on the steering wheel. 'Come on...places to go, people to see,' he muttered. Winding down the window and leaning out as far as he could he saw a flashing blue beacon ahead. Was it police, ambulance? 'Not an accident ...please,' he groaned. He turned up the radio. The local news was just about to start. In his experience local radio was always fantastic at keeping people up to date with traffic news. There was no alternative route though, whatever the problem, so he'd no choice but to wait. And he did; what could have been only minutes seemed like an eternity.

'Bloody hell,' said Dylan as he banged his hand hard on the steering wheel, accidentally causing his horn to blare out which triggered a chain reaction from the other drivers.

'Damn.' That wasn't his intention. He knew only too well car horns did nothing to ease a situation such as this and he immediately felt embarrassed.

'Police are advising motorists to avoid the Stan Bridge area of the A581 as they are dealing with an incident of a man threatening to jump off the bridge. There could be long delays.' The words came from the rich, calm voice of the broadcaster who was obviously sat in his cosy office. The last thing Dylan wanted was to get involved, but what could he do? Sit tight and hope a police negotiator was on the way or the person jumped? He, like the rest in the queue, simply wanted to continue on his journey. He picked up his mobile. Their phone was engaged. If he knew her, Jen would be ringing her dad with an estimated time of arrival. This message from him he knew was going to go down like a lead balloon.

'Slight delay love...I've got a jumper. I'll be with you as soon as I can.' He switched his mobile off, threw it on the passenger seat, retrieved his jacket and eased himself out of the car. Dylan locked the car and set off to walk past the stationary vehicles and their frustrated occupants.

Jen picked up his message smiling and ended listening to it in tears of frustration, kicking the suitcases that stood like sentries on the doorstep.

'Ouch,' she screamed as she stubbed her toe. Max cowered. Jen hopped up and down the hallway, moaning.' Flaming work, why do I bloody bother?' She seethed, flopping dramatically down on the sofa in the lounge. She looked towards the ceiling pulling her hand through her hair in frustration. Max settled amongst the bags in the hall like a brindle suitcase – to be sure he wouldn't be forgotten. She picked up the pamphlet of the beautiful, picture postcard thatched cottage in Luccombe she had rented. The pictures showed far-reaching sea views but it was nearly three hundred miles away and they were now not going to see them today, it would be dark by the time they arrived. Although the few days away was a chance to escape the rat race, it was also an opportunity to check up on her dad and see how he was coping since her mum had been tragically killed as a result of a road accident a few months earlier and she couldn't wait to see him. His neighbours had been kind, keeping an eye on him and updating her, but she was desperate to see how he was for herself. Although her Dad had always seemed the stronger of the two, in fact it was her mum who had always been the housekeeper and his rock. Jen couldn't believe he was cooking for himself these days, since he'd never so much as made a cup of tea when her mum was alive. She shook her head and sighed, poor dad. She felt so guilty leaving him after the funeral but he had insisted that his life was on the Isle of Wight and he had no intention of leaving. It had been her home too until a few years ago when she'd felt she had no alternative but to move away.

'Please hurry Jack,' she said, and Max barked as he rose and came to her side. She was never surer he understood everything she said as she stroked his strong, soft head.

DI Dylan's pace quickened as he passed the toll booth. 'Of all the bridges in all the world, why did it have to be this one, kid?' The bridge he knew was no stranger to disasters. The present structure, built from Yorkshire stone, had two semi-elliptical arch ribs that were supported by stone piers. An earlier stone bridge on the site had collapsed on Rogation Day in the seventeen hundreds, during a beating of the bounds ceremony, causing many injuries. It had partly collapsed in a flash flood in recent years and was a place that Dylan had become a regular visitor to as a Negotiator where he attempted to talk people out of jumping to their deaths. Dylan reached the police car and beyond it at its highest point he could see the would-be *flyer*. The fragile figure of a young man stood like an Olympic diver, peering over the edge.

Dylan recognised the young policewoman heading towards him.

'Do we know who he is, Tracy?'

'No sir,' she said, surprised he remembered her name. He looked upwards... 'Why's he up there?'

'Er. . . he's threatening to jump.'

Dylan raised his eyebrows.

'Oh, sorry sir, that's a bit obvious…' she said, blushing so intensely that her cheeks, brow and neck were suffused in crimson.

'Supervision is on its way and I've just been asked to stop traffic at this end. We've got another car at the Sibden end.'

Dylan nodded. 'Okay, let Control know there's a negotiator here, that's me. Now who's stating the obvious?' he said, as he smiled at her. 'Get them to divert traffic further back and make sure everything is stopped under the bridge. We could do with an ambulance down below, nearby. We'll also need HQ to mobilise the Operational Support Unit in case he goes in the river.'

'Yes, sir,' Tracy looked relieved to be given a purposeful task.

'I'm gonna try and talk some sense into him. When you've done, walk to within ten yards of me so I don't 'ave to shout if we need to pass a message to Control. At the same time I don't want him to be able to hear your radio transmitting.'

'Of course sir,' she said.

'Right, better get to him. He might go over before I even get there at this rate.' Dylan saw Tracy's face blanch. In an instant it was as though she realised that the man threatening to jump might actually do it and she'd be a witness to the incident.

Dylan strode out with urgency in his pace. He could hear the taunts and jeers from the crowd that had gathered behind him.

'Tell him to jump. Do us all a favour.' called one. Dylan cringed.

Dylan knew a lot of people hadn't time for suicides: their view being that some people frantically fought daily to save lives and people attempting suicide were throwing theirs away. Only one member of the public had stepped forward to help Dylan in a similar situation – the brother of a 'jumper'. Against the manual's advice Dylan had let him go forward. Within seconds the brothers were like bookends on the flyover both threatening to jump. Fortunately after a couple of hours of 'double talk,' they climbed down, but Dylan had learnt an invaluable lesson that day; to stick to the rules.

Thankfully, the further along the bridge Dylan walked the less coherent the voices of the frustrated motorists and on lookers were. He felt the wind in his face. St Peter's Park and the Sibden Valley came into view and in the far distance the bleak Yorkshire moorland: a spectacular sight, and one he realised he never truly appreciated as he drove over the bridge. Stepping up onto the pavement, he noticed the Victorian iron palisades which had been fitted after a man had been pushed to his death by an unknown attacker. Dylan was pleased it was there, boy did he detest heights. He'd almost reached the 'jumper' when he was stopped by shouting.

'Don't come any fucking nearer or I'll go over...I mean it.' he threatened.

Dylan instantly complied with his demands. He wished he had a penny for every time he'd heard that line before. Since becoming a negotiator he'd heard some horrific stories and personal tragedies from people who were threatening to end their lives, but if they were still there when he arrived, in his experience there was a good chance it was a cry for help; if they were serious they didn't hesitate. However, if the wind picked up it would take the 'jumper' over the edge whether it was intended or not.

This lad now had Dylan's total attention.

'I know you're serious, but I'm here to help,' said Dylan as clearly and as sensitively as he knew how. 'Will you let me? Whatever the problem is we can sort it out.'

'Just fuck off,' the 'jumper' insisted, stepping precariously from one foot to the other on the flagstone at the top of a pillar.

Dylan studied the lad, he'd have liked a closer look but he was sure he knew the face. He moved slightly forward hoping it would go unnoticed, and it did. Yes, it was Alan 'Chubby' Connor, local robber, burglar, and self-harmer, you name it, this lad had done it all before.

'Poor sod,' thought Dylan. He had spent his life in and out of institutions. Dylan pulled up the collar on his jacket. He could feel the cold seeping through his clothing; it was a hell of a lot cooler now. The northerly wind whistled by him sending a chill through his whole body. It might say March on the calendar but spring seemed a long way off to Dylan, from where he was standing.

Chubby's thin frame was clothed in a short sleeved, grubby t-shirt and jeans.

'You must be bloody perishing up there.'

There was no reply. However, he did adjust a baseball cap on his head.

'Perhaps it was an essential accessory these days,' Dylan thought, if you didn't have a hoodie.

'It's Chubby Connor isn't it?' Dylan took two further steps forward without reprimand.

'So there's nothing wrong with your eyesight then copper? And no I haven't done any jobs I want to admit to before I jump – so fuck off.'

Chubby splayed his left hand and Dylan caught sight of a small knife in his right.

'Don't do it Chubby, there's no need, I'm not coming any nearer.'

'Back off then.' Chubby held the knife to his wrist. Dylan took a step backwards.

'Okay, whatever you say.' Dylan's raised his palms to show him he was retreating.

A one man crime wave was standing right in front of him. A vote to save him or not, he knew, would definitely have got the thumbs down.

'Think about performance figures,' he heard his bosses say. 'What an opportunity you had.'

'What the hell is all this about, Chubby?' Dylan said. 'If you've done nothing wrong why are you doing this? You must be freezing your bollocks off up there for nowt.' He shivered involuntarily. Chubby remained silent. Dylan could see him shaking but whether it was fear, cold or withdrawal from some substance he didn't know. Dylan talked. Hands in his pockets he shuffled his feet in an attempt to keep warm. Chubby remained silent but studious, his pallor noticeably turning blue with cold. Detective Inspector Dylan couldn't tell whether his words were getting through, he could only hope.

'I'd rather go over than go back inside.' Chubby said.

Dylan remained silent but had gained eye contact.

'People think it's easy in prison, but it ain't,' he continued.

'Why should you go back inside, Chubby? What's happened to make you think that? Come on...tell me.'

He didn't reply but leaned forward to glance over the precipice.

Dylan took the step forward that he'd relinquished earlier and changed tactics.

'You might die if you go over... but then again you might just be badly hurt and in a lot of pain you know and still end up going inside. Let's try and sort it, eh?' Dylan pleaded.

'Life's shit...my life's shit...what's the point?' he whimpered.

'Of course there's a point...I bet you just haven't thought it through, 'ave you?...You're not ill are you?'

'Why, what you after? A bloody donor card? Tell you what get me one and I'll sign it for you before I go over.'

'No...do I 'ell,' Dylan back tracked quickly.

'What the fuck is she doing?' asked Chubby, nodding at something behind Dylan that had caught his attention. Dylan turned to see Tracy walking towards them and signalled her to stop.

'I asked her to see if she could get some hot drinks for us. I know I need one, don't you? She's probably coming to see what we want. Come on mate, you must be cold; you've got a purple glow about you. What about a sandwich . . .'ave you eaten today? What's the harm in having a drink and a sandwich, eh Chubby?' Dylan asked.

There was no response, but Chubby appeared thoughtful. By the look of his gaunt face and the sight of his pronounced ribs he probably hadn't eaten in days.

'Well, what do you think Chubby? I'm going to 'ave a drink, so shall I get her to get you one too?'

'Okay... just a drink...but I'm staying here...don't think I'm coming down...don't think I won't do it,' he said in a calmer less convincing voice.

'Coffee okay?'

Chubby Connor rubbed a grimy hand across his brow as he looked at Dylan and nodded. 'Three sugars.'

Dylan sighed; he knew he'd made progress. 'Tracy, radio up for some hot coffee as a matter of urgency... I don't care where it's from. Just reinforce its urgent,' Dylan said looking over his shoulder. He was feeling the cold; there was definitely no global warming in Yorkshire.

Tracy stared at him wide eyed and then screamed.

Dylan turned back. 'Shit.' he shouted, running to the railings. Chubby Connor had gone over the edge.

Chapter Two

Bartlett's Academy for girls was the cream of the schools in West Yorkshire, and Liz and Malcolm Reynolds were delighted when their only daughter, Gemma Louise had been accepted. Dropping her off in her new school uniform had been a proud moment and Liz brushed away a tear, wishing that Malcolm could have been there too. She'd stopped off at Tesco on her way home to obtain the supplies of champagne and strawberries for the afternoon tea party she'd organised for Sunday. Singing softly, she pushed the car door shut with her knee and juggled with a heavy box, as she walked the few yards to her front door. Fumbling with the key in the lock she could hear the telephone ringing. She wasn't expecting a call but the persistent jingle made her instinctively rush. Precariously, she rested the corner of the box on the telephone table and snatched the phone off its cradle.

'Hello?' she said. 'Damn. Why does that always happen?' she cried, and quickly rang 1471. Listening to the ringing tone, she smiled at her reflection in the mirror, running her fingers through her newly highlighted hair. She bent closer to the glass to look at her whitened teeth. Wearing the mouth tray of whitening gel had been a bit of a pain but the results were...wow. She giggled, inspecting them closely. Boy was she fortunate to have kept her looks from her photographic modelling days after all she'd been through.

'The caller withheld their number. Thank you for using this service.' Liz dropped the phone in its holder. She lifted the box and placed it on the worktop in the kitchen. The telephone rang again. Stopping in her tracks, she swivelled on one foot, glancing heavenward to the chandelier and totted back in her high-heeled boots to pick up the phone.

'Hello?' she said, resting the receiver between her jaw and her fur collar as she flicked through the post.

'That's better Lizzie...you've gotta be quick gal...you never know when it's going to be important,' said a man's mellow voice.

'Who is this?' No one called her Lizzie but Malcolm.

The caller dismissed her question.

'Gemma Lou looked very smart this morning in her smart new uniform, didn't she? Mmm...just lovely.'

'Pardon?' she said, as her gut involuntarily clenched. A hot flush crept through her body and her hand tingled. The man's voice was quiet, thick but crystal clear. She racked her brain to put a name to it or a place to the accent. He didn't reply but she could hear his heavy breathing. Liz realised she was squeezing the phone tight and saw the reflection of her white knuckles in the mirror. Who was this creep, this loony? Some 'paedo' they warned people about? How did he know their number, her name and, more to the point, Gemma's? In his silence questions ping-ponged around her head. The mirror in which she had just admired herself now showed her frightened expression. She turned her back on it.

'What?' she said, her mouth dry. 'W...what did you say?'

'You.' Liz jumped at the growl. 'You heard what I said. Listen, I'm not a crank. Gemma must get her looks from you coz it definitely ain't from Mal.' He sniggered. 'At the moment, she's at school. Do as I say and she'll remain there.' Goosebumps appeared on Liz's arms.

'What do you want?' she asked, not recognising her own voice as it rose in pitch. 'Speak to me...or I'll hang up,' she demanded.

'Don't fuck with me....' he snapped, 'or, little lady, you might just live to regret it. I'm watching you.' Liz's eyes flew around the room. There were no windows in the hall, which was the centre of their opulent Georgian home. So where was he watching from? She ran to the door and turned the key with desperate, trembling fingers. Had she opened any windows in the house? Were the deadlocks on the back door? She couldn't breathe.

'Liz...Liz look, just be a good girl; take off that fur coat...it does nothing for your figure love. Go into the lounge and sit down on your nice new leather settee. You need to calm down.' She stood rooted to the spot in disbelief. Where the hell was he?

'Do it.' he screeched. She jumped.

'I'm sorry...please, please, just don't hurt us.' She keeled over as if she had been punched in the stomach, trying to disentangle her self from the coat's sleeves. She was sobbing now, quietly. She staggered, dropped the fur coat to the floor in the sitting room wanting so much to just hang up the phone, but not daring to disobey.

Liz loved her lounge. An elegant Chinese rug sat in the middle of the solid oak wood floor, and upon it stood three huge beige Italian soft leather sofas. She'd chosen gilt Laura Ashley light fittings and lampshades with crystal droplets. The sun coming from behind a cloud suddenly burst through the full wall of windows that were framed with plush deep red velvet curtains making the room feel snug, until now. She stumbled like a zombie and sat on the edge of a cushion. Should she hang up? Drive to the school? Ring the police? Thoughts raced through her head, but she was under his control.

'I've done what you've asked.'

'I know...' he whispered.

Liz's eyes scoured the room out through the windows to the garden beyond. Where was he?

'What do you want? Why are you doing this?' she asked.

'Be quiet and listen.'

Liz held her hand to her forehead trying desperately to think what would be best to say. She daren't move; like a rabbit in a car's headlights, she was frozen.

'Firstly,you tell nobody about my call, do you understand...no one at all, because I'll know.'

'Yes...yes,' she said. She gulped. Tears threatened. Where was Liz, the strong, confident woman who had coped with so much, she asked herself.

'Later this morning you'll contact your bank manager at Lloyds.'

'Yes...but...but how do you...which?'

'Never you mind,' he interrupted, '...you just tell him that you're calling to warn him that you'll be with drawing a substantial amount of cash...soon. The amount and the day you'll confirm, when I've decided.'

'But...I can't. My husband deals with the money... you'll have to speak to...'

'You stupid, stupid bitch,' he shouted so loud in her ear that she almost dropped the phone. 'Don't try playing games with me. We both know that he won't be home for a long time yet, now don't we? Not even on day release.' Liz gulped hard. Who the hell ...? How did he know so much?

'Do as you're told, or next time it won't just be the Koi. I'll be in touch. And remember, I'm watching you.' The phone went dead.

'What do you mean? Wait.' she shouted. The dialling tone burred in her ear. Liz raced along the hallway to the downstairs bathroom and bolted the door. She was safe. Her head was reeling. She leaned forward, grasping the basin and looked into the mirror. What on earth was she going to do? She felt nausea rise within her.

'Gemma,' she said as she lifted her head remembering what he'd said. She turned and threw up in the toilet bowl.

Wiping her mouth of vomit and still gasping for breath from the retching, she realised she had to pull herself together.

Liz unlocked the door, her stomach swirled, she felt dizzy and her heart pounded. Thoughts raced around her confused head. What if he'd already got to Gemma? Why the hell hadn't she noticed someone watching her? There was no time to try to work it out, Gemma was her priority, and first and foremost Liz had to find out if she was okay and still at school. Her senses on high alert, her maternal instincts taking over, she headed for the knife block that sat on a worktop in the kitchen and snatching a stainless steel meat knife from the stand with one hand, she picked up the phone that was hung on the wall above.

Calm down, calm down, she told herself, as she stood in the corner that had full view of the doors and windows. Giving in to her shaking legs, she slid to the floor, her back resting against the kitchen units. She desperately needed to control her breathing or she knew she would faint. Was he still watching her? Her lips trembled, her eyes stung with hot tears that jumped afresh into her eyes and carried the remainder of her mascara down her face, and with them the make-up she had applied so perfectly, earlier that morning. Hanging her head, she could see her hair was tipped with vomit and her clothing was crumpled. She looked as she felt;

no longer did the thirty-six year old look a million dollars in her expensive designer outfit, far from it. Hugging her knees to her chest she bent her head in between her legs and stared at the marble floor as if she had never seen it before.

'Get a grip...come on, ring the school'. As she looked up, the brandy bottle opposite drew her like a magnet. She clambered to her feet. Leaving the phone on the work surface she fumbled with the screw cap of the bottle with shaking hands - Dutch courage.

'Shit, come on.' She struggled with the cap. Liz gulped the cognac, spilling more down her silk blouse than she managed to swallow. Coughing and spluttering, she slammed the bottle down and heaved a sigh. It seemed to bring her to her senses, or dull the pain, she was unaware which. She pressed number 5 on the phone, which she'd programmed, for Gemma's school. 'Come on, come on,' she tapped her foot impatiently, tightening her grip on the handle of the knife.

'Good morning, Bartlett's Academy for Girls', said a high pitched, beautifully spoken lady.

'It's...its Mrs Reynolds from 'The Grange.' I'm ringing to see if my daughter's...okay?' Liz's teeth were chattering. 'When I dropped her off she wasn't feeling well...too well...you see. I can... do you want me to come for her?'

'I'm sure if she was ill we would have contacted you Mrs Reynolds. It's probably first day nerves...but wait, one moment. I'll go and check to put your mind at rest.'

The line went dead for what seemed like forever. Liz could hear children's faint, muffled laughs and squeals in the background.

'Come on...come on...come on ...' she said, prodding the tip of the knife into her leg until she drew blood. 'Ouch.' She jumped and hit the button on the oven with her head. The timer beeped loudly. Her heart leapt.

'Fucking hell.' she screeched.

'Pardon? Mrs Reynolds...are you there?'

'Ouch, er...yes...sorry,' Liz grimaced.

The Secretary continued nonplussed, 'Gemma's fine. Whatever it was that was troubling her this morning seems to have passed.' Liz exhaled loudly. The words spun in her head 'She's fine... She's fine.' There was a buzzing in her ears.

'She's painting away at the moment, not a care in the world.'

Tears of relief streamed down Liz's cheeks and she let out a cry.

'Mrs Reynolds, are you okay?'

Liz bit her lip. She placed the knife on the floor and put her hand over her mouth to smother the sobs. 'Yes, yes thank you...thank you ...Oh...it'll be me who picks her up this afternoon...no one else.'

'You have a nice day now.'

'Wait...don't...please don't let her go with anyone . . .' Liz sobbed into the mouthpiece but the phone had already been replaced at the other end.

The house was still; Liz could hear a train rattling in the distance, the burr of a motorbike, a siren; the normality of the outside world. Strangely, she was soothed by the familiar noises that usually annoyed her living on a main road. Above her the small window in the kitchen was open and she thought she heard the latch on the gate click. Liz held her breath and again sunk to the floor. The wind chime tinkled; usually a sign someone had nudged it as they passed on the block paved path to the back door, or was it just the breeze? Eyes staring and hand once more tight around the knife, she crawled on all fours across the kitchen floor. She cowered on her haunches for a moment slowly daring to raise her head above the worktop. She was sure she could hear footsteps outside. Her hand holding the knife shook uncontrollably and she grabbed her wrist with the other to steady it. A tingling sensation trickled through her upper limbs as her heart banged in her chest.

'Who is it?' she called. Straining, she could hear a dragging sound. 'What the hell...oh, my God, oh, my God,' she whispered.

'I've got a knife.' she shouted. She stopped. She listened. 'I've got a knife,' she screamed.

Chapter Three

Dylan's stomach flipped as adrenalin rushed around his body. Before peering over the wall he prepared himself to see Chubby's body splattered on the ground below or floating down the river.

'Fucking hell'. Dylan's heart pounded and his whole body trembled. Chubby Connor was squatted on a ledge on the other side, clinging to the railings.

'Next time I won't jump onto the ledge.' Chubby said, seeing Dylan's face. 'You care don't you?' he continued, surprised.

'Care, I'll bloody kill you myself when I get my hands on you. You...you bloody fool...course I care. You nearly gave me a frigging heart attack.' he stammered.

Chubby sniggered. 'We used to do it as kids, as a dare.'

'Well you're not a kid now, get back over here.' Dylan said, leaning heavily on the wall.

'You okay? You look terrible?' Chubby said pulling himself back onto the bridge. Instinctively, Dylan reached over and grabbed him like a striking snake...breaking all the rules of negotiation, adrenalin undoubtedly giving him the strength to drag Chubby to the floor beside him, where he landed with one almighty thud.

'Don't you ever fucking do that to me again...do you hear, you stupid, fucking bastard?' Dylan said, straddling Chubby, his clenched fist was centimetres from his nose.

'Shall I handcuff him, sir?' shouted Tracy. Dylan nodded, unable to speak momentarily as he took a deep breath. 'Yeah,' he said, eventually. 'We don't want him back up there do we? There's a knife of his just over there too,' he said pointing to the offending object lying yards away from them on the road.

Dylan rolled off Chubby and sat with his back to the pillar, his head in his hands between his knees trying to stop his body from shaking. Reality had hit home and Dylan knew only too well that Chubby's body weight, light as he was, could easily have pulled him over too, if he'd decided to leap.

'We'll sort things out Chubby, there's no need for all this,' he said, lifting his head.

'You think so? You wouldn't say that if you'd found your girlfriend in bed with yer best mate.' Chubby said solemnly as a tear rolled down his cheek.

'So that's what all this is about?' Dylan stood. Emotionally charged, Chubby told Dylan how he'd gone to court to see about his suspended sentence and the community work he'd been expecting to get as punishment for his crime, maybe even an ASBO. The hearing had been cancelled so he'd returned to the flat, which he called home, when he wasn't 'inside'. When he walked in the bedroom he'd seen his best mate Billy in bed with his girlfriend, Carly. He'd lost it big time and given Billy a good hiding and Carly a slapping as she'd tried to intervene. The police had been called so the neighbours had screamed, as they banged on the flat's door, so he'd legged it. Chubby knew he'd broken his conditions and he wasn't prepared to go back inside, which is why he had ended up on the bridge. Dylan let him talk.

''Ave they complained about the assault?'

'Police were called...so I 'aven't a cat in hells chance 'ave I?' he shrugged.

'You sure they've complained? If they 'aven't you've been up there for nowt.' He could tell he was giving Chubby food for thought as all three walked slowly towards the police car.

'Tracy, will you check with Control and see if Chubby is wanted for anything, or if any complaints 'ave bin made against him this morning? He'll need a new place to stay, perhaps a probation hostel.' Tracy turned and spoke into her radio. The men were silent. Beneath his calm exterior Dylan was still in shock at seeing Chubby 'go over'. Minutes later Tracy confirmed.

'He's not wanted and there's no complaints been made against him. When I get back to the nick I'll make some phone calls to his probation officer and see what can be sorted out, sir.'

'See...everything's alright. Now go with Tracy back to the nick, and you behave for her,' Dylan said, sitting beside him for a moment with the police cars door open wide. Tracy brought a blanket out of the boot and placed it round Chubby's shoulders. The kid was shivering uncontrollably.

'I don't want to see or hear of you threatening suicide again. Do I make myself clear young man? Nothing or no one is worth it.'

'I can't face going back inside,' Chubby said, shaking his head.

'Well you don't 'ave to worry about that today...so keep your nose clean from now on and it won't be an issue will it? Look, I've got to go, so do as you're told.' Dylan put a reassuring hand on Chubby's shoulder before Tracy gently closed the door.

'I'm sorry I screamed sir...it wasn't very professional but I thought he'd jumped,' she said.

'You and me both Tracy,' Dylan said shaking his head. 'Let Control know the outcome will you. I've got to get home,' he said looking at his watch. 'We're supposed to be setting off early for a weekend away.'

A few people stood out of their cars as Dylan walked back along the line of traffic. A stocky man in a leather 'bomber' style jacket leant heavily on his open door.

'About bleedin time...you should've thrown the sad bastard off,' he said, as Dylan came alongside. Dylan pushed the door closed, trapping the man against his car.

'And you should learn to keep your thoughts to yourself if you want to finish your journey,' he said, giving the door an extra shove. He would complain about Dylan – he was the type. Did he care? Right now...did 'e hell.

Sitting back in his car seat he checked his watch as he waited for the traffic to move. Dylan sighed and looked at his watch again; two hours had passed since he'd left work. Jen would be livid and the Divisional Commander wouldn't be impressed either, but Dylan was satisfied. He was sure it was the right result. He acknowledged Tracy, who was talking into her radio as he passed the police car, before he put his foot down and headed home, better late than never, he thought.

Dylan pulled into the driveway. He walked past the toppled suitcases that lay on the hallway floor and into the lounge where Jen stood staring out of the window. Turning to him, the look on her face spoke a thousand words. He walked towards her and she turned away. He grabbed her to him from behind, circling her waist with his arms and nuzzled her neck. He was pleased she didn't pull away.

'Before you say a word, he was on Stan Bridge so I was stuck in the traffic. The only way to get home was to talk him down.'

She knew he was right, she'd heard the report on the radio that a diversion was in place. He kissed her shoulder.

'Come on, let's go...just you, Max, and me,' he said softly. He could feel her soften, but she wasn't ready to give in just yet.

'You don't know how lucky you are I'm still here,' she said, her voice could have cut through steel but her expression portrayed the softness within her. He looked into her eyes. 'Oh, yes I do,' he said, slapping her bum playfully. 'I'll get changed.'

'Do you want a quick coffee?' she shouted after him. He smiled, knowing her anger had subsided.

'No thanks,' he called.

Max jumped up with excitement and Jen managed a half smile.

Minutes later he was locking the door behind them.

'Switch that damn mobile off,' she called as she walked to the car.

'Yes boss.' he said.

She sat in the car waiting for him to put the cases in the boot. It was a long journey south and it would take them at least six hours, but at last they were on their way. Max stretched out on the back seat, rolled around for a moment or two until he was comfy and moaned with pleasure as he settled. Dylan knew how lucky he was that Jen didn't give him any hassle. He couldn't decide which would be worse - the tongue-lashing or the silent treatment.

'I bet you could have strangled him Jack.' Jen said, when Dylan recalled the incident.

'I'm not kidding I thought he'd gone...it really threw me...God, what a strange feeling it was,' Dylan shivered. 'In the past fifteen years I've had some close scrapes. I've been spat at, had bottles thrown at me, stitches to my face and fought for my life but none gave me the feeling I had when he went over the wall,' Dylan said, as he replayed the scene over again in his mind. He felt his body drain and he closed his eyes.

'Well, for the next few days you're mine Jack...no bodies, well, only mine and believe you me, this one is very much alive,' she chuckled, as she turned to him to see his reaction. He was fast asleep.

'Please God for a few days of peace and quiet,' she uttered into the darkness, not too sure if it was Jack or Max she could hear snoring. She was quiet and content as she negotiated the traffic to the Isle of Wight, her special place.

Chapter Four

Liz Reynolds flirted on the telephone with Mr Beckwith, the bank manager, in a nervous way, informing him that she was considering purchasing a work of art. He caught her off guard, asking her questions she hadn't considered. How did she want the money, cash, banker's draft? She didn't have a clue. As she waffled on the reality of being blackmailed suddenly hit her.

'I'll let you know if I decide to buy it,' she said, as she put the phone down.

She worried, had she managed to comply with all the caller's instructions?

The comfort, serenity and security she'd always felt in her home had disappeared. Liz ambled into her bedroom and perched on the suede window seat, looking out over the beautifully striped lawn. For an instant the slight glimmer of sun through the window felt unwillingly soothing. She looked up at the clouds racing across the sky. Liz placed the knife and phone next to her, finally feeling able to release them from her grasp. She looked down at the fishpond and beaming up at her were the floating koi carp, their scales catching a glimpse of sun that momentarily burst through a cloud. She drew her hand to her mouth and gasped.

'Oh, my God.' she squealed, jumping up. Her movement in the wardrobe mirror caught her eye and she went towards it to take a closer look, she didn't recognise the image she saw before her.

Liz switched the shower onto full power and turned the heat up to as hot as she could bear. Scrubbing feverishly, she desperately tried to clear her confused mind as if cleansing her skin would somehow clear the fog in her head. Changed and focused, she set out to dispose of the dead fish so that Gemma wouldn't see them on her return from school. The fish had grown to a good size over the years under Malcolm's tender care, and as she knelt on the flagstones at the edge of the pond and netted their lifeless bodies into the bin her sporadic tears dripped into the water and her feelings turned to that of helplessness.

Later, sitting in the kitchen with a hot, strong, cup of tea she tried to make sense of what had taken place, wondering what on earth she was going to do next. She needed help but who could she turn to if the caller was really watching her? She analysed what he had said, he knew what they were wearing, where Gemma went to school. He had killed their fish so he had been in the garden. He knew the bank they used; would he know if she rang someone? And who the hell did she know who might be able to help her...'Larry,' she said, out loud. 'Larry Banks, he'll know what to do.' It must have been two years since she had seen him, how time flew.

For the few days Dylan was away Detective Sergeant Larry Banks was Acting Detective Inspector. Dylan wouldn't have chosen Larry as his deputy but it was part of his personal development plan. Dylan's hands were inexplicably tied. He had raised his concerns to the Chief Inspector Personnel but they were ignored.

'It will make him or break him,' he had said. 'We'll review his performance. He must be given the opportunity like anyone else. We cannot be seen to show favouritism. We have a force policy of equal opportunities.'

Larry strutted about Harrowfield nick 'like a dog with two dicks', in his Adonis-like way. The egotistical Chief Superintendent, Walter Hugo-Watkins, would have been proud to wear the same, new, designer suit Larry had bought for the occasion. The CID staff loved to mimic Larry's performance. Dylan hoped the responsibility would temporarily curtail his alcohol consumption, which on occasions was Larry's Achilles heel. One of the team's more experienced DC's Vicky Hardacre had pointed out to the others that he was wearing socks...he really was taking the role seriously.

Liz had met Larry through happier times with her husband Malcolm. Where had it all gone wrong? She'd been married to Malcolm for six years. Inheriting the well-known local scrap yard from his dad had meant they had no money worries. Malcolm was a popular guy, in fact it was often said he was the life and soul of a party. He knew a lot of people and was ruggedly handsome, although she hated his hands being ingrained with dirt and the stink of Swarfega he always used. She screwed up her nose at the memory of the smell. His arrest and prison sentence had rocked her world. Why had he got involved with a wrong crowd? Or had he always been involved and she just hadn't been aware? Maybe she had been naïve. For two years of Gemma's short life he had been locked away at Her Majesty's pleasure and little Gemma hardly knew her daddy. Looking back, there had been signs. He had begun to drink heavily, stayed away from home, and on more than one occasion had hit her, as he became controlling in his behaviour, which escalated. If she didn't write to him weekly or was late for a visit, he'd be livid with her. She tutted. Rumours had begun to fly that he'd had other women, and one even came to the door heavily pregnant, professing it was his child but Malcolm had dismissed her as a crank and she had heard nothing more. At the time Liz had been daft enough to believe him.

Malcolm had brought Larry home one night. She'd thought he was nice; he'd had a sparkle in his eye which ignited an instant connection between them. Malcolm told her later that Larry was a copper and he'd got him out of a tight spot. She didn't pry, as ignorance was bliss by this time. Malcolm had started spending more and more time away, and she and Larry had got quite close...well, they'd had moments of pure lust. Larry never wanted more, and she liked that. When they'd talked, they'd talked mostly about Malcolm, she conceded it was the only thing they had in common. When Malcolm got locked up Larry stopped coming round...she wondered why? His number was still in her phone and she toyed with the idea of sending the text she'd typed out, as she read it over and over again. Liz closed her eyes and said a prayer as she pressed SEND: what had she got to lose? She needed help and she needed it quickly.

Larry was busy fiddling with his new mobile as he sat with his feet up on the desk in the general CID office. *'Urgent. A blackmailer who says he is watching me is threatening my life and Gemma's. I need your help. Please. Liz.'* To onlookers as he walked to Dylan's office his stride changed from a strut to a scuttle, and he slammed the door behind him. He needed to think. He needed a drink. He thought Liz was history. She was attractive though, he sneered. They'd had great sex but he didn't want commitment and he thought she knew that. The text sounded like a problem, not fun...but he was intrigued. He wondered if he should ignore it. Then again, perhaps she was feeling needy and bored with hubby away.

'Well I can do the sympathy shag if that's all she wants,' he said chuckling. He decided to reply.

Reynolds Scrap Merchants was started in 1916 and was respected for miles around until Malcolm Reynolds got greedy and saw a money-maker in stripping stolen cars. Neglect and knocking his wife, Liz, around had been the start of his downfall. She'd unintentionally told the smooth talking DS Larry Banks one or two things during their affair, which he used to ensure CID, could target her husband and bring about a prosecution. Larry got enough information to put Malcolm inside for receiving stolen goods. Still looking at the text, considering his reply, he continued to reminisce. Thank God Malcolm had never caught them together and Liz hadn't told him either. There was once a very close call, he recalled, when he'd left his socks under their bed when Malcolm had come home unexpectedly, hence his resistance to wear them at all now. Either way, if Malcolm had found them Larry thought he'd have probably killed them both. Malcolm was into power lifting and was built like a 'brick shit house' as were his close associates. Larry smiled to himself, for some strange reason he got a buzz out of it and the excitement made the effort all the more worthwhile. Gosh, he'd had some close calls when he thought about it, but with Liz he'd got a result. Good job Dylan didn't know he'd been sleeping with a villain's wife. What a martyr Dylan was. He laughed out loud. It might actually be fun to see her again he thought, as he typed the text.

'Hi Liz – I'm in charge here these days so I can meet up anytime and see what can be done. Leave your house at 11. 30 and head for the car park at the Tandem Bridge side of Dean Reservoir - When I've checked nobody's followed you I'll come over. Stay in your car, leave the passenger door unlocked.'

They'd been there before...at least he thought it was her. Larry freshened up by applying the Anherb aftershave gel that he kept in his drawer. He read the bottle. 'A macho deep blue aftershave gel for the man who keeps pace with time. 'Yeah, that was definitely him. He shrugged smugly as he tossed the bottle back in his drawer and locked it. Vicky coughed to draw Lisa's attention to Larry as he strolled through the office, talking on his mobile, leaving without a word. Lisa raised her eyebrows, 'A woman,' they mouthed in unison, holding their noses and laughing. The smell of his aftershave lingered long after he had left.

Liz felt some relief now that she had contacted Larry; at least it was someone to share her problem with. She'd convinced herself that he would know what to do; after all he was a police officer wasn't he? Her mind was focused on the meeting. She changed into tight black leggings and a baby pink cashmere jumper, purposely leaving off her bra. He liked it that way, if she remembered correctly. Passing the hallway mirror she checked her appearance. Happy, she picked up her car keys, took a deep breath and went out to her car. Conscious that someone could be watching her, she tried to act as normal as possible as she climbed into the pale blue Renault sports car, with a personalised plate beginning LR3. She checked her watch, and at precisely eleven thirty she pushed the key card into the ignition, but the car's engine didn't turn over. Confused, she took out the card and tried again, scanning the information on the dashboard. Put your foot on the clutch...oh, she was stupid. How many times had she started this blessed car? Hands shaking, she pressed her foot on the clutch and inserted the card again, the car purred into action, only to stall. 'Grr...what's wrong with you, woman?' she said, as she tried again. This time it started and she turned left onto the main road. She knew the journey would take about twenty minutes. Constantly she checked her mirrors to see if anyone was following. At every junction she stared at men in their cars. Any one of them could be her blackmailer. 'Then again,' she thought, 'what did blackmailers look like?

No one appeared to be in the car park when she arrived. The weather was seasonal for Yorkshire, the wind was rushing across the heather and rippling the water in the reservoir below. She instinctively locked the doors, and dropped down the vanity mirror, scrunching her hair in her hand as she did so. She wanted Larry to like what he saw, otherwise she knew he wouldn't be interested and she was desperate. After all, she and Gemma's life may depend on him. Deep down she'd no doubt, unless he'd changed, there were only two things on Larry's mind, sex and drink. The quietness of the purring car felt eerie in this spot that time had forgotten. So many years before the scene could have been the one the Bronte sisters looked upon. Through the window, Liz searched for a slight movement that would indicate Larry's arrival. There was none. Surely he'd turn up, he wouldn't let her down, would he? She turned the radio on and flipped channels for something to do. It was no use she couldn't concentrate. She turned it off. Suddenly there was a loud bang on the boot. She jumped, but to her immense relief it was Larry, she hadn't seen his car or heard it. She looked around, where was it?

'Come on, open up,' he ordered at the passenger door, holding his lapels on his suit to keep his jacket fastened in the wind.

'I told you to leave the passenger door unlocked.' he scolded.

'I'm sorry...you frightened me. I never saw you. Where's your car?' she gasped, her mouth was as dry as a bone as she tried desperately hard to control her breathing.

'Over there,' he said pointing to the dark blue Audi that could just be seen tucked into the hillside. He rubbed his hands together. He turned his eyes towards her and she noticed the appreciative look on his face.

'So you remembered,' was all he said as he leered at the sight of her. No, he hadn't changed.

'You're looking really good, Liz,' he said.' What's happened? How can I help?' He was a smooth talker. Liz didn't need to think, every last word the blackmailer had said was imprinted on her mind and she relayed it all to him very quickly.

'What do I do? I'm scared stiff. Should I tell Malcolm?' Her eyes, although unnoticed by Larry, were pleading and frightened.

He whistled. 'Slow down,' he said, laying a reassuring hand on her leg.' He's done nothing at the moment apart from kill the fish, has he?'

'Well no...but you know they were Malcolm's pride and joy,' she wailed as tears welled up in her eyes.

'How did he leave it with you? Did he say he'd be back in touch?'

'Yeah, he didn't say when, just to tell the bank I'd be going in to withdraw a large amount of cash, and I've telephoned the bank manager,' she swallowed.

'You 'ave? Good. Did he say how much?'

'No,' she sniffed.

'Right, so all he's after is money is he? We'll play along with him. Keep in touch with me by text, he can't trace that. I imagine his next call will be telling you how much he wants, what denomination he wants it in and where he wants it leaving. Can you draw a large amount of cash from your bank account?'

'Within reason, it's a joint account...our nest egg from his dad's estate. He told me not to tell anyone. He watched me take Gemma to school, he described what she was wearing...he suggested he'd hurt her...I'm really frightened,' she said. 'I don't want to annoy him. 'God, what do I do, Larry? What about Malcolm? He'll go mental if he thought someone was threatening us, especially Gemma. You know what he's like.'

'Don't tell him for the moment then. There's no point upsetting him, yet. He can't do anything from where he is, can he? Look, let's see what happens. Let's take it slowly, step- by- step, play along and I'll put a team on it. On your way home, call at a shop for a carton of milk or something.'

'What?'

'That way, if the blackmailer is watching your comings and goings you can use it as an excuse for going out. Calmer now?' he asked.

'Yes a bit, thank you,' she said forcing a smile, and retrieved a tissue from her handbag. A team of police watching out for her, yes that did make her feel safer. She exhaled, wiping her nose.

Larry leant forward, moving in for a kiss, his hand automatically reaching out for her breast. Liz held her breath, gritted her teeth and closed her eyes. His mobile rang, and he leaned back and a long moan escaped from his lips. Liz heaved a sigh of relief.

'Okay, I'm on my way. I'll be there in ten minutes,' he said.

'Sorry kid...must go...maybe next time eh? Armed robbery at a petrol station to deal with,' he said, by way of an explanation, as he got out of the car.

'Shame.' she said, rather too enthusiastically, even to her own ears. He leaned back in the car and pecked her on the cheek. At the same time he slid his hand underneath her jumper and squeezed her breast hard. It was so expertly done; so quick, so brief she never anticipated it.

'Keep in touch...everything will be okay.' He winked and was gone. She locked the door behind him. Stunned, she realised he had come for sex. Nothing could have been further from her mind, although she was quietly pleased he still fancied her. If he got it sorted for her perhaps she would reward him, she thought. After all he was being very good to her. They'd been close at one time. Larry had seemed so confident he knew how he could solve her problem, that it gave her strength. She didn't feel so alone. If Malcolm knew, however, that she'd be drawing money out of their account he'd go ballistic. She shuddered, knowing how violent he could be. She steered out of the car park and a car pulled up on her tail. It couldn't pass on the single track road, but continued to be right on her boot. She had two choices; she could either pull into the next passing spot or continue on the road. What the hell was she to do?

Licking her dry lips, she clutched the steering wheel hard and pressed down the accelerator. What if it was the blackmailer? What if she stopped and he pulled in behind her? Ahead she could see a white van in a viewing spot and as she approached it was obvious her follower had seen it too, as he backed off. It was a police dog van, thank the Lord. She indicated to pull in behind it and the car tailing her passed in a blur, sounding his horn. Was she being paranoid or was it the blackmailer telling her he'd seen her meeting Larry?

Chapter Five

Larry skidded onto the petrol station forecourt where uniformed officers were already in attendance. An instant response firearms car passed by as it toured the area. Everything appeared to be under control he thought, as he climbed out of his vehicle and strolled across to where four 'uniform' were talking to a pale young female, wearing the petrol station's brightly coloured clothing. The door to the petrol station was open and the bright lights made Larry screw up his eyes.

'DI Banks,' he announced to his audience. 'I'll be outside directing the theatre of operations when you're ready to update me.'

'Yes, sir,' replied one. The others looked at him with their mouths open, lost for words at his remark and his dramatic entrance.

Larry contacted Control, 'DI Banks – just to let you know I'm at the scene and I've taken charge.'

One of the officers joined him in the yard.

'How much did they take?' asked Larry, as he rubbed his chin thoughtfully.

'Oh...only about a hundred quid, she thinks. She'll know the exact amount when she's checked the till, but for now I've asked her to let SOCO examine the kiosk.'

'Yes...good...do we 'ave a description?'

'She describes the robber as a young, thin, tall, white male, baseball cap pulled down over his face, no car. He came in on foot...she believes she saw a gun.'

'Had he been in the garage before?'

'She doesn't think so but I've seized the CCTV tape, just in case there was anyone on it that resembled her description.'

Larry took the video cassette offered by the officer. 'Thanks, I'll get it checked,' he said, stuffing it into his pocket.

'It's not good quality and the camera's set a bit high up on the building, sir,' he said, sounding disappointed.

Larry tutted as he shook his head, 'I'll 'ave a look at it and see what we can do and record it as a theft, it'll keep the violent crime figures down,' he chortled. 'Anyway, I'll leave it with you kid as they say,' Larry called out to the officer and his probationer as he walked back to his car. 'I'm on the mobile if you need me. It's time for a drink,' he shouted.

'As who says?' Asked the young rookie. 'Is he joking about a drink?' he whispered as the officers watched him go.

'Who Acting Inspector Banks?' mocked his mentor. 'One thing Larry Banks never jokes about is alcohol, son.'

The nearest pub was the King's Head and that's where Larry was heading. He found decision making thirsty work. He knew a couple of pints of hand - pulled Tetley's would go down a treat. Staring at his pint in awe as it stood on the bar, he was mesmerised by the froth that spilled over the rim of the glass and trickled down the side. He reached in his pocket to get the money to pay, not taking his eyes off the pint of beer that he picked up delicately, like a long lost treasure. He could feel the cool, wet glass in his hand and savoured the thirst-quenching nectar that had the smoothest of heads.

'Ahhhhh,' he sighed, it sure was good he thought, as he drank it dry and ordered the next. It stopped his hands shaking. Free bread and dripping decorated the bar. What more could a man want he thought, as he tucked in. Police officers knew the pubs in the town long before the street names: not because they were all drinkers but because that was where trouble was most prevalent. Larry propped up the bar in such a place, where he felt at home, and his thoughts went back to Liz Reynolds and her situation. Let's face it; he'd nobody else on the go at the moment. He smiled as he wiped the froth from his lips with the back of his hand, deciding there and then that he would keep quiet at the nick about the blackmail. He'd sort it himself. It'd be a good collar and she'd be so grateful to him when it was all over, No one would have been any the wiser, especially Malcolm. He ordered another pint. Boy, he wasn't half beginning to enjoy

Dylan's absence. Detective Inspector Banks – now that sounded good...very good. He really should go back to the office, he thought. He would, after another.

Larry was dozing in Dylan's chair, after snagging up the tape from the garage in Dylan's machine, when, late that afternoon, a familiar face appeared at his office door.

'Hell fire...no, it can't be? Is this the same Larry Banks...a bloody pen pusher?' Gary Warner guffawed loudly as he walked in the office. Larry staggered from behind the desk and shook his hand vigorously.

'It must be five years since I've seen you.' said Larry, yawning. 'What brings you to Harrowfield? Are you still with the Regional Crime Squad?'

'Yeah. I've come to speak to Jack Dylan about a dealer on your patch that's starting to feature in one of our operations: 'Operation Whirlwind' would you believe?'

'Who the hell thinks up the bloody operational names, eh Gary? Jack's away so I'm your man,' Larry said, red faced, shoulders back and chest out.

'Right then,' Gary grinned.

'Come on, let's go talk over a jar, shall we? Walls 'ave ears that pubs don't.' Larry patted Gary on the back as he steered him into the general office and out of the nick.

'It smells like you've had a few already mate.'

'Just the one. I had to meet a snout at lunchtime, you know what it's like. I couldn't order an orange juice now, could I?' he laughed.

'We've got good information from an 'undercover' that Frankie Miller is importing heroin and cocaine on a regular basis,' Gary told Larry, whilst they sipped their lager in a quiet recess of the Armitage Arms. 'He's not been out of prison long. Him and his brother own Millers Haulage, so if you've got any intelligence no matter how trivial we'd be grateful if you passed it on,' he said, taking a sip of his pint, 'especially with an undercover officer being involved.'

'Yeah, I know of the Millers, they're loaded. We're obviously in the wrong business.' Larry said thoughtfully.

'Only joking mate, there's no need for that look. You still married?' Larry quickly placed his pint glass down on the table as quickly as he'd changed the subject.

Gary studied his drinking partner carefully. 'Yeah. I'm well looked after. What about you? Still playing the field or 'ave you settled down?'

'Not likely. Although I've got myself a very demanding attractive, wealthy, married woman after me,' Larry said beaming.

'Well there's nothing urgent with this job at the moment so it's for your and Jack's ears only, for the safety of the undercover cops, if you'll just update him for me when he gets back?'

'No problem. One for the road?'

'No...I'm driving.'

'Go on, just for old time's sake.'

'Just half a Coke then,' Gary said, as he handed his glass over the bar to the landlord.

'Two more pints please my good man.' Larry roared, slamming his glass on the bar.

'I said Coke.' Gary yelled above the noise of the pinball machine, as he walked towards the toilets.

'Ah, come on...I'm not ordering bloody Coke in here, they'll think I've gone soft.' Larry bellowed.

'No mate, I'm driving,' Gary firmly reiterated.

'Okay.' Larry said, picking up one jar and downing it in one. 'Waste not, want not.' he gurgled, his mouth full of beer.

'A half of Coke it is for my colleague, please landlord,' Larry said.

As Gary walked back towards the bar he felt uncomfortable. This was supposed to be a quiet drink; the last thing he wanted was for attention to be drawn to them.

'When's Jack back? Is he off for a while?' he asked, making a mental note to give Dylan a call on his return.

'Next week ...'till then I'm in charge of his patch.' Larry shouted, proudly, for anyone to hear.

Gary left shaking his head in dismay. What had happened to Larry since he'd last worked with him? He was no longer the great thief taker he had once been.

Back at the station, Larry sat in the office with his feet up. It was Dick Foster's retirement do that evening; the buffet would be his meal and after a few pints in the bar, that would be Larry sorted for the day. His life these days seemed to take him from one public house to another. He hardly knew

Dick, a PC from the front office, but that didn't deter him. After all, the poster did say ALL welcome, and anyone who'd done thirty years in the job definitely deserved a toast to them. Thirty years in the job, Larry dreaded the thought he was looking for a much easier option. A wealthy widow with her own pub, he contemplated. Not too much to ask for, was it? He smiled at the thought, and as he did so he pulled the drawstring of the blind and yanked hard, although he regretted it instantly as dust flew down on him. Waving his hand in front of his face and coughing fitfully he took the wedge from under the open door and employed it to keep it shut. Pulling up a visitors chair to rest his feet on, he made himself comfortable, in Dylan's chair. A smile crossed his face as he remembered the conversation he'd once had at his local.

'What happened to that lovely young barmaid you were knocking off?' Larry had asked the barman, pulling a face at the woman now behind the bar, he could only describe as being as ugly as a bucket of frogs.

'Ah, she went off with a punter.' He said pulling Larry's pint. 'So, I married the landlady,' he nodded in the direction of the unfortunate looking lady.

'Why?' Larry had gasped, paying the barman.

'Well, my favourite drink is on tap. I'll never be frightened of her leaving me - I can have sex when I want it, and she's ever so grateful...do you want me to go on?' he'd said, chuckling.

Larry remembered him saying, as he fell into a deep sleep.

About an hour later he woke up. He needed a clean shirt for the evening. On the way he'd change out of his new suit at his flat, and have a couple of shots of Jack Daniels as an aperitif.

Someone has put on a good spread he thought, as he headed straight for the buffet. It was early, so there was hardly anyone about as he overloaded his platter. Why the hell didn't they give out bigger plates? He thought as he ambled to the bar.

'The first drink's on me,' someone shouted. The day was getting even better. Larry stuffed his face with pies, sausage rolls, scotch eggs, what a rare treat. He looked around the room. No one else was eating. He chuckled; perhaps the food wasn't supposed to be eaten yet, he thought as he discreetly slid his empty plate and dirty napkin along the shiny bar surface. Now, which 'wooden top' can I blag the next drink off, and where was Dick Foster he wondered, as he looked around the room? At the end of the bar people were handing presents and hugging a kind faced man with laughing eyes...Dick Foster. Larry grinned knowingly...he wasn't a detective for nothing now, was he?

He swayed as he sat on the bar stool, surveying the crowd as he overtly nodded to people as they passed, and in doing so toppled off his seat and into the chest of a large buxom woman.

'What the fuck?' came the shout. As he knocked her to the floor she screamed. A big strong arm yanked Larry to his feet by his collar in one fell swoop. Before he knew what was happening, he was staring into the shirted chest of the lady's husband, and was bounced out of the bar like an abusive, drunken teenager.

'Fuck off home. Otherwise you'll be investigating your own assault, you plain clothes wanker.' the man shouted.

Larry wasn't one for doing as he was told and no way was a 'wooden top' going to talk to him like that he thought, as he picked himself up off the gritty, tarmac driveway and dusted himself down.

Chapter Six

Jack Dylan was quick to resume work mode, as he hurriedly got ready to go to court for a bail shout, and Jen was a lot more relaxed arriving home from the Isle of Wight than when they'd left. Immediately after she'd made breakfast she was stuffing clothes into the washing machine, whilst making a mental list for the supermarket.

Max stretched out on the kitchen floor, moaning contentedly as he watched them mill around him.

'Don't work too hard,' Jen shouted to Dylan, as she rushed to catch up with him on his way to the front door. Holidays were okay, but you had to come back.

'I won't,' he called over his shoulder in his 'I know' tone.

'No, promise me. I'm serious,' she pleaded, as she stood with him at the open car door. Jen brushed the front of his jacket with the palms of her hands, and stood on her tiptoes for a kiss. Jack smiled and hugged her tightly.

'After the relaxing time I've just had on that beautiful Isle, I'm going to find it very hard to get motivated love, never mind working too hard,' he said as he flopped down into the driver's seat and wound down the window.

'Good. Love you,' she said, touching his cheek. 'I couldn't bear to lose you Jack.' Jen's eyes filled with tears.

Max's bark from inside the house broke their gaze. They laughed at him clambering on the settee; watching them from the window seat, he eagerly awaited Jen's return. She brushed away a tear spilling onto her cheek, which didn't go unnoticed by Jack.

'You'd better go back in, someone wants to go out for his walk,' Dylan said, as he watched Jen bite her bottom lip. She nodded and smiled.

Dylan breathed a long sigh of relief as he quickly drove away she nearly had him going there. It had been tough getting Jen to agree to come back with him from the Isle of Wight, and who could blame her. She loved the Island, her birthplace. He was selfish, he knew, but he needed her and he truly meant all the promises he made to her before they left.

The clock chimed eight a.m. as Dylan arrived at the nick. His inbox was overflowing.

'What the fuck?' he groaned, pulling the paperwork out onto his desk. The least he'd expected was for Larry to have kept up with it.

'Coffee, sir?' Vicky called cheerily, as she stuck her head round his office door.

'Thank you. I'd love one,' he said eagerly, as he started to prioritise the paperwork. What the hell had Larry been up to? This stuff hadn't been touched whilst he'd been away.

'It's good to 'ave you back, boss,' said Vicky, strategically placing Dylan's coffee cup on the corner of his littered desk. Dylan pointed to the pile of work. 'By the look of this lot, it must 'ave been busy whilst I've been off, I hope Larry's looked after you,' he said, looking down at a report.

'And I thought you knew everything, boss,' she commented flippantly, as she quietly closed the door behind her.

I wonder what she meant by that he thought, but was distracted by the phone ringing.

'Jack, its Ralph, I'm sorry, I'm afraid Dawn won't be in today. She's feeling a little under the weather, probably something she ate. You know what she's like. Eats anything,' he laughed.

'Oh, tell her I'll manage somehow without her. Just, tell her to get well soon. I hope it wasn't something you cooked for her or you'll never live it down.'

'No, no...it's nothing like that. Thanks Jack...she'll be back tomorrow, I'm sure. Look after yourself.'

Ralph, Dawn's husband owned a restaurant in the Sibden Valley called 'Mawingo' and food was her Achilles heel. Although she denied emphatically that was what first attracted her to him.

Dylan knew some of his male colleagues hated having a woman as their partner, but he enjoyed Dawn's company. Not only did she look like Dawn French but she also had the sense of humour to match. Dawn laughed at herself when he teased her about her habit of dabbing her mouth when she was hungry, and made fun of her beautiful embroidered hankies she carried around with her for that purpose.

Draining his coffee cup, Dylan cursed Larry. Through the glass partition of his office he saw Tracy, the young policewoman he'd last seen on Stan Bridge. She was in a smart suit and was standing by a desk in the CID office; she looked thinner out of uniform, he thought, her light brown, curly hair hanging neatly over her shoulders. What a smart, clean looking young lady she was. It made a change from casually dressed youngsters, with their tattoos and piercings. How on earth could anyone think that was attractive? He was getting old, he thought, as he eased himself from behind his desk and walked towards the general office.

'Morning you. How's things?' he said cheerily. She blushed, ferociously. 'You decided to become a detective, then?'

'On attachment for two weeks sir and I'm really, really looking forward to it.' She drew back. Her grin reminded Dylan of an over excited child. He remembered his first CID attachment. In the 'olden days' he'd been shoved and pushed around the CID office as an aide, by the older detectives, who insisted he called them Mr and he got a clip round the ear if he answered back.

'Nervous and excited, I bet?' Dylan said, smiling.

'Yeah, something like that,' she said, shrugging her shoulders.

'Good, it'll be a bit different from guarding 'scenes' and stopping traffic, that's for sure.'

Dylan got the impression she was uncomfortable talking to him. Unfortunately, he felt that was the uniform mentality. Uniformed bosses, inspectors and sergeants tended to be officers who gave orders to be complied with. They didn't, in his experience, stop for a chat to get to know the individuals under their command. No, perhaps that was unfair, he reflected, these days attitudes were changing.

'Sit down and make yourself at home, it's a much different style of work in CID to what you've been used to. Did 'Chubby' behave himself for you after the episode on the bridge?'

'Yes sir, thanks for that. I don't know what I'd have done if you hadn't been in the traffic, waiting to cross the bridge that day. I've seen him since and he's living with a mate and his girlfriend. She's got a small boy. You never know, Chubby might settle down now.'

'Who knows? Leopards and spots do spring to mind though,' he said, grinning, as Vicky walked in the room.

'Vicky, this is Tracy, sorry I don't know your last name,'

'Petterson, sir,' she said, smiling apprehensively at Vicky.

'PC Tracy Petterson is with us for two weeks secondment. Look after her will you DC Hardacre?'

'No probs, I'll treat her as if she were one of me own,' Vicky mocked jovially, putting Tracy instantly at ease.

'Don't know if I've done you a favour there or not,' Dylan said grimacing playfully as he retreated back to his office, feeling very much his age once more. Vicky threw her pen at his closing door. Laughing at her through the window, he picked up his phone to text Jen.

Lovely lady, missing you already... Dawn's gone sick and Larry hasn't surfaced yet. But by God when he does he has a lot to answer for.

'Gosh, how dare you do that?' Tracy whispered to Vicky.

'Because Dylan is okay; he's a good boss and he's got a good sense of humour but don't be misled, he's nobody's fool. Keep him supplied with coffee and you'll be his friend for life though.'

Two hours later, Larry casually strolled into Dylan's office looking worse for wear; the smell of stagnant ale accompanying him, which only confirmed to Dylan that he'd slipped back to his old ways. Was that a black eye he was sporting? After his dad died suddenly, Larry had gone on a bender but after a while he seemed to recover. Had someone or something knocked him back again Dylan wondered? He would have to have a chat with him, and not in a pub.

'Morning Boss,' he slurred. 'Good break?' Larry just about managed the words, before slumping into the chair opposite Dylan, his hands deep in his trouser pockets.

'I've been south for a few days actually, to see how Jen's dad's coping since her mum died if you remember, Larry, not exactly two weeks in the Bahamas.' snapped Dylan.

'Er...er...yeah...sorry boss.' He shuffled uncomfortably in his seat and sat up straight.

Dylan placed his empty cup down on the desk and studied Larry. 'Well, what's been happening then? Any messages or updates for me?'

'No...no, it's been dead quiet. Bit of a theft from a garage, but the young lad only got away with about a hundred quid, and would you believe it, the CCTV tape we retrieved is jammed in your cassette player.' Larry yawned, pointing to the offending video player.

'What the hell is it doing there? It should 'ave been copied and the original kept, Detective Sergeant Banks. Even you know that.'

'I know... just thought I might know the lad and get a quick I.D,' he whined.

'We don't need to cut corners, Larry, and there's no doubt the offender will try again if that's all he got. Did you put his description on the ring around, for petrol stations to be on alert?' Dylan asked, staring hard at Larry. There was something different about him. Have you 'bin in a fight?'

Noting he was under scrutiny, Larry made a display of coughing and spluttering, avoiding any eye contact. 'Nah, I'm too old to scrap. I walked into a door. By the way I've got a dentist appointment at eleven so if I'm missing for a while, you know where I am.'

Dylan knew he was lying about his eye. Walking into a door? What a lame excuse, but Larry was an adult after all. He knew what he was doing, or at least Dylan hoped he did. He'd make sure he'd cover Larry's appearance and his attitude when they had that chat.

'Dentist? Rather you than me Larry' he said, looking down at a report he had started writing. Larry stood to leave and farted loudly.

'Larry. For God's sake.' Dylan said as his phone rang. 'Be here at one. There're a few things I need to talk to you about; one being this untouched bloody paperwork and another, your conduct.' Dylan looked up as he put the phone to his ear. Larry was gone.

'Hello Dylan? Harriet Anderson from the Child Protection Unit.' Dylan could tell by her voice she was smiling, but then again, she always did.

'Gosh, Harriet, long time no see...It can't be long now can it before you go on maternity leave? How the hell are you?'

'I'm fine, that's why I'm ringing. I'm going at the end of the week and no one has got a replacement for me. Do you know of anyone who I could suggest would like to take on the role?' she enquired tentatively. 'I'm too big to sit behind this desk now, in fact if I get any bigger I think I'll explode,' she said.

Dylan's heart sank, they would miss her. If ever there was a round peg in a round hole it was Harriet and the CPU.

'I just thought I could show the cover the ropes before I go.'

'I'll be honest with you I didn't realise you were going to be off so soon, these last few months have flown. Look, let me 'ave a think and I'll get back to you,' Dylan had known about Harriet's pregnancy since the day she'd took the test, because she'd sent an e-mail to everyone she knew, with the good news. So, his opposite number in Child Protection was going on maternity leave, one DS was off sick and one was heading for...Larry's future didn't bear thinking about. If not much had happened whilst he'd been away, then what the hell had Larry been up to, so he couldn't manage the paperwork he wondered, as he fired up his computer. He needed more coffee and stood up to stretch his legs, to catch someone's attention. The CID office was empty, which was a good sign everyone must be out working.

Larry was having a mouthwash, but not one you'd get at a dental surgery. He felt like a kid bunking off school, which was becoming a familiar feeling. He hadn't always been like this, but after being overlooked for promotion again, he'd lost his focus. He caught sight of the pub clock, twenty past eleven. 'Come on,' he muttered impatiently. What was it about women and time? There was nothing polite about being late, although he knew he always was he thought grinning to himself.

Dylan sat alone in his office, with his door propped open. The large, general CID office that he looked out on was quiet, apart from the odd telephone ringing. He was concerned with his e-mails. HQ was drawing his attention to a recording of a robbery that had been reduced in severity to a 'theft from a garage'. This must be the crime Larry had mentioned to him. Dylan researched it on the CIS computer system and looked at the 'I' screen for the MO. *'Single male walks into garage believed in possession of handgun, demands cash from female cashier. In fear she hands over money from till.'* He immediately changed the crime to robbery. What the hell was Larry thinking of? Since when had he been concerned with crime figures? Manipulating numbers was downright stupid, he knew that. Dylan went on to read the description of the robber. It sounded like a typical 'Chubby.' No, surely not. Chubby didn't want to go to prison again, but Dylan decided to give Tracy the job to investigate, since she had recently dealt with the youths in the town while in uniform...it was a start. Dylan smiled, thinking about some of the nicknames of local youths. 'Scarface' was obvious, 'Bandit' because the guy had only one arm or 'Jaws' because the kid had it broken a few times, were more tongue in cheek. Often, as officers found out to their dismay in interviews, they were the only names the youngsters knew each other by. His smile froze as he caught sight of the mangled tape in the video machine. Hell Larry; that might've lost us vital evidence. He'd get one of the techno bods to deal with it. He didn't want to damage it further by trying to yank it free himself.

'What's happening?' Larry texted Liz, as he drained his pint glass. A right pain in the arse this was turning out to be. He just hoped it would be worth it in the end. He needed to pull a good job out of this bag. Sort himself out.

   'I need to see you now,' came the text back.

'Boss, I've had a call to see an informant,' Larry told Dylan over the hands free, as he put his Audi into gear and skidded in a half circle across the pub car park. He stopped abruptly, and without looking reversed back to allow him to face his exit. He heard a loud thud. Larry hung up. Dylan snarled into the receiver.

'Shit, shit, shit.' Larry shouted, slamming the palm of his hand on the steering wheel. Climbing out he saw the crumpled figure of an old man on the ground. He jumped back into the car, rammed the gear stick into first and raced out of the car park in a cloud of dust, causing a car to skid to avoid him. Car horns blared in his wake. His heart raced. His head banged. What had he done? He could hear sirens.

'Think...think Larry,' he said out loud. 'Get off the road.' He drove into the supermarket car park. It got him out of sight and in a crowd. Reversing into the garage forecourt he got out and inspected the damage. Bending down on his haunches, he sighed. That was a fair dent the stupid old git had made in his car. 'Urgh', he thought, pulling a face. Was that blood he could see?

'Why hadn't the silly old sod looked where he was going?' he muttered as he walked to the kiosk. He queued up; picking up some mints and a car wash token.

'Six quid? I only want to wash my car love, not buy a new one,' he moaned to the cashier.

'There are two cheaper programmes, love, if you want one,' she snapped, oblivious to his attempt at a joke.

'Don't do cheap, love.' he winked before walking out.

He sat in his car as the heavy brushes pummelled the roof, and water lashed at his windscreen. It wasn't his fault. The daft old git should have looked where he was going. Larry felt warm and clammy, panic engulfed his body. Oh, my God, what was he going to do?

An ambulance with flashing lights faced him as he pulled out of the entrance to the supermarket car park. Unbeknown to Larry, paramedics were struggling to keep the elderly man alive. Fred White was a well-known local boxer in his time but was now facing the biggest fight of his life.

Larry drove slowly back to the station and parked his car on a side street nearby. Striding into the station, his mind was working overtime. The old man had been alright, he hadn't run him over. Dylan was heading towards him down the narrow corridor. Thrusting his hand in his pocket he found a handkerchief and held it to his mouth.

'Thought you were off to see an informant,' said Dylan. 'Good- grief you look dreadful. What on earth did the dentist do? You're as white as a ghost.' Larry leaned against the wall, pressing the hankie tighter over his mouth. He'd only hoped it would cover the smell of ale but, trying not to smile, he quickly jumped on Dylan's unexpected reaction.

'He's only gone and done a bloody extraction.' Larry groaned. 'I thought I was okay...the informant never showed and I didn't feel like hanging about. Ah, God it kills.'

'You better get home,' Dylan said, deciding to postpone the reprimand he had intended to deliver. Dylan felt for him; probably because of his own phobia of dentists.

What a morning Larry had; he needed some more anaesthetic, which he knew he could find at the Kings Head. His face hurt all right, not from the dentist, but from the copper who'd had a swipe at him the previous night. *'You deserve a pint after pulling that one off,'* he told himself, but maybe he should go to the Armitage Arms on the other side of town.

Back in the office, Dylan asked Vicky and Tracy to try and find out what Chubby Connor was up to. He wanted to see if there was any evidence that would connect him with the garage job.

'No problem.' said Tracy, turning to the crime on the Crime Information System, on her computer. 'I'm on with it now, sir.'

'Were we that keen when we started, boss?' asked Vicky gloomily.

'Probably,' he leant closer. 'But your coffee's better for practice,' he said.

'Hint taken,' she said. 'You're such a smooth talker and' she whispered in his ear, 'that aftershave you're wearing boss is...heavenly.' She breathed heavily.

Dylan laughed as he texted Jen. *'Hope your days going better than mine. Just had to send Larry home he's had a tooth extraction. No DS's now.'*

'That's strange,' she texted back. *'I could have sworn I'd just seen him going into the Armitage Arms. And there's me thinking you were the Detective.'*

'I am... He went home.'

'He certainly didn't... go see for yourself. He's probably still there.'

'Sir, there's been a hit and run; an old man called Fred White. He's critical and in A & E, we're just being told.' Tracy called from the office.

'Forget Chubby, Vicky. You and Tracy go to the scene to see if you can assist, in case it's a stolen car or a deliberate knockdown.'

Dylan could have done with a DS at the scene but he knew Vicky was quite capable. He needed to get to the Armitage Arms to see with his own eyes if his officer had lied to him. On the one hand he hoped Larry was there, then he could get the help he needed for his drinking. On the other, he hoped Larry hadn't lied to him. But he was going to confront him about his issues.

Chapter Seven

Liz paced the floor. 'What's the twat playing at?' she said, her nerves turning to anger. Desperately she tried the controlled breathing she'd been taught at Pilates, knowing she needed to be focused and calm when the blackmailer rang again. What was it Larry had said? She had to get details and delay matters so that she could discuss it with him before she made any rash promises. Her eyes flew to her pen and paper on the work surface. *Write it down so you get it right,* he'd said.

Although she'd been expecting the call, when the phone rang she nearly jumped out of her skin, snatching it off its cradle.

'Hello?' she said, her voice wobbled with emotion.

'Listen very carefully. I'll say this only once. Do you understand?' Liz nodded, silently. The voice of the blackmailer was surreal- like something out of a movie. 'Yes,' Liz finally managed. Her mouth was so dry, she struggled to speak.

'You'd better not have told anyone about our chat.'

'I haven't...I wouldn't...Look...I just want this to be over.' Her hands were shaking so much she could hardly hold onto the phone.

'I believe you, but if you've lied to me you won't live to regret it. Do you know what I'm saying? It's not a game.'

'I haven't...I won't...I promise, please...trust me.'

'So, let's get it over with,' he said quietly. 'You will go to the bank and withdraw five hundred thousand pounds.'

Liz gasped, 'I...'

'Don't bother,' he snapped. 'I know you've got the money so don't fuck me about, otherwise I will enjoy the consequences. You will get it as soon as they open. In fifties, and take it home. I'll call you with your next instructions.'

'But ...'

'Just...do it.' he shouted. She held the phone away from her ear. When she put it back, he'd hung up.

Larry was on his second pint. *'just had a call, he wants half a million. Do I call the bank now?'* Liz texted.

'Can you raise half a million?'

'Yes' she texted back.

'Then ring.' He could see the smile that crossed his face reflected in the mirror, magnified through the bottom of his glass as he drained it.

'Wow.' he gasped, slamming the empty glass on the bar. What he could do with five hundred thousand pounds; that was ten times more than his pension. He knew the Reynolds' had a penny or two, but he never knew they were able to lay their hands on that kind of cash. Well there was an old Yorkshire saying: *Where there's muck there's brass.* Liz Reynolds was looking more attractive to him by the minute. He'd have it all sorted before he went on holiday. His mobile home was booked and Larry was more than ready for a break this year, out of the country. 'Maybe she'd like to come along,' he mused.

The pub was getting busy and he decided it was time to move on. There was a CID course at training school, so he thought he'd have a drive over and see if any would-be detectives felt like buying him a drink. If he got lucky he could always blag a room for the night, or use Dylan's old one now he was living permanently with Ms Jennifer Jones from the admin office. He'd cajole the reception staff into letting him in, no problem.

Dylan drove to the Armitage Arms. Larry had long gone, if it had been him? For now he would give him the benefit of the doubt. Jen was impressed when she heard Dylan's key in the front door; he was on time for once. He'd no cover with all his DSs out of action, so although there was a high risk of a call-out, at least for the time being he was home; and she knew he would have a warm meal inside him tonight.

'Did you catch Larry, Jack, or was he only there for a swift one?' she said as he walked in the kitchen. Max fussed around Jack's feet.

'If it was him, Jen,' he said, putting his arms around her and resting his chin on her shoulder, as she stirred the liquid in the pan. The delicious smell of soup was overwhelming as it reminded him of his childhood and his mother's kitchen. He sneakily reached from behind her, grabbed a homemade warm bread roll from the basket and dipped it into the liquid.

'Hey you.' she tapped his hand. 'It was him. What about poor Fred? He's gravely ill it says on the news. What an awful thing to happen to such a lovely chap. Just tell me how anyone could knock someone down and flee like that?'

That night they snuggled up on the sofa. Pretty Woman was on TV, for what seemed like the zillionth time to Dylan. Jen never tired of it. Dylan watched her lovingly as she tilted her head and smiled at the screen, playing each of the actor's parts, in her head. Her long blonde hair caught the light from the lamp, and it shone. Her skin looked peachy soft and beautiful, almost glowing in the firelight. He felt for her hand as she savoured her favourite moments and Dylan knew, as always, she would cry at the end; this time just as the phone rang.

'Sod's law.' Dylan said, raising his arm. Jen sat up to blow her nose on the hankie he'd struggled to extract from his trouser pocket.

'Good evening, sir. It's the duty officer at force control.'

'Where am I going?' he said, reaching for a pen and paper from the coffee table.

'Nowhere sir. I've been asked by the Deputy Chief to inform you of the arrest of one of your officers.'

'Who?' asked Dylan, startled.

'DS Larry Banks.'

Dylan's jaw dropped. Jen looked at him puzzled. It wasn't Jack's usual expression when he got a call-out. Her tears quickly halted. She blew her nose noisily.

'You still there, sir?'

'Yes' he said quietly, staring into Jen's eyes, and for once, he was lost for words. 'What the hell's happened?'

'He was arrested for drink-driving and failing to stop, as well as driving off from an injury accident, just before lunchtime today. An eighty-two year old man, by the name of Fred White, is seriously ill in hospital.'

'You've taken the wind out of my sails. I mean he went to the dentist and then I sent him home, but my other half did say she'd seen him...and ...'

'His car is damaged and has been impounded for further examinations. We have a witness who saw it leaving the pub car park where the accident occurred. At this time he's about four times over the legal limit, so he'll be staying in custody overnight. That's about all I can tell you at the moment.'

'I understand...thank you,' Dylan said, as he slowly replaced the receiver. He shook his head and lay back on the settee's cushions, closing his eyes. He sighed. Jen sat on the edge of the sofa and looked at him, waiting patiently for an explanation.

'Larry, the stupid, stupid man has gone and got himself locked up for OPL.'

'Driving over the limit, you can't tell me that's a surprise Jack?'

'Not only drinking and driving but he's the one who knocked down Fred White.'

Jen shook her head sadly.

'I believed him,' he said.

'And what else has he been lying to you about, if he can lie about something like that?'

'I don't know but I'll bloody well find out. If I'm completely honest with you, I knew he had a drink problem and I didn't do anything about it. I was too wrapped up...He'll lose his job and his pension and I'll be served with forms for failing to supervise. The press will 'ave a field day. What a nightmare.'

'For heaven's sake, Jack. If you must worry, worry about Fred lying in hospital, and his wife and family. Not that bloody idiot. He might have killed...Larry's only himself to blame...I've no flaming sympathy for him,' she said, standing up briskly. 'Do you want a drink?' she snapped, her hand on the doorknob of the lounge door. Dylan stared passed her.

'He might get help now.'

'Help? And he might have killed Fred, so the help he needs might be time inside.'

Jack said nothing.

'He could have stopped, tried to help Fred, Jack. But he went for yet another drink, I saw him. I told you I did. Do you want to blame yourself for everybody's mistakes? Does that make you feel better? Jesus Christ, he ran somebody over who might yet die,' she shouted.

Jen managed to hold back the tears as she opened the door and marched to the kitchen. Memories of the phone call to notify her of her mother's accident, all too raw. Dylan followed her.

'I know. I know what you're saying. I'm sorry love, but maybe I could've prevented it all from happening. I was gonna talk to him today about his behaviour, but he looked in so much pain. So I thought it would keep.'

With tear filled eyes, Jen reached into the cupboard for the mugs. Dylan leaned on the breakfast bar opposite her and reached out his hand for hers. The kettle whistled as she brushed the top of his head with her hand and leaned forward for a kiss, not bothering to wipe away the tears that ran down her face. She knew no matter what she said, he'd have a restless night until he'd spoken to Larry.

'I trusted him Jen, like I trust all my officers. He used to be so dedicated. Where...when did it all go wrong?' His stomach churned. He pushed aside a piece of Jen's homemade parkin that she offered him and she tutted.

'It's not your fault, Jack. Put it to bed, 'till tomorrow at least, and pray for Fred; that would be more use than worrying about bloody Larry.'

Dylan hung his head.

'He conned you as well as everyone else, and he's old enough and big enough to know what he's doing. Please let's just go to bed and see what tomorrow brings.'

Jack ate his porridge in silence the next morning, and Jen knew only too well how much he'd tossed and turned.

'Hindsight's a wonderful thing love,' she said as she kissed him goodbye. 'Keep in touch, eh?' He smiled, but had a look of distraction.

'What a dismal start to the day,' Dylan thought, as he drove into the yard at Harrowfield. It could only get better though. He sighed as he extracted his briefcase from the boot and went into the office. The rumours he'd heard about Larry were exaggerated; Chinese whispers, surely? Talking to the Custody Sergeant, Dylan found out Larry at six fifteen a.m had been bailed after a further breathalyser test showed that he was no longer over the prescribed legal limit. He desperately needed to speak to him. Larry had hit rock bottom, Dylan was concerned for his welfare but it was also now out of his hands. He tried his mobile, fully expecting him to have it turned off, but surprisingly, he got an instant response to his call, in the form of a text.

'*Sorry Boss. Don't worry. I'm okay.*'

'*Sure?*' Dylan texted back.

'*Just give me a few days to get my head round things. I'll call you.*'

Larry knew his clock was ticking; time was running out. It was going to be goodbye to any pension. He poured himself a vodka. His own car impounded, he flipped through the phone book trying to find a place to hire one. He wasn't banned yet; he could hire a car and get the camper van delivered for his holidays, before he was. He just needed to decide what to do then.

Dylan sat studying staffing at sergeant level. The job had to go on and he'd have to check with HQ personnel to see who was on the list. There was a knock at the door and as it opened slowly, he saw Dawn struggling with two steaming cups of coffee.

'Come on in, you've just made my day.' He said, as he smiled at her warmly. Dawn looked pale and drawn; in fact, rather green around the gills. She put the coffee on his desk and after closing the door she sat down opposite him.

'Dawn?'

'I need to tell you something...in confidence.' She looked down at the floor, holding her cup with one hand and stroking it with the other.

'Are you okay?'

She looked up, tears in her eyes. 'I'm pregnant.'

Dylan breathed a sigh of relief, 'Dawn, for goodness sake that's wonderful news. I bet you and Ralph are over the moon,' he said smiling.

'Well yeah...but no one thought to warn me about how bad morning sickness is,' she said

Dylan chuckled.

'It's not funny. I'm told it can last for sixteen weeks. Sixteen...bloody...weeks.'

Dylan couldn't contain his laughter; it lifted him but he realised how much he'd miss her.

'You may laugh but I've tried everything from standing on my head to the BRATT diet.'

Dylan's eyebrows rose as he sniggered. 'The what?'

'Bananas, rice, apple sauce, toast, tea, and cabbage, ginger nuts and crackers, but nothing seems to be working. Oh, I wasn't going to tell anyone. I don't want it to change the job I'm doing, but as you can see, I'm wrecked.' she said, splaying her arms.

Dylan looked thoughtful his face full of concern. 'Well now you have told me there's no turning back, you do realise don't you? My hands are tied; your role has got to change. I'm sorry but I can't 'ave you doing anything that would jeopardize yours or the baby's health...you do understand?'

'I know, but Jack,' she pleaded.

'No buts, Dawn. I know you'll hate me for it but I can't 'ave it on my conscience. If anything happened . . .' Dawn's chin dropped to her chest sulkily and he tried to lighten the mood.

'So how many weeks are you then?'

'Thirteen, I think.'

'So, it could go on for another two weeks? When do you go for the scan? Or 'ave you 'ad one?' His interest was genuine and excitement rose in his voice.

'I'm booked in at the antenatal clinic next week, so I should know more when I've been. Even so, I'd rather people didn't know just yet, if that's okay with you.'

'Well, let's just think about that one, Dawn. I've got an office full of detectives; a building full of police officers...you're throwing up in the morning. Don't you think they might just guess at some point? You can't carry on doing what you've been doing either...so it might just be easier if you told them.'

Dawn frowned.

'Look, I might 'ave a solution that'll be right up your street,' he said smiling.

Dawn scowled. 'I'm all ears.'

'What about Acting DI in charge of Child Protection?'

She lifted her head and stared at him, disbelieving.

'This must be serendipity. Believe it or not I've just had a call from Harriet, and she's off on maternity leave in a week, which would give you chance to shadow her before you take over. Deal?' he said grinning, obviously thrilled with himself.

'That would be fantastic.' Her face beamed. I was dreading you putting me in the control room.'

'Well, at least this way you'll still be operationally involved but you won't, and I repeat you won't - be involved in any arrests or enquiries where you could pick up something nasty or get injured. Right?'

'Yes sir.' Dawn nodded, still wide-eyed with surprise.

'You've got to look after number one and two now. Child Protection is busy, and it's good lateral development for when you go for the DI boards in the future. Or are you going to shock us all and become a full-time mum?' Dylan said.

'Heavens, no. We haven't thought that far ahead. I'm just concentrating on getting through one day at a time at the moment.' Dawn felt in her pocket, and produced, not only a beautiful embroidered hankie to dab her mouth with but a half - eaten packet of arrowroot biscuits. She took the one off the top, blew it and offered one to Dylan from the pack.

'Are you sure this is not just a good excuse for eating biscuits Dawn?' He took one, smiling.

'I wish it bloody was. Do you really think they'd be plain ones?' she said grimacing.

''Ave you heard what happened to Larry?' Dylan said looking sombre.

'Yeah, it's sad but why aren't I surprised?' she said, absentmindedly trying to fish a half dunked biscuit out of her cup with a spoon. 'He was always an accident waiting to happen with his drinking habit, all his own doing, no self-control, no sympathy.' She gave up and stirred it in. 'How's the elderly gentleman doing?'

'Fractured hip, a bit like Jen's mum. It's not good.'

'Poor Jen, it must have brought it all back.'

Dylan nodded. 'You know Larry lied to me. He told me he was going to the dentist, and when he came back holding a hanky over his mouth, he said he'd had a tooth out. How gullible was I to believe that?'

'If you can't trust your own team Jack, who can you trust?' she said. She stood, lifting his empty cup off his desk.

'Well at least you're sorted, Dawn. I'll just 'ave to square it with personnel, but there should be no problem. Does Ralph realise all the problems he's caused?' he said, teasing her.

Dawn's smile was broad and her eyes danced happily.

'I know you don't want people to know, but best get it over with, eh?' he said, screwing up his nose. 'Can I tell Jen? She'll be thrilled.'

'Yeah sure,' she said.

'Would you two like kids one day?'

'I'll tell you a secret, Dawn. I'd love 'em, but it's not fair to any woman, especially Jen. I'm married to my job,' he said.

'Thanks Jack.' she beamed at him as she left.

Dylan's smile soon left his face. He needed a replacement for Larry and Dawn now, and as soon as possible. 'Trying to get through to the personnel department often took longer than reaching call centres abroad he thought,' as he drummed his fingers impatiently on his desk and listened to the persistent ringing.

It was better than the constant interruption of, *'your call is important to us, please hold the line…'* though he conceded.

Oh, he hated the music too. The best recorded message he'd come across on an answer machine had been for the Underwater Search Team the noise being the sound of bubbling water, and then the 'glug' of a voice saying all the officers were out of the office at the moment. After the sound of the bubbles someone said, 'please leave your message'. The 'hierarchy' had made them remove it pretty damn sharpish.

'About time,' Dylan muttered, as someone eventually picked up the phone.

'Lucy Kate, personnel.' The voice sounded high pitched and agitated.

'DI Dylan, Harrowfield,' he said brightly, and quickly explained the predicament he was in and the urgency of the situation.

He couldn't believe it: only one person on the list selected for Detective Sergeant. Dylan groaned loudly, resting his elbow on the desk and his head in his hand. Not only was it probably someone no one else wanted, as they were still on the list but he also needed two sergeants. It was no good, he'd have to get involved in promotion boards for CID. This wasn't a good situation to be in for the Force.

Lucy agreed to Dawn's move to Child Protection; she fitted the criteria for Force Regulations and therefore there was no need for Harriet's post to be advertised. Dylan felt a flood of relief, the deal, however, was that he would take the uniformed sergeant on the list.

Dylan agreed, cringing as he did so.

'Go on who is it?' Dylan said, closing his eyes and holding his breath.

Chapter Eight

'What did five hundred grand look like? How would she carry it? Would her weekend suitcase with the wheels be big enough? It would look less suspicious than a holdall.' Liz was thinking, as her phone vibrated in her pocket.

'I'm worried about you being on your own with all that money overnight. What if he turns up?' Larry's text read. 'Oh, God she hadn't thought of that.' *Do you want me to stay over? I could photograph and mark the money at the same time, which will prove it's yours.'*

Liz hesitated. Did she really want Larry staying? She'd arranged for Gemma to be collected from school by her gran and gramps and have a sleepover, so at least she knew she'd be okay. What had she got to lose; there was nothing stopping the blackmailer turning up at the house like Larry said, and if he did she would at least have some support at hand.

'Okay, whatever you think best. I'll leave a key in the gas meter cupboard, on the wall out front. Let yourself in when I've left for the bank'. She was secretly pleased she wasn't going to be on her own.

Her trembling fingers fumbled with the big yellow plastic key, as she crouched on her haunches to see the keyhole of the gas cupboard.

'Argh.' Liz moaned as pain seared through her finger. She cursed under her breath as, in the shingle at her feet, she saw a perfectly painted acrylic nail that had pinged off. She picked it up and held it in her pained hand. Tears sprung in her eyes. She went down on her knees as she heard a crunch behind her on the gravel. Not daring to turn, she felt the hairs rise on the back of the neck. She listened. The key fell to the floor as the cupboard door silently flew back.

'You okay Mrs Reynolds?' said the postman, who towered over her as he held out a pile of junk mail. 'I thought I heard you shout.'

Liz swallowed hard as she closed her eyes tight. A wave of nausea and a hot flush ran through her body. 'I'm fine, just fine,' said Liz, her heart in her mouth. 'I've just broken a nail,' she said, as she stood up and offered the postman her hand, which displayed her own nail, which was lifted slightly and bleeding under the nail bed. He took it in his.

'It's not going blue, I'm sure you'll live,' he said, kindly.

'But, you're as white as a ghost and shaking like a leaf. You sure you're okay? Can I get you a drink of water?' he said, holding her by the elbow and guiding her to the bench beside the front door.

'No I'm fine, honestly.' She smiled, reassuringly taking her mail from him.

'Well, if you're certain,' he said as he retreated down the driveway backwards, unconvinced by her reply.

Twenty minutes later, nail stuck back on, door key in the cupboard and case on the doorstep, she locked the front door. Liz couldn't count how many times she'd struggled with the very same case, bulging with clothes, when she was going on holiday, as she threw it, empty, into the boot of the car. But this was no holiday. She checked in her bag for her passport and ID for the bank, as she paused at her open car door. The blackmailer thought how very lovely she looked in her designer, beige, two-piece suit. She locked the doors immediately, although she was sure no one was watching her, and with butterflies in her stomach, she set off.

A warm blast of air emerged from the bank as she walked through the doors but as she strolled through the foyer, a welcome rush of air conditioning blew in her face, sweeping her hair up from her sweating neck. She headed for the sign saying customer services that hung above a desk, pulling the suitcase behind her. Liz was sure people could hear the blood pumping through her veins. She could feel it gushing through her heart and hammering in her chest. The noises in the bank echoed as if the room was a hollow capsule and although her trolley glided silently across the floor, the heels of her shoes clicked on the marble. She licked her perfectly pouted lips and brushed away the sweat beads that she could feel appearing on her eyebrows; glad for her Estee Lauder Double Wear stay-in-place make-up. Moments later she was in the manager's office. It was a great relief when she was told that Mr Beckwith was away for the day on a course, but had left the paperwork ready for her to sign. She sat staring at the money as if in a trance, as it was counted and placed into her suitcase. The deputy manager was a young man, fussing over a lady who could afford to draw £500,000 from the bank in cash.

'Security – wise, are you okay Mrs Reynolds?' he asked.

'Yes, thank you,' she said. 'I have an escort outside.'

All he needed was three signatures and the deed was done.

Liz had never been so happy to see a traffic warden at her car in her life as she emerged from the bank. The sight of the uniform settled her nerves, as she unlocked the boot with the loud beep of her remote key, which flashed the car's lights, making the warden flinch.

'Nice car, lady,' he said, resting his hand upon the roof.

'Thank you,' she said coyly, as he moved towards her to help her lift the cash laden case. She suddenly had the notion he might be the blackmailer; she hadn't got a ticket, there was no mention of yellow lines, - was he protecting his money?

'Wouldn't mind one of these myself,' he said, stroking the paintwork of the car lovingly. 'But on my wages I'll be a long time waiting.' He grinned a toothless smile, as he tapped the top of the closed boot and walked on.

Sitting in the driver's seat with the doors locked, she sighed with relief. She looked round, was he still watching? She had the notion someone was, but from where she had no idea. 'Larry hadn't mentioned he'd have a tail on me but surely he would have,' she thought as she feverishly glanced in her mirror. Whoever the blackmailer was he could have the bloody money; good riddance, as long as he left them alone. Fleetingly she worried she'd have no option but to tell Malcolm on her next visit. He would go mental, but the wardens would be there, so she knew he couldn't hurt her, and right now the blackmailer could.

At this moment in time Malcolm was definitely the lesser of two evils, she shuddered.

Liz pulled onto the driveway, slowly scanning her garden, but nothing seemed untoward. Stopping the car as near to the front door as possible, she turned off the engine. In the comfort and security of the locked car she sat still, craning her neck to see if there was any sign of life inside the house, but there were no twitches of curtains or a face at the window. If Larry was inside, thankfully he was keeping out of sight. She climbed out of the car, walked quickly round to open the boot, and struggled to lift out the case. Slamming the boot shut with one hand and pulling the case handle out with the other she took quick, short steps to the front door.

Liz leaned the small of her back against the inside of the bolted door. She was shaking, but a warm flood of relief washed over her. She closed her eyes, putting her hand to her mouth. Thank God that was over. Her phone beeped, the text said, 'Bring the case to the bedroom.'

What did he think she was? she thought to herself, as she fought to drag it up the stairs.

Larry was sprawled out on the bed, a large holdall by his side. He didn't know if she was being watched but he was gambling that the blackmailer was only following her enough to make sure his demands were met, and today wasn't one of those days. Blackmailers, in Larry's experience, used the fear factor. He wasn't too concerned but wouldn't be stupid either: he was prepared for every eventuality.

'Don't worry,' he said grinning, as he saw the look on her face. 'I'm not moving in. It's just some gear to enable me to mark and photograph the money in case he gets away with it.'

'He won't, will he?'

'Oh no, will he heck. So for God's sake smile, woman. Blackmailing goes on all the time.'

Liz managed a nervous grin in spite of the situation. She hadn't thought of that. 'Are you gonna mark it now?' she said, reaching for the zip.

'Later,' he said, reaching for her hand and pulling her towards him.

'Look, you're doing really well,' he said.

'Am I?'

'Yeah, and hopefully the money will be back in the account before you know it,' he said, as he nuzzled her hair. 'You'll be able to tell Mr bank manager that you didn't need it after all. He's not going to mind now, is he? Women change their minds all the time don't they?'

'Oh Larry, do you really think so? Just think no more threats.' She sighed into his chest; at least she had someone to share the burden with. 'I'm so frightened.'

His hands started to wander from her waist to her bottom. She pushed him away gently, the last thing she wanted to do was upset him.

'I'm starving, aren't you?' she called, her voice sounding more cheery than she felt, as she made her way towards the stairs. 'I haven't managed to eat yet today. Do you want anything?' It was true, she was feeling light headed. Yes, it was an excuse to get away from his clutches, but she knew she was only stalling the inevitable and before that she needed a drink.

Larry wasn't in a hurry; he knew he had all night.

'A sandwich would be nice. Tell you what I could do with though...a drink,' he said, strolling down the stairs, passing the windows with a cautionary glance.

'Coffee, tea?' she said, getting the bread out of the breadbin.

'Anything stronger, a beer?' he said, popping his head around the kitchen door.

'Thanks Larry. I mean it,' she said, as she took a can from the fridge and walked over to him. She took a gulp of white wine. 'I'm really grateful. I don't know what I'd have done without you.'

'What're friends for eh?' he said, slapping her backside gently. She cringed.

Larry was tempted to open the case and have a look at the money.

'Five hundred grand, five hundred grand,' he whispered. As he sat down on the bed he noticed that the light had began to fail. A slither of lamp light shone directly on the case, from the landing, through the doorway. Liz walked in with a tray of sandwiches, more cans and a bottle of wine. She placed the tray on the bed between them and took off her jacket. The white blouse beneath moulded to her body.

Larry gulped his beer from the can. He wasn't particularly listening as Liz talked; he had other things on his mind. Was she wearing stockings? She always used to. Occasionally he gave her a sympathetic nod and grunt as she chatted away. He decided; he wouldn't invite her on his holiday; she talked too much.

'I don't remember you being such a good listener,' Liz said, as she refilled her glass. They'd had the most amazing sex in the past, she recalled, pulling herself closer to him. In her drink induced fuzzy haze, he looked decidedly handsome. Confusingly, he didn't respond to her advances though, and she was still sober enough to feel clumsy and foolish. But it was just Larry's game.

'Can I get you anything else?'

'Pass me another can.' He kicked off his shoes and eased himself up onto the pillows. He would make her wait just a short while longer, and then he knew she'd be gagging for it. He might as well enjoy himself. After all, he was doing her a big favour, he thought, as he watched her totter out of the room in her stocking feet.

Giggling, Liz stumbled back into the bedroom from the ensuite. The wine had undoubtedly gone straight to her head.

'Having a nap, eh?' she slurred.

'No...thought I'd make myself comfy. It's gonna be a long night.'

'You're right,' she said nonchalantly, sitting on the foot of the bed and rubbing his bare feet. He could feel the sexual tension between them.

'You could always come up here,' he patted the bed beside him. 'Can't promise I'd behave though,' he said.

'I just think I might do that. Sitting on the edge of the bed gives me backache' she said, stretching. 'Move over.' She finished her wine and placed the glass on the bedside cabinet.

They lay next to each other, silently looking up at the ceiling. 'It wasn't as if they were strangers to each other was it,' she thought. But then again, it had been a while. Liz's skirt rose up her leg as she bent her knees and the slit in the side showed off her suspenders in all their glory. Not one for missing opportunities, Larry propped himself up on his elbow and looked down at her face. Her smile was the only invitation he needed to find her lips, and his hand crept between her legs and rested at the top of her stockings. Within seconds they were both naked, clawing, biting and scratching each other's bodies, as if punishing each other for the situation they found themselves in.

'I didn't realise how much I needed that,' panted Liz, as she touched her damp brow with the back of her hand. They'd both used each other, there was no doubt. Was it the alcohol or the circumstances? Neither of them knew. What they did know was that it was pure lust, and for an instant Liz hadn't thought about the blackmail. Tears stung hot in Liz's eyes and ran down the sides of her face, wetting her ears and running onto the pillow.

'I feel so guilty now, I should be thinking about Gemma.'

'Don't beat yourself up. You've done nothing wrong,' he said, leaning over and grabbing another can.

The phone rang and Liz's face froze. She lifted the receiver, sighing with relief as she heard Gemma chatter on gaily. About school, Gran had made her jelly, they were going to watch a DVD with Gramps when she was ready for bed.

'After the past few days you needed some comfort,' Larry said, when she'd said goodbye and blew kisses down the phone to her daughter.

'Maybe,' she said, trying to snuggle up close to him; but the moment had passed.

'I really do need a shower,' she said, rolling off the bed and stumbling to her feet. Larry swigged his beer, nonchalantly.

Her absence gave him the perfect opportunity to take a coveted look. His eyes nearly fell out of his head as he stared at the wads notes. He was stunned; he'd never seen so many fifty pound notes. Hearing the shower stop, he closed the case slowly and quietly tiptoed back to the bed. She didn't return to the bedroom immediately.

With her hair wrapped in a towel and wearing a soft towelling dressing gown, she toured the house, checking all the curtains were closed properly before switching on the lamps.

She decided she'd leave the lights on all night. In the kitchen she drew the blind and started to prepare pasta. She was still hungry and she was sure Larry wouldn't say no to some hot food. She could hear the shower and wondered about the sleeping arrangements. Should she sleep with him? It made no difference now. What would tomorrow bring? She hoped and prayed for an end to it all.

Refreshed and wearing Malcolm's dressing gown, Larry checked all the curtains were drawn, before he ventured through the hallway and into the kitchen. He watched Liz opening another bottle of wine.

'Not for me thanks, I need to keep a clear head and I'll have to get started on photographing the money.'

'Please yourself,' she replied with a shrug, swaying slightly. 'I need it for my nerves, purely medicinal. If it's okay with you I'll probably go up and watch TV in my room after dinner. You okay using the back bedroom?'

'No probs.' Larry was ecstatic. He'd decided what he was going to do. There was no need to mark or photograph the money, and this way he didn't need to waste his time keeping up the pretence.

Liz was tucked up in her bedroom, her television loud enough for the street to hear, and she was still drinking. Larry placed his camera on the floor for authenticity if she should come in, removed the old law books he'd brought with him in his holdall and started to replace them with the money. He put the money to his cheek and ran it under his nostrils, smelling the crisp, clean notes. He took a wad and put it in his wallet. Covering the cash with a change of clothes, he zipped up the holdall. He then placed the books in the case; he wasn't going to need them where he was going. Sweat bubbled on his brow, and ran down the side of his face. He wiped it with the back of his hand. Once the contents had been switched, he lifted the holdall and the case. The case felt a bit heavier, but she wouldn't be any wiser.

'Cheers Liz, cheers Mal,' he whispered, as he raised another can to his lips and drained the contents. He walked back along the landing to the main bedroom where Liz was laying down; the flickering light from the TV shone on her body and from the doorway and he could see her clutching the neck of the wine bottle beside her. She was asleep. A glass full of wine sat on her bedside table. He picked it up, surveyed her semi-naked frame and gulped the bitter liquid from her glass. He shivered. Slowly he took off the dressing gown and he laid on top of her, entering her body whilst she lay in a drunken stupor. He wasn't concerned about her, he was just satisfying himself; he could do anything he wanted now. Spent and satisfied, he flopped beside her on the bed. He'd set the alarm on his mobile for four thirty a.m. and pulled the duvet up over him. He needed to be away early. He didn't need Liz anymore, in fact he didn't need anyone.

Chapter Nine

'What the?' Larry's mobile beeped, insistent of attention. He pulled himself unwillingly from his slumber. The TV was the only source of light in the darkened room but it was bright enough for him to see.

He raised himself onto his elbow and turned off the alarm.

'What time is it?' Liz mumbled in sleepy confusion; her head pounded as if a pneumatic drill was drilling inside. Her body ached, feeling battered, bruised and sore. She tried to moisten her lips with her tongue, and wiped the saliva from the side of her mouth.

'It's early,' Larry said, flopping back onto the pillow. He stared, wide eyed, silent for a moment, watching the patterns the TV's light made on the ceiling. 'I've set a dye capsule inside the case, so whatever you do, don't open it.'

'Why should I open it?' she said, turning to face him, lines furrowing her brow.

'Well, just in case he asks you to transfer it to his bag. The blackmailer won't know about the capsule, but let's say he'll struggle to use any of the money after he's opened the case.' Larry held his breath, waiting for her reaction. Had she bought his lie?

He needn't have worried; it took Liz all her time to focus on moving her body, let alone think straight. Using the mattress for support, she levered herself from the bed and hobbled unsteadily to the bathroom.

'I'll leave before it gets light,' Larry said. 'You must text me as soon as he rings you with your instructions. We'll have this all sorted today, don't worry.' Not getting a response, he jumped out of bed, sneaked up behind her and grabbed her round her waist as she brushed her teeth. 'I'll be back for my thank-you's' later.' He leered at her in the mirror. She spat out the toothpaste and, holding onto the sink, she closely inspected her swollen lips in the mirror. Her eye ball ached. How'd she got those bruises, she wondered, as she gently touched her face?

Thirty minutes later, Larry picked up his holdall. He had no intention of letting it out of his sight from now on. Draining his coffee cup as he stood at the breakfast bar in the kitchen, his heart beat fast as he shouted his goodbye. Was it the caffeine that caused the palpitations or the excitement?

The suitcase was stood at the bottom of the stairs. Liz could see it from the gallery landing. She headed for the shower. The water was hot, powerful and searching as it pierced every pore of her body. She let the force hammer her aching bones and sensitive skin as she washed herself in the moisture rich foam. The water rinsed away the suds and in the bright light she could see the red marks that were prominent on her skin. Towelling her hair, she tried to erase the heavy ache inside.

Larry returned the hire car, putting the keys through the garage letterbox. It was a brisk mile walk to his flat, but he felt as if he was walking on air. The streets were still and he could hear the odd bird sing out its morning call. The town was quiet; most people were still tucked up in their beds. Outside his flat, the mobile home looked huge as he turned the corner into the courtyard, but it was the latest edition of the one he usually hired: a Carloca four berth that had GPS navigation. 'Freedom' he whispered and whistled quietly to himself. Larry secreted the money around the van. He realised he was now in charge of his own destiny and financially he was sound. His first call was to the petrol station to fill up his 'wheels' to the brim. Then he would head for Dover and the P&O ferry to Calais. He wanted a drink to calm his jangling nerves but he'd wait until he boarded. Nothing was going to stop him now. This was his chance to start over and he wasn't going to blow it.

At the petrol station he went straight to the pump. The only other driver on the forecourt was a lady with a Spaniel in the rear of her car that caught his eye as it poked its nose out through the partially opened window, sniffing frenziedly. Its tail wagged frantically. Larry nodded.

'Nice dog.'

'Better than some people,' came the tardy reply. Larry couldn't argue with that as he swaggered to the kiosk to pay with a crisp, clean, fifty pound note.

The lady watched Larry walk into the garage. Hadn't she seen him before somewhere?

Minutes later he was on the M1 south, foot to the floor, humming to the radio, eager to reach the port. The onboard Club Lounge beckoned him for his first stiff drink of the day.

At ten minutes to nine, dressed in a towelling leisure suit and slipper boots, Liz sat on a stool at the breakfast bar watching the telephone and willing it to ring. She tapped her beautifully manicured false nail on the worktop, the other nine now non-existent. She inspected it closely and proceeded to peel it absent-mindedly from its bed. Her scalp hurt where she had unconsciously pulled her hair by its roots; her nerves were undoubtedly shot. She glared at the phone. Part of her was terrified that it would ring, and the other part wanted it to do so. Every now and then she looked at the clock. Her eyes hung on the dials, which didn't appear to move. She stroked the bruises on her arm that had started to turn blue. Pressing them made her wince. Had Larry taken advantage of her or had she dreamt it? She drummed the work surface. Usually her nails made a tapping sound but now, instead her finger ends made a beating noise on the wood, she noticed.

The phone rang and she jumped, it was exactly one minute past nine. Her heart leapt into her mouth. It began thumping, faster, faster as if it was going to race right out of control. Her breathing was erratic; her hands shook as she lifted the receiver and inhaled a gulp of air.

'Hello,' she said. She felt a damp patch appear under her arms. Liz didn't recognise her own voice.

'You've got what I asked for?' the caller snapped.

'Yes. I've got it. It's here. Please, I just want it to be over.'

'Then don't fuck me about.'

'I'm not, I won't, I...I...I wouldn't, please... just don't hurt us. I've done everything you've asked. I promise. . .'

'Listen.'

'Yes.'

'St Peter's Park. The bottom car park, one o'clock. Park at the far end near the woods. Have the money on the passenger seat and the passenger door unlocked. Have you got that?'

'Yes, yes I know where that is.'

'Oh, I know you do,' he sniggered. 'Sit in your car, engine off. If you're followed or I see anyone or anything that looks like the old bill sniffing around, you're dead. Do I make myself clear?' The dialling tone rang in her ear.

A wrong move and she was dead. Thank the Lord she'd confided in Larry. She could hardly pick up her mobile. All fingers and thumbs she was thankful for predictive text. Breathe, or you'll faint, she reminded herself. Swaying, she bent over and leaned on the work surface. Breathing in fiercely through her nose and out through her mouth, to the count of six, she put her head between her knees. She could feel the blood running to her head as she struggled to finish typing the message.

Larry's phone vibrated; he'd check it when he stopped at the services. Things could wait, everything could wait; nothing was more important than catching the ferry. A sign at the side of the road read, **'NEXT SERVICES 20 MILES'.** That would do him nicely.

Twenty minutes later he was sitting waiting for a full English breakfast when his phone rang: the estate agent, what did they want?

'Mr Banks?'

'Yeah,' he drawled, smiling at the young waitress who brought him his pot of tea and toast.

'As instructed we've managed to rent the room in your flat to a student who is studying at Harrowfield University.' Larry listened absentmindedly as the waitress hovered around the table with the condiments.

'Mr Blake's parents will pay in advance to the end of the academic year, so you won't have any problem getting your asking fee.'

'Full amount?'

'Yes. Mr Blake is leaving home for the first time, although he's not keen, so they're insistent that he's got somewhere decent to stay, and with your police background, they think you will be an excellent role model.'

Larry stifled a laugh.

'Of course, good call.' Larry beamed at the waitress as she bent over to clear the table next to him.

'Thank you Mr Banks, we'll deal with the paperwork and give him the key, since you're going away, aren't you?'

'Yeah, I'm on my way now as it happens, thank you.'

Larry sighed contentedly as he put the phone down and looked out of the café window. When the contract was finished he'd instruct the estate agents to sell the flat for him. He'd make a new start, abroad.

'Someone looks as if they've just won the pools,' said the waitress, as she put a plate of eggs and bacon in front of him.

'Mmm, sommat like that.' The salt he threw over his breakfast spilled all over the table and the young waitress picked up a pinch and threw it over her shoulder.

'That's for good luck according to my Nan,' she said to him as he raised his eyebrows at her.

'Tell you what, it could be your lucky day too. How about coming with me and I'll show you the world,' he said, pointing to his mobile home in the car park.

'Sorry mister, I've got a boyfriend who might not be too happy if I took you up on that,' she said, nodding towards a scruffy young man putting money in a slot machine beside the counter.

Larry smiled. 'Your loss little lady, your loss,' he sniggered as he picked up his mobile phone to read the message shown.

'He's called. I've got to meet him in St Peter's Park at one o'clock. Where are you?'

Liz paced back and forth. Where the hell was Larry?

'Don't panic, everything is under control. We'll be watching and waiting. Did he say anything else?' Larry texted back, as he gulped the tea from his mug.

'Yes, to have the money on the passenger seat and make sure the door is unlocked.'

'Good. He's most likely going to try to snatch it and run. My advice is to keep your doors locked though; once he finds it locked he'll probably run away and give our team time to arrest him. It'll all be over soon.'

Larry winked at the waitress who was at the till, and turned his phone off as he mopped his plate with the toast. Yes, in a few hours he would be over the water. Larry paid with a fifty-pound note.

'Keep the change love.'

'You sure, mister?' she squealed. 'See, I told you throwing salt over your shoulder was lucky,' she laughed loudly waving the note in the air.

'Hey, shh...don't make such a song and dance of it kid, it's only a few quid.' Larry gasped, looking around him. The services were getting busy and to his horror, across the tables he saw a PC Hannah Jordan from the nick heading in his direction. That stupid, noisy waitress. What was she thinking, making such a spectacle. He stepped to the side, pretending to read the menu on the blackboard, waiting for the tap on his shoulder, but it never came. As he dared to glance sideways, he saw Hannah sit down at a table occupied by a man dressed in black. It was Inspector Mark Baggs. Fortunately for him they were oblivious to anyone else in the room.

Liz lay on her bed. The white linen duvet cover felt cool to the touch as she tried her best to stay calm. She waited. She'd never be able to thank Larry enough. Just knowing the police would be in the park gave her great comfort. The blackmailer's voice and threats haunted her and she shivered. Time after time se replayed the phone call in her head. St Peter's Park, she and Malcolm had done all their courting there. In fact it was where he had proposed to her, but that was years ago. She allowed herself a brief smile, despite what was happening. Oh God, how could she have such thoughts now, of all times? She'd felt safe when Malcolm was around; he was her protector, her 'man mountain'. Nothing could hurt her when he was with her. Why, oh why did he have to go and involve himself in crime? What had made him do something so bloody stupid? She sighed, and threw her legs over the side of the bed. The next few hours were going to feel like an eternity.

Having put the suitcase on the back seat of the car, and listening for the grandfather clock in the hallway to chime half past twelve, she locked the front door. Adrenalin pumped around her body, and her head buzzed. All the traffic lights seemed to be at red. She braked hard at one, making the suitcase slide forward, and with a thud it went into the back of her seat. She instinctively locked all the doors.

Larry was aboard the ferry. Upstairs in the Club Lounge he was enjoying his complimentary glass of champagne and gazing out to sea. Soon he would be in France, and as he sat in a window seat, he stared at the picture in his passport. He looked like a criminal, he thought, smiling, but then, he supposed he was. Fiddling with his mobile, he wondered about his new life. He contemplated the wonders of technology. He couldn't believe he could actually type a resignation letter to work on his phone, and headquarters in Harrowfield would receive it within minutes.

'For the attention of Police Personnel,' *his note began.* 'Due to recent events, which have caused me personal trauma, I find myself needing time to recover and regain my personal health. I am at present on leave and will be in touch in due course. Please pass my sincere apologises and kind regards to Detective Inspector Dylan. DS Larry Banks – Harrowfield CID.'

After sending it, he dropped the mobile over the side of the ferry, all too aware how easy they were to trace.

It was one o'clock as the ferry sailed from the harbour. The voice of the captain over the loudspeaker informed passengers of the safety procedures. The journey would take approximately ninety minutes. Larry raised his glass to Liz. His dinner was served.

Chapter Ten

'Go on Lucy, tell me who's left on the list?' Dylan scowled, as he waited for the name.

'A Sergeant Patrick Finch...he transferred to us from the Met. In fact he's been working in uniform over your way ever since.'

'Come again?' he enquired.

'Patrick Finch. Are you deaf?'

'No, no...that's marvellous...I thought my ears were deceiving me. He sealed a murder scene for me last year, he'll do nicely. Can I 'ave him as soon as possible.'

'Well, since we've sorted the Child Protection post out, and as long as you take Sergeant Finch, you can act up from Division in the role of DS for development purposes, as long as the Divisional Commander agrees of course.' Lucy said.

This was turning out better than Dylan could have ever hoped. He didn't need asking twice.

'Good, I'll act up John Benjamin as Temporary Detective Sergeant, please.'

'You'll need 'the nod', but I'm sure you'll sort that bit out, won't you?'

Dylan knew the Divisional Commander wouldn't pose him any problems.

'Lucy, you've been very helpful. I'll pass on my gratitude to your Supervisor.'

'Oh... thank you Inspector Dylan, I'll send it on e mail to you with the confirmation of what we've discussed this morning,' said a seemingly highly delighted Lucy. 'That's very kind. No one has ever done that before.'

'Well there is always a first time for everything, Lucy. Thank you.' Dylan smiled smugly as he replaced the receiver. Why, he wondered was Patrick Finch still on the list, what was wrong with him? Dylan looked at his personnel record on screen. Fast tracked for promotion, young and bright. No negative comments.

Dylan deliberated as he sat in his office waiting for the arrival of his two new Detective Sergeants. He'd only made one phone call, and without the usual blocks or delays, they were on their way. Would there be a catch though?

Dylan was comfortable with the seemingly very capable Sergeant Patrick Finch, and the keen and gentleman like young DC John Benjamin. Most of all he needed to be sure he could trust them after what Larry had done. By lunchtime he was able to give them the good news regarding the agreed moves within the office by personnel as well as an outline of what he described as the sad events in respect of DS Larry Banks, and the exciting news of Dawn's impending new arrival. He went through what he expected of them, the rota they would work, the on call cover and the fact that they could always call him, night and day. All he needed from them was proof that his selection had been the right one.

There were no other vehicles in the car park. Liz stopped her car near the woods. The silence was deafening. Tentatively she looked around, but there was no one to be seen. She wound down her window slightly and felt the welcome rush of a cool breeze. A siren's whine was loud and clear, the brakes of a lorry screeched nosily in the distance; all surprisingly comforting to her. She leaned over to the back seat and struggled to heave the case onto the passenger seat next to her, as she had been told. Pressing the button to unlock the passenger door, she followed the blackmailer's instructions to the letter. Then she remembered Larry telling her to keep the door locked. What should she do? She flipped the button again feeling her heart hammering in her chest as she gripped the steering wheel tight and realised her shoulders were raised, her arms rigid. Shaking her head to relieve the fuzziness within, she craned her neck to and from side to side, and it cracked loudly like a stick snapping. All was now still. Two pigeons strutted on the grass in front of the car cooing happily. She could hear the low drone of distant traffic but above that birds singing and an aircraft overhead. Liz concentrated on the new shoots on the branches of the willow tree, which dangled before her; new life. A bee hovered before her eyes. Suddenly birds took flight. A shadow fell on the windscreen. She gasped, but it was only a black cloud covering the sun, weak as it was. Her mouth grew dry as she waited; she attempted to swallow and her parched throat made her cough. She shuffled in her seat. Peering behind her through the rear window she expected to see a car approaching down the driveway. As she turned she saw, stood before her at the front of her car a man wearing a black balaclava. In what seemed like a flash he'd made his way round to the passenger door and tried the handle. She screamed. He ran to the driver's side, brandishing a weapon in the air. Without warning, there was a loud crash and her window came smashing through. She turned away and ducked instinctively as the tiny glass particles showered her.

'No, please no,' she screamed, hiding her face in her hands, 'take the money.' The man pulled at the handle and opening the door, yanked her crumpled body by the neck, from her seat to the gravel floor. Repeatedly he kicked her.

'I told you to leave the fucking doors unlocked,' he yelled, panting aggressively.

Liz was only semi-conscious as she lay motionless. She could feel warm urine run between her legs. She heard the man retrieve the case from within car and she saw its wheels bounce on the floor beside her. 'Please Larry, please help me,' came the gasp from her lips. 'Where was he?' She thought. 'The police, where were they?' She caught sight of the case springing open.

'You stupid bitch, you've tried to trick me,' the hooded man shrieked at her as he tipped the contents over her prone body. Books rained on her from above and she cried out. He lashed out at her foetus like, postured frame with the empty case.

'What? No, no please,' she cried through her sobs. The taste of blood filled her mouth and she spat it out with saliva.

Suddenly there was silence. Then Liz heard the scrunch of his shoes on gravel which made a crunching sound. He was walking away. What was happening? Was he leaving her like this? She opened her eyes and could faintly see his outline by her car, through a fuzzy haze. Her boot 'popped' open, her senses were heightened. Hearing his footsteps marching towards her, she curled up as tight as she could, sensing him standing over her. All she could see clearly was his white training shoes. Again, silence. Was he opening a bottle? She dare hardly breathe, but gasped involuntarily as cold liquid trickled over the trunk of her body. Petrol fumes engulfed her lungs. Coughs ravaged her chest. She couldn't catch her breath 'Quick.' She shouted. Her mind raced. 'Stop him.'

'Your husband won't think you're beautiful now will he Lizzie?' he sniggered. 'Banging on about you day after day he did. I looked after him you know, and for what? Nothing.' He jumped. The gravel sprayed. There was a flash, made by the ignition of the petrol. Both Liz and her car almost instantly became a fireball. Flames rushed towards him, lapping at his feet and he jumped backwards.

Frankie Miller was no stranger to murder. Money was his priority, money and drugs. He owed it, he owed lots of it and his supplier wouldn't wait any longer. Liz had been his ticket but she'd failed him. He'd warned her what would happen, the stupid bitch.

Liz's murderer ran out of the park and through the woods, to the main road, discarding his headgear to the bushes. The scorched sole of his trainer flapped annoyingly, catching on each step up the snicket. Sweat ran off him. Reaching his stolen car, he was met with pandemonium, as emergency vehicle sirens alerted his fellow road users of their presence. Moving vehicles stopped and pulled over in front of him to let them pass.

'Fucking hell.' He punched the car's console and revved the engine wildly. Yanking the steering wheel to the right, he put his foot to the floor and flew around the stationary cars, clipping the wing mirror of one. Without stopping, he glanced at the blonde woman within and flashed one angry finger.

Dazed, but with disregard for the glass that had shot into the car along with the wing mirror, Jen stared frantically at the number plate G470 RSR.

'G470 RSR. Oh, God...what was it?' she rhythmically repeated the registration number over and over in her mind, and pulling a receipt and a pen out of her bag, with shaking hands she scribbled it down. Her heart beat frantically. She scrawled over the letters to make them as clear and bold as she could. It was red; the car was red. What was the make? It was no good, she was useless with makes and models. It was big. What an idiot she thought, how dare he poke one finger at her. It was his bloody fault. Tears sprang into her eyes but she knew it was shock and anger that brought them.

Detective Sergeant Patrick Finch left Dylan's office, pleased that at last he'd not only been given a DS's post but he was also looking forward to working with Jack Dylan. He'd heard a lot about him.

'Tracy, the Detective Inspector says he would love a cuppa. I didn't know he was sexist,' he said.

'He's not, the kettles over there Sarge. I'm sure he'll enjoy a drink made by you just as much as Tracy,' Vicky said, temporarily stopping typing a report.

'Okay, worth a try though,' he laughed. 'Do you two want one?'

Vicky pushed her chair back on its wheels and stood up, 'Oh, go on, I'll make 'em Pat,' she yawned, as she stretched lazily and shook her long blonde hair. She stuck out her expansive chest. 'I don't want you upsetting the boss with your bloody awful coffee.' DS Finch wasn't looking at her face, she clocked him and smiled. Her breast enlargements were the best, she knew, thanks to the money she managed to save from working overtime, and even Patrick 'perfect' Finch as he was known in the Met, she'd been told, couldn't resist breaching his own politically correct code of conduct.

'I'd rather you call me Sergeant or Patrick,' he said.

'Whatever,' she replied, nonchalantly shrugging her shoulders.

An outside line was ringing on Dylan's phone. He was just picking it up when John tapped at his office door and entered. Dylan smiled and beckoned him to sit in the chair opposite.

'Hi Jen ...' he started, 'calm down...what on earth's happened?' Dylan said, sitting bolt upright in his chair.

'Some idiot nearly wrote me off,' Jen sobbed. 'He smashed into the wing mirror of my car and he never even stopped. He was driving like a maniac.' Jen's voice was shaking.

Dylan's mobile nearly leapt off the desk with the vibration, and it made John jump. Dylan pointed at it for John to answer.

'Boss it's a job, it's urgent,' John said, quietly.

'Look love...I've gotta go...an urgent job's just come in. As long as you're okay and the car is driveable, go home and ring the traffic office to report it...I'll ring you as soon as I can.'

'But Jack, I'm ...' Jen cried. It was no good, Dylan had hung up. His lack of empathy broke Jen's heart...what would it take for him to make her his priority?

Chapter Eleven

'Inspector Dylan,' he said, as he replaced one phone and took the mobile from John.

'Hello Sir, Force Control. Your attendance is being requested at the bottom car park of St Peter's Park. Uniform personnel and fire brigade have attended at the scene of a car on fire and they have found a woman's body nearby, they're sealing the scene. There's a strong smell of accelerants and it appears suspicious.'

'Thank you. Inform them I'm en route. I'll be approximately thirty minutes,' he said, glancing at his watch.

He stood up, grabbed his suit jacket from the back of his chair and threw it over his shoulder. 'Come on John, job on. Vicky, grab an exhibits bag and bring Tracy with you,' he called from his doorway. 'See you later Pat.'

'Sir, I'd rather be called Patrick...' Patrick Finch said, to the back of Dylan's coat tails.

'Baptism by fire, John,' Dylan said, as they screeched out of the yard. He could see John's young, large, athletic, black frame fill with nerves as he sat beside him and remembered how he'd felt on his first job as a DS, heading for an unknown death scene, whilst being under the spotlight of the boss, his every move being watched.

'Confirm with Control that the Scenes of Crime Supervisor is on their way, will you please, John?' Dylan instructed.

'Your first murder maybe, Tracy?' Vicky grinned, excitement in her voice as they drove to the scene in the CID car. 'This is what all the training's for, girl.'

'Yeah,' Tracy said holding her stomach. They whizzed past cars going in the opposite direction. Her mind was racing as their sirens wailed. What would it be like? How would she cope? Would she show herself up and be sick at the sight of the body?

'Don't look so worried love, I'll look after you,' Vicky said kindly. 'I've told you before, Dylan's a good boss. Think yourself lucky it's not one of the others.'

'Thanks,' was all Tracy could manage to say; words were no comfort. Nerves seemingly forgotten on their arrival she ran to keep up with Vicky, who was striding out as she headed towards what looked like their rendezvous point at the scene. She'd cope no matter how bad it was. Wouldn't she?

St Peter's Park was a large and rambling estate, just off the A518, which lead from Harrowfield towards its neighbouring town of Bradford, and the M62 motorway network. Although there were numerous entrances for pedestrians, there were only two means of access for vehicles; one to the Manor House and its car park at the top, and one directly to the lower car park. The acres of lawns from Sibden Manor and its fortress walls sloped down in a steep gradient to include the park, its boating lake and children's play area. Rough wooded terrain steeply sloped back up to the main road on one side. The park was well used during the summer months but in the winter dog walkers were the main occupants. In fact it was a place Dylan and Jen quite often walked Max.

A fire engine stood shrouded by trees. Its lights turned as the water pipes hung from it and snaked along the ground. The fire tender was masking the burnt shell of a vehicle, and a police car alongside. Dylan tentatively stepped into the water that had been discharged to dampen the flames. It looked like there had been a torrential downpour, 'evidence washed away'. He reached in the boot of his car and opened the packaging of a protective coverall, handing another one to John as he did so.

'You'll end up with a boot full of these John, one for every scene, don't rely on SOCO to 'ave your size, mate.'

Dylan noticed a small area around the car that had been sealed off with cones and rope, and a uniformed Inspector came towards them.

'Hello Jack,' Dylan nodded as he joined him. He turned back to the scene. 'We were called to a report of a vehicle on fire,' he explained, as Dylan, now suited up, walked beside him, John close behind. 'We arrived about the same time as the Brigade. They quickly extinguished the fire but you'll see the vehicle is just a shell, and there's a body...or what's left of it on the floor, at the driver's side. I've kept the Fire Officers here just in case you need to speak to them.'

'Good, 'ave they also pronounced life extinct because of the state of the body?'

'Yes,' the inspector replied.

'Thank-you.' Dylan raised his eyebrow at the young officer. 'We'll need their details and a copy of their report. Can you get a unit to the entrance to stop anyone coming in? I'm expecting the Scenes of Crime Supervisor. Can you also arrange for a dog man to attend?' Dylan directed. He made notes in his pocket book and noticed John doing the same. There was an overwhelming smell of fuel, and the remains of a petrol canister and a suitcase lay next to the body. 'I hope the fire officer in the cab pressed the record button to capture video footage. The recording of the route to the scene may 'ave recorded a car or a person leaving the scene that we can focus on for further enquires. We'll also need it for disclosure purposes.' Dylan called to the uniformed inspector.

With the movement of the fire engine, the devastation could be seen more clearly. Dylan squatted as close as he could to the burnt corpse, without touching it. He had always been taught to keep his hands in his pockets at a scene; that way he would never instinctively touch anything and he never broke the rule.

It was a mangled black skeleton with little flesh left on its frame. Fragments of clothing and flesh still clung to it. The jaw bone was dropped, as though the person had been screaming or shouting. The smell filled his nostrils, it was acrid, like hair burning or burning plastic. The smell of burning flesh was not a smell anyone forgot in a hurry. Dylan kept himself busy, scanning what was before him; the sight of other burned bodies etched on his mind. It never got any easier. In fact he seemed to get more sensitive, the older he got. Or was it the accumulation of tortured souls he'd witnessed. Corpses burnt or hung were always the worst for him.

'Everyone okay?' Dylan asked, sensing in the air, quiet initial shock of seeing carnage.

'Well let's just say, it's enough to put me off barbeques this summer, boss,' Vicky said, glancing back at Tracy who was grey, and held a hand to her mouth. Dylan could feel their reluctance to approach the body, and wondered if she was already regretting her attachment to CID?

The smell of petrol seemed to be diminishing, but the aroma of burnt flesh hung heavy. SOCO supervisor Phil Turnbull arrived. It was apparent to Dylan that he needed a specialist from the forensic laboratory to attend too. He would have to remind them to use specialist bags, so the inflammable liquids didn't evaporate. He wanted to know, if it was petrol, what type? Where had it been bought; a nearby garage possibly? Would there be CCTV there? A 'to do list' ran through his head.

The barking and rocking of the police dog in the van that had pulled up on the car park, told Dylan that Trojan was ready and eager to start the sweep search.

'Trevor, can you look for a trail that suggests whether anyone has been through here earlier today, please,' Dylan asked the police dog handler. A few minutes later, Trojan pulled Trevor unceremoniously into the woods, by what Dylan could only describe as a tow-rope thrown over Trevor's shoulder and around his waist. Dylan thought it was a bit like the anchorman in a tug of war being dragged along.

Thinking aloud and giving instructions to John, Dylan reeled off his thoughts.

'We'll need aerial photographs of the area if we ''aven't already got them on the database; a search team for the area once the body is moved, and we'll 'ave to consider how we lift the shell of the vehicle.' Dylan shook his head. Everything was as black as a silhouette. There were no tyres left on the car. The body was melted to the tarmac. Was it a man or a woman, he pondered? There were no visible clues. The remnants of a suitcase could be made out nearby but it was mostly ash. Dylan needed an investigation team. What sort of car was it? The fire had been so fierce it had mangled it so badly, that at the moment it didn't give any clues away. Once forensics arrived he knew they would take a closer look. His priority was to identify the deceased, the vehicle and what had taken place. Experience told him he had a murder on his hands not a suicide, and it wouldn't be long before the press descended.

'Get me a better cordon around the immediate vicinity of the park to stop all access. We need to keep this crime scene as sterile as possible,' he told John.

Waiting for his instructions to be acted upon, he texted Jen, *'How you doing, love?'*

'Speaking to 'Traffic' at the moment. They're hoping I got a current number plate.'

'Good. Sorry I had to dash, picked up a murder in St Peter's Park x I'll speak when I can x'

Jen sighed and got back to the job in hand. To Jack, her car accident was trivial and she knew it, but so soon after her mum's accident, it would have been nice for him to look out for her, just this once. Tears streamed down her face. Oh, God what did she sound like? He'd have a fit if he thought she was so dependent. She was acting so irrational. What on earth was the matter with her?

'What colour was the car, if you don't know what make it was?' asked the young, impatient, PC Dale. Jen thought hard; she'd never been a witness before. ' Red...I think.'

PC Dale sighed audibly. She was just beginning to realise how difficult it was for those witnesses that she typed statements for nearly every day of her working life. How could they be so sure of their evidence they signed, to say was a true account of what they saw?

Dylan put his mobile back in his pocket as he walked round the scene. Somebody wanted rid of the evidence and they'd made a bloody good job of it. He scratched his chin. The obvious signs told him that this was going to be a 'runner': there would be no quick solution to this one.

Jacob Rhodes from the Forensics Laboratory was called in for his expertise in arson cases.

'Should I arrange for the hot flasks, sir?' Tracy interrupted Dylan's thoughts.

'Yeah, please. John, can you make sure Control is keeping a log of the attendees at the scene, etcetera.' John told Dylan that the pathologist had been contacted, and would be attending at the mortuary.

'Do you think it looks like rain, Vicky?' Dylan asked looking towards the sky.

'How would I know? I ain't one of those glam weather girls. Even though I might look like one.' Vicky posed. Dylan frowned.

'I'll organise an inflatable tent, just in case it rains,' she sighed.

'You've too much front for a weather girl, Vicky.' Dylan called, as she walked away from him.

She stopped and turned. 'Somewhere for you to shelter under if it does rain though, eh?' she laughed. 'Good job Finchy isn't here, eh?' she said.

Dylan tutted and smiled as he turned to John, 'We'll make the most of the time whilst we're waiting for Jacob. All CCTV in the area will need seizing, or 'ave I already mentioned that?' He didn't wait for a reply. 'We need to organise a HOLMES incident room as well as the investigation team.' John nodded as he scribed away in his notebook.

'Boss,' Trevor shouted. 'Trojan has followed something on the footpath that leads up from the woods to the main road. There are possible recent footprints in the mud.'

'John, estimated time of arrival for the Police Support Unit please? I need them to prioritise searching that route.' He shouted, as he ran towards Trevor.

'On their way, sir, fifteen minutes max I'm being told.' John called back.

'It could be nothing...just a dog walker,' Trevor deliberated. But anyone who knew Dylan knew that he left nothing to chance, he'd have it photographed for the pattern and size but a plaster cast would give him a three- dimensional impression.

Wheels in motion, Dylan studied the body once more. What would the small, perhaps female skeleton tell them? The open jaw showed fear, he was sure of that but it was so charred and burnt. The blaze had been intense there was no doubt. Was the person in the car when it ignited?

For a moment the skeletal hand, seemed to reach out to him. Fingers splayed, quite a reasonable sliver of flesh hung from one. Was there enough for DNA or a fingerprint? Was he losing it? Dylan stared unblinking as he stepped back, soaking up the image and considering the possible motives. Upset lover? Revenge? What was the body doing here? What did he tell others to do? Find out who the victim is...find out how they lived that way you'll find out how they died.

'Tent's on its way, Boss.' Vicky called. 'You'll be glad it's self- erecting,' she said. 'Did I tell you I once went out with a guy who...' Seeing Tracy's face, she shook her head, deciding not to continue. Tracy dropped the flask and bent down to pick it up.

'It didn't last long...and neither did he,' she contemplated sadly.

'An inflatable I think you mean Vicky,' Dylan chuckled.

'Yeah he'd one of them as well I think,' she answered back.

Chapter Twelve

Jacob Rhodes wore slim, black, designer spectacles, which made him look sincere and intelligent. He greeted Dylan and John as he eagerly took his protective suit from the back of his dark blue Range Rover. It was obvious by his manner he was keen to get started.

'I'll need copies of any photos as exhibits for disclosure,' Dylan told him.

'No problem Jack, both Phil and I will take samples and I'll get copies of them for you from the memory card.' Dylan watched them as they quietly busied themselves, sifting carefully and meticulously over the scene.

'I've asked for a low loader to collect the vehicle shell and take it up to the forensics lab, but I'd be grateful if you could try and identify a chassis or engine number before they take it,' Dylan said, leaning over the men.

Jacob didn't raise his head or make any comment.

'Anything? Anything would be welcome. That'd give us a head start.'

'We'll do our best and it'll be priority at the lab. We'll bag the remains of the suitcase and take it back with us once we've finished with the car. My first impressions though...,' said Phil Turnbull reaching out to poke the ash, '...are that the contents of the suitcase were paper, not clothes, this certainly wasn't an accident or suicide.'

Dylan stood staring at the burnt remains, wondering what Tracy was thinking. He remembered one of the first bodies he'd been called out to, which just happened to be on the fourth floor of a hotel. A suicide note had been left at the scene. He'd offered to help the elderly undertaker place the body into the body bag and together they'd precariously carried it from the bedroom to the lift. Dylan had only then realised just how heavy dead bodies were. The dead man was around 6ft 10 in tall and they had struggled repeatedly to squeeze the man's stiff frame inside, so that the lift doors would close. The undertaker of some years experience came to Dylan's aid, as he showed him how the body would fit in diagonally. Doors closed at the last ping of the lift, and signalled that they had arrived at their elected floor. Last in, and without further ado, when the doors opened Dylan proceeded to walk backwards out of the lift, straight into a wedding reception. Red-faced, he'd realised they were on the wrong floor. Fortunately, the body went quickly into the lift that time. Looking back, to observers it must have looked like a farce out of a silent movie. He chuckled to himself; it had caused a few laughs back at the nick but at the time he'd been horrified.

Jacob stood up from his hunched position to face Dylan. 'It's the remains of a female and she was outside the car when she was set alight...no question. I've moved the body slightly and look,' he pointed, 'there's a white patch unsoiled beneath. I should be able to identify the accelerant no problem. It's most likely petrol, but I'm certain of one thing; the car, suitcase and body were all heavily doused in it. I might get you the type of petrol, too.'

'That would be great,' Dylan said, as he walked with Jacob to where John was talking to Vicky and Tracy.' Then we might be able to locate where it was bought.'

'Sir, best I can do I think is a partial finger-print from flesh on the finger of the right hand,' said Phil.

'Bugger.' said Dylan, scowling.

'Low loader confirmed boss and en-route. Tracy will help with the packaging of all the other exhibits, boss.' John said, as he approached the men. 'I've elected Vicky as the Exhibits Officer.'

Dylan was pleased that John felt confident enough to act on his own initiative. He'd listened to what Dylan had said and got on with the job in hand. Dylan felt sure he was going to like working with his new team.

All the photographs and samples had been taken, and the removal of the body to the mortuary was next on Dylan's agenda.

'Sorry Dylan, I'm not able to find an engine or chassis number for you here but I'll be able to examine it more thoroughly back at the lab,' said Jacob.

Everyone held their breath at the lifting of the fragile skeletal remains. There was flesh under the body and a clump of hair at the base of the skull. Because it was stuck to the tarmac, it needed John, Dylan and the undertakers to release it.

'You wouldn't have thought a skeleton would be so heavy, would you?' John groaned, as he struggled to help lift the charred remains. Dylan smiled knowingly.

The Operational Support Unit transit van driver waved to Dylan as the Operational Support Search Team arrived in the car park, just as he was about to leave.

'Can you believe we've been at the scene for three hours?' said John.

'It's not something that can be rushed is it? And let's face it, the body's not going anywhere is it, so the investigation might as well be as thorough as possible,' Dylan said as he made his way to speak to the sergeant in charge of the team.

'Search the route first taken by the dog handler before you start the fingertip search of the car park, will you, and make sure the area remains sealed to the public.'

'Will do, sir,' replied the OSU Commander who, in Dylan's absence, was now in charge of the scene.

'Tracy, you go with Vicky to the mortuary in the CID car and follow the hearse for continuity. Phil Turnbull is already en route and one of his colleagues from SOCO will join us there.'

'Yes, sir,' Vicky and Tracy replied together. Dylan smiled as the ladies walked away, chatting amiably.

'I don't know about you John but I'm bloody starving. It'll be an hour or so before the pathologist arrives at the mortuary, so if you want to go back with Vicky and Tracy for some food and bring me a sandwich back to the mortuary, I don't mind. I'll see you there, eh?' Dylan said, as he opened his car door.

'You sure?'

'I'm certain. Jen is bound to 'ave slipped some snap in my briefcase to put me on until my dinner tonight, if I know her. It'll give me chance to write up the Policy Book.'

'Okay, boss. See you at the PM,' John said as he raised his hand to catch the girls' attention.

Dylan watched from his car, at what looked like a vacant hearse being driven away by the undertaker. The CID car containing John, Vicky and Tracy was close behind. He had never known before joining the police, that in the rear of the hearse, underneath the platform where the coffin rested, there was a void where bodies in body bags were transported, out of the view of the public. Although some funeral directors had started to use black transit vans, which these days were more economical.

PC Dale had very kindly taped up the remaining arm of Jen's car wing mirror but had kept the rest of the debris for evidence. Alone now at home, she cried. Why? Goodness knew. She was safe. The police were doing what they could to find the person responsible, and with the statement, identification and number plate she had given them, they had a good chance. So what the hell was up with her? Max sat beside her, resting his head on her lap, and she looked into his deep brown eyes as she stroked his head and he leaned his body heavily against her leg. Jen had watched Max grow up and grow wise, and she felt that he knew at that moment what was in her heart: she needed Jack, just a brief cuddle would do.

The post-mortem was about to commence, and Dylan could see Tracy's jaw clench and her hands shake as she twisted them in her lap.

'You can go in the police room behind the glass screen if you want, you know,' Dylan whispered.

'No, sir, I'm fine thanks,' she smiled. Her determination to get through it was written all over her face. She looked around. If the others could cope with a post-mortem, so could she. Who was the victim here? Didn't she want to help catch a killer?

''Ave a mint then, I always find it helps,' Dylan said, as he searched for the extra strong mints in his suit pocket.' And if you need to go out to get a breath of air go; it's okay. Most of us 'ave disappeared in our time.' He smiled, offering her the packet of mints. 'John, don't you forget to call home, you're gonna be late tonight.'

John nodded as he saw Dylan retrieve his own phone to text Jen.

'I'm at the mortuary. How'd it go with traffic? X'

'I'm fine – don't worry x' Jen texted straight before throwing her phone back in her handbag.

'Come on Max, I need some fresh air, fella' she said, as she held his head in her hand and gently removed the sleep from the corner of his eyes with her finger. Max didn't flinch, nor did he need asking twice. She was sure he smiled at her, and focusing on Max's needs made her feel less sorry for herself. She didn't know how Jack coped; it was just one body after another. The last thing he needed was to worry about her.

Sitting quietly and writing quickly, Dylan had only managed to eat a little of his sandwich before Donald Jefferson, the pathologist, arrived. Putting the sandwich back in the paper bag, Dylan started to give him the background regarding the discovery of the body.

Mr Jefferson examined the corpse, 'Female, 5ft, 4in.' There was no hesitation.

'That's surreal; - it's just a skeleton, how'd he know that?' Dylan heard Tracy whisper to Vicky. Dylan shook his head; even he never ceased to be amazed by the professionals with whom he came into contact in his work.

'There are no signs of broken bones,' Jefferson dictated into his Dictaphone.

Mr Jefferson took samples, along with the clump of hair. Hopefully the root would give them her DNA. The victim had died by asphyxiation from inhaling smoke and carbon monoxide.

'I'll arrange for the orthodontist to get her teeth impressions.'

'That'll be great. Then we can start making enquiries with dentists in the area.' On completion of Mr Jefferson's examination, there were no other signs of injury. Dylan was more than pleased that they had a line of enquiry to pursue, and he shook the pathologist's hand.

The incident room was buzzing. Dylan walked in with a purpose; he had the press office to update and an enquiry team to arrange.

'Earlier today,' the statement commenced, *'emergency services responded to the report of a fire in the lower car park of St Peter's Park. On arrival they found a vehicle and a female at the side of it. Both were totally engulfed in flames. The fire brigade managed to extinguish the fire but unfortunately the body of the female was burnt beyond recognition. The vehicle is also unidentifiable at this time.'*

The announcement incorporated an appeal for any possible witnesses in the area at the time of the incident, or anyone whose sister, girlfriend, daughter, partner or wife had gone missing.

Dylan searched for the ringing phone underneath the mountain of paper on his desk that he and John were wading through.

'Sergeant Delvers, sir, PSU. We've found a black balaclava along the route. It's been photographed in situ, bagged and tagged.' Dylan raised his eyebrows at John.

'Sounds interesting; how far from the scene is it?'

'Er...'bout quarter of a mile, just off the snicket up to the main road.'

'Can you tape the route from the car park, and we'll include it in a more detailed search tomorrow? Thank your team for me and pass on my compliments to Trevor, the dog handler, will you?'

Dylan felt excited; it could be nothing but it was something to work with.

The HOLMES team was established; enquiries at garages for purchases of petrol in canisters were ongoing, arrangements had been made for the balaclava to go to forensics, and the CCTV was being examined. The basics had been done: it was time to go home. A briefing was arranged for eight a.m. the following day.

'It's not an easy one,' Dylan said later that night as he nuzzled into Jen's neck, hugging her tight. 'Are you okay? Tell me all about your day; the accident?'

'It's nothing,' she yawned. 'Sorry, I don't know what's wrong with me, I'm so tired,' she said. 'There's glass all over the seat and footwell of my car. The wing mirror flew straight past me, luckily.'

'What was the twat doing?'

'God knows. He was obviously in a hurry to get somewhere; he went around a line of traffic at one hell of a speed.'

'Where were you?'

The phone rang, 'Dad, how lovely to hear from you, lovely.' Jen smiled at Dylan as she took the phone into the lounge and settled on the settee. 'Later,' she mouthed to Dylan, who followed her. Dylan lay down and rested his head on her lap. Closing his eyes, he listened to her soothing tone and fell asleep.

Jen could smell a hint of mortuary on his hair as she stroked his brow and listened to what her dad had been doing throughout the day.

Chapter Thirteen

The day started dry and cold, but by mid-morning the blue skies had become grey and the rain fell like stair rods. It was as if day had suddenly become night. Dylan briefed the team and made sure items prioritised for examination were taken to forensics. Sitting at his desk, he was engrossed in establishing the priority lines of the enquiry. Once the female or the car was identified, he knew things would move at a pace; but for now he had to be focussed and patient taking one small step at a time. He undid his tie and released the top button of his shirt. God, the weather was so depressing, he thought as he looked out of the window at the tall, dark puffy cumulonimbus clouds.

The ringing phone broke his concentration. The message from personnel didn't do much for his heavy mood; Larry was to lose his job, there was now no doubt. After all the good work he had done in the past, the drink had been his ruin. Dylan felt sad. It was true what they said, you were only as good as your last job, and in Larry's case it couldn't be worse. There had been no response from Larry to Dylan's repeated phone calls, so he decided to visit his apartment as soon as he could, to discuss the future with him. Dylan rose from the desk, and stretching his back, he stood staring out of the window at the copious amount of rain that was being swept by the strong westerly wind, across the back yard. The next minute hail hammered at the window snowflakes stuck to the sill and ribbon lightning lit the sky. The weather was more like winter than spring, even for West Yorkshire. Could Dylan have done something to help Larry? Could he have done anything at all? He'd not even managed to see or speak to Larry since it had happened. Had he let him down as his boss and friend? He sighed heavily. Perhaps saying he was going away for a few days to personnel had just been Larry's way of saying he didn't want visitors. He should have at least gone and knocked on his door. Whatever, Larry must surely be back now and the least Dylan could do was make the effort to go and see him. Find out what had caused him to start drinking heavily again, and what he planned to do now.

Acting Detective Sergeant John Benjamin shifted from cheek to cheek on his chair. He played with his tie and pulled his jacket around his ample body, unfastening and fastening the buttons on his jacket as he sat beside Dylan, preparing himself for his first press conference. The pressure he felt at the hands of the media, being the deputy on a major investigation, was apparent. He listened and looked at Dylan for guidance, watching how he controlled them. Dylan's sole objective for the conference was an appeal. It was a chance available to him to glean any information at all about the car, the woman or the motive for the murder. He spoke directly to anyone whose daughter, girlfriend, wife or mother hadn't arrived home last night, or anyone who was in the area at the time.

The one-to-one television appeals were eventually over and a live radio appeal was planned from the phone in his office, after which he could return to the normality of the incident room. Vicky and Tracy had left for forensics when he arrived. Tracy had been so excited at the opportunity to see the laboratory and the work that they did. Dylan was like a cat on a hot tin roof waiting for information from them. Would forensics be able to identify the car, engine or chassis number, which would then lead them to a registration number? God, he hoped so. It hadn't been possible at the scene and his patience was waning. He closed his eyes and put his head in his hands, rubbing his face with vigour. He remembered the poor woman's body; burnt, distorted, blackened, her mouth wide open. He stood up, shook his head and took his jacket from behind his chair, as he walked towards the door. He needed some fresh air. It was time to visit Larry.

Fifteen minutes later Dylan parked his car in the car park next to the electric substation, by the riverside development where Larry lived. He rang the doorbell and pounded on the door of Larry's flat but there was no reply. He went back to his car. He couldn't believe the weather; the sun was now shining and the water remaining on the pavement glistened, mesmerizing him. He wondered momentarily if there was a rainbow. He called Jen to cheer himself up, but she wasn't answering either.

'Good news and bad news Jen,' PC Dale said, as he stood at her desk.

'Go on. Give me the good news first.'

'We've identified the car that hit you.'

'Fantastic.'

'The bad news is that it was reported stolen and yet to be recovered.'

'Mmm. So now it's a CID job, then?'

'No, we're on with it. You can tell Dylan we'll get there; it's only a matter of time.'

'Thanks, anyway.' Jen was savvy enough with the criminal fraternity's way of thinking that if it was a stolen car and had not yet been recovered, it would probably be burnt out somewhere by now.

It was the end of the day before the first call from forensics came through to Dylan.

'The balaclava, although slightly singed by the fire, actually did contain remnants of saliva and hair. It's very hopeful that a DNA profile can be obtained over the next few days,' said the official voice at the other end of the phone.

Dylan grinned. 'But that's great, and the vehicle?'

'It's a Renault. The chassis plate is being treated at the moment but it'll be this evening at the earliest, most likely tomorrow, before we will have a full number for you.'

'That's excellent. I'll await your call, thank you,' Dylan said. It was a great start and something positive he could give to the team in the debrief.

His phone rang and as he picked it up the smile must have been apparent in his voice. 'Dylan.' he said, chirpily.

'Sir,' the PC at the help desk said morosely.' I've a lady in the front office wanting to report her daughter missing.'

'Start taking the details, will you. I'll be down in a minute.' Dylan marched along the corridor to the front office. Tracy was heading towards him. 'Now then, how's it going?'

'Oh, gosh, it's so busy. I'm sorry, sir I haven't even had the chance to check up on Chubby for you yet. But there's no intelligence come in about him to LIO, since he attempted to jump off the bridge, so that must be positive,' she said grinning.

'No, I 'aven't heard his name mentioned either. Listen, don't worry; remember you can only do one job at once. He'll wait, he's alive and he can thank you for that.' He smiled as he continued on his way.

'No, she called after him. You saved him, sir. I just stood and watched.'

'DI Dylan, I think the woman, the woman you've found, might be my daughter.' This was the shocked confession of the middle-aged lady who stood with a child at the counter. 'My daughter, Gemma's mum,' she said, picking up the girl, placing her on her hip and kissing the top of her head. 'She's not answering her phone and she's not rung to speak to her daughter, my grand-daughter. Something's wrong. I just know it is.'

'What's your daughter's name?' asked Dylan, smiling kindly at the little girl, who was trying to hide her face behind her hands.

'Elizabeth. Liz Reynolds.'

'And when did you last see her?'

'The day before yesterday, but she should 'ave been back by now. She didn't ring...she always rings, always.'

'The body we've found can't be identified by normal means due to the damage by the fire. Neither can the car. It might not be your daughter. I don't want you to worry unnecessarily. We are doing everything we can to identify the person we found at the scene.'

'She isn't at home. I've been there,' she continued. Her voice faltered. 'I've a horrible feeling inside, that's why I'm here.'

'I know how hard this is for you, Mrs. . .'

'Platt.'

'Platt. But if you could continue to help the police constable at the help desk fill in the necessary Misper forms that we have to complete when a person is reported missing, then I'll get back to you as soon as I can. I promise. We are checking all reports of missing females and your daughter will now be included. Thank you for coming in. If in the meantime your daughter makes contact with you, can you please let us know immediately?'

'Of course,' Mrs Platt said, turning to leave.

'Before you go. You do know who Liz's dentist is don't you?'

'Yes,' Mrs Platt replied.

On the way back to his office Dylan's shoulders stooped and he could feel his feet dragging. His head ached and he knew it was time to go home. 'Elizabeth...Liz.' Her name was going round and round his head in a whirr. It was the only misper report to come in during the last twenty-four hours. Could this be her? He'd get the team on this line of enquiry, as a priority.

The kitchen felt moist and warm. The vegetables for their tea were boiling away on the hob, but there was no sign of Jen. Looking through the open door to the back garden, Dylan could see her, heavily laden with clothes from the washing line. She was still in her coat, which meant she couldn't have been home long. He walked onto the patio.

'Hiya, how's it gone today?' she called, as she unhooked the peg bag from the line and placed it on top of the damp clothes in the basket. Max bounded towards him from the bottom of the garden in the darkness, to be fussed.

'Some guard dog you make,' he said, as he cupped the dog's ears in his hands and ruffled his fur. Jack walked over to Jen, gave her a quick kiss and picked up the overflowing basket from the wet grass.

'When am I going to learn and watch the weather forecast?' she said, smiling, tiredness etched all over her face.

'Why don't you use the tumble dryer that's what it's there for?' he shivered. She shrugged her shoulders. 'Come on let's get inside before we get pneumonia.'

'Oh, I don't know. I love the smell of clothes dried outside, and using the tumble dryer costs a fortune.' Jen said, following him into the house. Dylan stopped at the door to let her go in the house first.

'The woman, she's called Liz, I think. Her mum came in with Liz's daughter to report her missing just before I left so with luck we might get an I.D.'

'Oh,' she said, sighing. 'It always seems...real when the body has a name, doesn't it?' she said, as she took the basket from him and placed it on the worktop in the utility room.

'Liz...the skeleton...it was awful, like something out of a horror movie,' Jack reflected, sometime later, as he pushed his broccoli to one side of his dinner plate. Jen normally gave him a hard time about eating his vegetables but tonight wasn't the time to tease.

'Poor love...I really don't know how you stand to see...and ...well all the things you do. I'd be ill,' she said as she slid her chair back, scraping the tiles. 'Literally.'

'Neither do I, sometimes. The cigs...at one time I'd smoke one after another to calm the emotions. Now, now it's the strong mints and chewing gum that helps. D'ya know, sometimes I can taste the smell of death for a long time afterwards...if that makes any sense at all?'

'It makes you wonder, doesn't it, if that's why detectives drink, to try and forget the sights and the smells. Talking of drinking, I spoke to Dorothy, the Duties Clerk Supervisor today, and according to Larry's Annual Leave Form he was going 'abroad' on his holiday,' Jen said, as she wiped the table. 'She's sent you a copy.'

'Yeah, I know he'd booked time off, I signed his application form. I went to his apartment today. I thought I should, just to see if he was back...he wasn't there.'

Jen shook her head in disbelief.

'I 'aven't heard from him since it all happened,' he said to her. 'He's definitely lost his job you know, and if Fred does die, he could face a charge of causing death by dangerous driving and go to prison.'

'And, he deserves to have the book thrown at him, don't you think?' she snapped.

Chapter Fourteen

Dylan could feel in his bones that it was going to be an eventful day. Every time his office door opened, the electrifying buzz of voices encroached into his space. The 'unknown body' enquiry was ongoing and expectations were high that the burned corpse would be identified. Checks at Liz Reynolds home had proved inconclusive and the house was secure. Door to door enquiries had drawn a blank. Her car was now known to be a Renault.

'Hello Jack,' Dawn greeted him warmly at the end of the phone.

'Gosh, you're up and about early. Morning sickness passed?' he asked, as he reached for his pen and writing pad.

'Umm...sort of.' He could imagine her grimacing and dropping her shoulders; he knew her gestures well. 'I've had a call from A & E at the Royal Infirmary. They've a 'dead on arrival'. A small child called Charlie Sharpe, and he's not quite four years old.' Dylan made notes. 'The poor little mite's got numerous non-accidental injuries. The cause of death's not known at the moment but he's got recent head injuries.'

'Where are the parents?'

'Mum's at the hospital with him. I'm told she's not married. They're taking the little boy's body down to the mortuary.'

'I'll see you at the A & E in ...' Dylan looked at his watch. 'twenty minutes? Make sure an officer stays with the body for continuity. If we 'aven't got anyone at the house, get someone there to preserve the scene.'

'They're en route, boss.'

Dylan placed the phone on its cradle and closed his eyes as he tried to gather his thoughts. No matter what procedures authorities put in place; children always ended up murdered. John tapped on his door as if he'd been summoned by telepathy, and walked into the office.

'Good timing, you'll 'ave to take the morning briefing. I'll be on my mobile; Dawn's just rang. She's at A & E; we've got a suspicious child death.' Dylan stood up, straightened his tie and put his arm in the sleeve of his suit jacket. 'I'm off to the infirmary, so I'll give you a call later.'

'No problem,' John called out over his shoulder, as he walked back into the main office, glad that he was on this murder enquiry; although it was horrific, at least it wasn't a child.

Dawn's eyes were red. Dylan knew she'd been crying. Nevertheless, he thought she looked well, as he smiled at her kindly.

'Hormones,' she said, shrugging and with a tissue, wiping away a tear that had escaped the corner of her eye.

'No beautiful hankie?' Dylan said, in mock horror.

'I'm pregnant; I'd be washing all day, every day, if I used a hankie every time I cried,' she replied; a huge smile crossing her face.

'That's more like it,' Dylan said, as he steered her to a chair in a quiet recess of the hospital corridor.

'The mum's been taken through to a private office with the coroner's officer. It's awful this one Jack,' she said. 'Poor little soul, his face is badly bruised but he still looks so angelic.' Several tears easing out of the corner of her eyes and she let them run down her cheeks unchecked this time. Dylan put an arm around her shoulders and squeezed the top of her arm. She looked up at him, 'I'm sorry, I'm all over the place,' she said, blowing her nose, loudly.

'Don't apologise. It shows you're caring and sensitive. Tell me, what do we know already?' Focusing on the job in hand was the only way to cope with this one; that was for certain.

'Mum's twenty-one years old. Susan Sharpe and she lives in a two bed-roomed council house on the Drighton Estate, 14 Peel Street. She says she's lived there alone with Charlie, the boy until recently, when she let her boyfriend and his mate move in.' Dylan listened intently.

'Do we 'ave a name? Who's the dad?'

'Don't know yet. She doesn't appear to be awkward, just genuinely devastated. She tells me that she found Charlie this morning and called the ambulance.'

'Okay,' Dawn got her pen and notebook from her handbag to take down the list of enquiries that needed to be done as, Dylan reeled them off.

'Statements need to be taken from the ambulance crew as to what they saw and did at the scene; also what the mother said to them. We need to find out if the mother has any relatives. Do social services know the family? Is Charlie on the 'at risk' register? We'll need to hear what she says under caution. Somebody's responsible for his death...and it may be her.' Dawn didn't lift her head, only too aware that the murderer more often turned out to be someone the victim knew. 'We'll need SOCO at the house, and a search team. Find out who the boyfriend and his mate are and where they are now. There'll 'ave to be a post-mortem of course.'

'She must've been aware of so many injuries. You can't miss them on his tiny body,' Dawn said.

Dylan saw the tears welling up in her eyes again.

'I want you to deal with her but I don't want you anywhere near the post-mortem in your condition.'

But I'm fine Jack,' Dawn protested.

'And that's the way I want it to stay. It'll be bad enough for you, dealing with her. It sounds to me like she's tried to cover up his injuries, and I won't hear anymore,' he said, walking away from her without a backward glance. Dylan didn't want the argument that he was sure would follow. 'I'll go down to the mortuary and see what timescale we're working to,' he called back over his shoulder.

'Don't take this one away from me Jack. I want the bastard that did this to Charlie,' she cried, running after him.

He stopped and turned. 'My decision's been made Dawn. I won't change my mind.' She stood and watched him go. Tears once again stung her eyes and she stamped her foot in anger.

Dylan looked through the head-high window of the door and saw Charlie's mum sitting at a table. He was slightly shocked by the sight of Susan Sharpe. She was skinny, pale and sobbing helplessly into her hands. He studied her body language as she spoke to the coroner's officer; mother's seemed to get younger. Susan Sharpe looked but a child herself. 'How difficult it must have been for such a young girl to bring up a child on her own,' he thought, as he turned and carried on down the corridor to the mortuary.

'Hello Sir,' PC Hannah Jordan greeted him. Dylan nodded. 'Mr Lacy, the coroner's officer, has arranged a pathologist with paediatric experience. He's due here at one.'

'You okay?'

'Yeah, fine thanks - plenty of paperwork to be getting on with,' she said smiling at him.

'In that case I'll get onto headquarters for staff.'

As Dylan walked out of the office, taking his mobile from his pocket, he saw the small body on a stainless steel trolley, wrapped in a green hospital blanket.

'Little Charlie Sharpe,' he whispered. The trolleys were designed for adults; each could have carried eight 'Charlie's.' He felt so very, very sad.

Chapter Fifteen

Dialling HQ, Dylan knew for a fact he was going to be a thorn in everyone's side. Once again he was requesting staff from the divisions, which already had stretched resources but for once he didn't care. Baby deaths, baby murders and attacks on small children always tugged at his heartstrings. You would have to be numb for them to have no effect at all. The line was engaged and he ended the call. His mobile rang instantly.

'CID will meet you at the scene, boss.'

'Thank you, Tracy,' he said.

Dylan was in his protective clothing. The house was a potential murder scene, and with that in mind he entered the front door that led from a busy main road, into a small, square living room. The immediate wall of darkness from the daylight outside slowly started to lift, to enable him to see. He shivered. The smell of sweat and cigarette smoke mingled with a food odour he couldn't quite identify. He saw in the centre of the room a well worn, soiled, burnt orange coloured settee and a fading blue blanket lay haphazardly on it. Did the occupiers sleep there, he wondered? A very large flatscreen TV stood proudly off the wall, too big to fit in the corner of the lounge. On the floor was a filthy, threadbare, old-fashioned, patterned carpet, which his protective shoe covers, stuck to in places, as he walked upon it. Pulled to one side across the window, was an old, tatty, moth-eaten curtain. The walls were painted purple, and the paint had bubbled and was flaking around the window frame and below. As he made his way towards the kitchen door he stopped to take in his surroundings. He walked into the bare light bulb that hung from the ceiling and ducked instinctively, brushing it to one side with his gloved hand. His eyes caught sight of a neat pile of electrical goods against the back wall and he went over to look; there were DVD players, mobile phones, the odd laptop, a PSP and other handheld games consoles.

'Someone's been busy thieving,' Dylan muttered under his breath. Like the television, he would bet the shirt on his back they were the proceeds of crime.

The kitchen was what Dylan would have expected; there were unwashed dishes and cups, doors hung off cupboards and there was no sign of any food. A filthy dishcloth had been thrown into the sink, which was littered with food debris and congealed grease. Crumpled clothes lay in an untidy heap on the floor, which was also strewn with empty cider bottles, tins of lager, beer and takeaway cartons. No wonder he couldn't identify the smell. He stooped to peer at the takeaway boxes which had remnants of Chinese, Indian, Mc Donald's and Kentucky Fried Chicken. Roll-ups overflowed out of ashtrays on the windowsill, and the ash was scattered like dust. Dylan lowered his mask and sniffed up close; was it cannabis? Yeah, for sure.

Dylan tentatively felt his way up the narrow, twisted, windowless staircase, onto a landing. An open door straight ahead led into the main bedroom. The room was almost in darkness because a blanket was pinned up over the window. Stale body odour hung powerfully in the air. Dylan adjusted the mask over his face to delay the smell reaching his nostrils. A dirty mattress covered with heavily creased, dirty linen and newspaper lay on the floor. A bed headboard stood against one wall and an old dressing table and wardrobe leaned against another, with the doors and drawers broken and open, clothing askew.

Bleach would have had little effect on the bathroom fitments; the toilet, sink and bath were encrusted with deep rooted grime. Empty toiletry containers had spilled over into the bath. A dirty towel was strewn on the floor amid pieces of curled up old lino and dirt-caked bare floorboards. There were some tiles on the walls, but most of them were broken on the floor. Dylan didn't cross the threshold but caught his reflection in the old cracked mirror above the washbasin. Turning away, he saw a rope had been pulled tightly over a peg on the outside of another door off the landing. He held the loose doorknob in his hand, before slowly pushing it open.

The smell of urine and excrement made him wretch. He fumbled in his pocket for his torch and scanned the dark room, to see the window had been boarded up with cardboard. There was a pile of faeces in the corner on the bare, damp floorboards, and more was smeared on the walls. The box room was no bigger than a large airing cupboard and the dangling light fitting had no bulb. Dylan could see a dirty piece of blanket strewn over the floor. He stepped inside and closed the door behind him, to sense the atmosphere. It was deathly quiet, more cramped than an animal's pen. Through adult's eyes, with a torch and knowing he could open the door and leave at any moment, to him the room felt like a dungeon or a prison cell. Moisture sat on his brow; he gasped for air and his heart began to race. Was this where Charlie had been kept? There were no toys, no books; nothing to remotely suggest a child had been there. Dylan's heart ached. This hadn't happened overnight, and the sad thing was that he knew this was not as rare as people liked to believe.

'How the hell does this happen? Someone must 'ave known,' he muttered. He needed some air; the atmosphere was overbearing. He reached for the door handle, there wasn't one there.

Stumbling down the stairs he could hear voices. SOCO had arrived.

'Jasmine. Good to see you. Can you do the usual, please; seize blankets, photograph the rooms, and the walls will need examining for blood splashes. The child's got recent head injuries.' Dylan's phone rang. Jasmine nodded, smiling knowingly at him as he turned to take the call.

'Boss, Patrick Finch. Where are you? Can't hear you. Signal's bad but if you can hear me; Division's letting me go, so I can meet up with you. Anything happening?' Patrick sounded eager and Dylan walked to the door to try for a better reception. 'That's great news. Apart from the burned body in the park, it looks like we've got a murder of a little lad on our hands.'

'A murder? Right boss, where do you want me then?'

'Here at 14, Peel Street, on the Drighton Estate ASAP.'

Jasmine was heading towards the stairs as he ended the call. 'We may need to place people in the boy's room. Can you give some thought to fingerprints please?'

'Will do,' she said.

Half an hour later, giving the DS a tour of Susan Sharpe's home, Dylan saw Patrick's face drain of colour. 'But it's no better than a kennel of an ill treated animal,' Patrick said, his voice choking as they entered the boy's bedroom.

'And that is exactly why every SIO should go to the scene. See how the victim lived and you will see how they died,' Dylan said, repeating his aged old theory. 'Then and only then can you get a feel for the circumstances surrounding the death. The hardest thing to do though once you've been there is control your emotions.'

From the scene they headed to the hospital, only to find the canteen was chaotic. Dylan had no appetite and he saw Patrick hadn't either, as he watched him toy with the food on his plate, but they both knew they had to force something down; there was a lengthy post-mortem ahead of them. Dylan felt angry inside and was quiet. How the hell could incidents like this continue to happen? So many people, including him, would count themselves blessed to have a little boy like Charlie.

Walking down the long half-glassed corridor of the hospital to the mortuary, always felt surreal to Dylan. The quietness made the hollow rap of shoes on the polished tiled floor echo loudly. The smell of formaldehyde hung in the air. The sun either blazed through the windows making it feel stuffy and warm or the rain beat heavily on the corrugated roof and it felt cold and austere. It was never just an ordinary day, for how could any day that involved attending a post mortem be ordinary? And this was not just any post-mortem, but that of a small, helpless child who had been beaten to death. Dawn walked alongside Dylan and Patrick. 'Lock up the mother on suspicion of wounding,' Dylan said. 'At least 'til we 'ave a cause of death, then we'll see where we go with her. Does she 'ave a photograph of the child on her? I didn't see one at the house.'

'I'll find out,' said Dawn. 'Shall I get her checked out regarding her fitness for interview? That way I can get a responsible adult if we need one,' she continued, panting as she struggled to keep up with him.

'Yeah, thanks. Video any interview and I want to know the whereabouts of the boyfriend and his mate as a matter of urgency.'

'Consider it done.' Dawn said, as exhibits officer DC Carter arrived with Phil Turnbull from SOCO in tow, who would cover the mortuary scene, whilst Jasmine continued at the house.

Professor Jefferson studied the unwrapped body of Charlie Sharpe. The little boy's clothing that had been removed in Casualty earlier lay folded, neatly on the trolley beside him. The professor looked at them before handing them to DC Carter.

'Dear, dear,' sighed Donald Jefferson. 'Let's weigh him please. Date of birth?' he asked Dylan.

'Born 8th July 2003,' he read from his notes.

'He looks underweight and malnourished for his age. Gosh,' he said and paused. 'Let's make a start shall we?' he said, as the infant's body was placed naked on the examination table.

Charlie's swollen face looked contorted with the bruising; like a broken doll. Dylan groped in his pocket for a mint, as he felt bile rising from his stomach. Popping it in his mouth, he offered the packet around, never taking his eyes off the tiny frame on the table. A picture of innocence, he thought.

Donald Jefferson spoke into his Dictaphone. 'Externally to the head are four cuts,' he said, measuring them with a twelve inch wooden ruler. 'Hair has been pulled out by the roots. There is severe bruising to the back of the head and petechia in the eyes, which suggests strangulation,' he said, turning the head and lifting the eyelids. 'Broken nose...both wrists have been broken for several days. Left leg broken and there are also welt marks to the backs of both legs, with burns to the feet.' The list went on and on. Dylan's chest felt tight with anger and his heart felt heavy with sadness. This little boy had been tortured badly. Charlie had led a painful, brief existence. Dylan heard a mobile ring and it was moments before he realised it was his own, consumed as he was by the horrific scene on the slab.

'Hello boss, John. Can you speak?'

The body was being opened up, the saw and knife slicing through the bones that weren't fully developed, as if through butter.

'Yeah.' Dylan swallowed hard.

'A couple of bits of good news. Firstly, forensics 'ave a DNA good enough profile, from the saliva on the balaclava found in the park. They're going to start searching the database. And on the burnt out car they've come up with a chassis and engine number. I've already been onto the DVLA and I'm waiting for a call back. The original plate has been changed for a personal one, so I should get that in the next twenty minutes. Shall I get back to you?'

'That's great John, thanks.' Dylan looked at the clock . 'I'll still be at the mortuary.'

'Is it bad?'

'Appalling. One of the worst, if not the worst case I've ever seen.'

Professor Jefferson shook his head as he pulled at his mask over his nose and mouth. His eyes were puffy and red and he looked pale and tired. 'Cause of death, inspector; severe fracture of the skull. He hasn't just been hit; he's been hit with a tremendous force.'

'And the cause of the other injuries?' Dylan asked.

'The burns on his feet...cigarette burns I would think. His wrists have probably been broken for about seven days. They have been bound at some stage; see the old bruising?' Professor Jefferson pointed out. 'The injuries to his wrists again suggest that he has been hit with something. Again, whatever caused the damage had to have some force behind it. When we've run further tests I'll probably be able to be a bit more precise with the timings.' He sighed before he continued. 'I can confirm what I said earlier; the fractures to the wrists and leg are around seven days old and consistent with being punched and kicked, and it appears he's had something around his neck.'

Dylan flinched.

'I've counted seventy-five independent injuries, all-recent, and in my estimation, within the last seven or eight weeks.

Some of the cuts to his head are similar to that caused by, perhaps ...' Professor Jefferson studied for a moment or two...'A razor. His heads been shaved, and none too carefully either.' He pointed to the gashes on Charlie's scalp. 'They would've been very sore for the poor little un. Death was probably a blessing in disguise after what he'd been through. He's been systematically beaten, that's for sure. Let's put it this way; to break his limbs wouldn't have been simple, it would've taken a lot of strength and determination and no doubt this has been intentional. You've got numerous injuries to support murder.'

'Thank you Professor.'

'Just find the animal that did this, Jack,' he said, as he shook Dylan by the hand. 'Good luck.'

The team stood rooted to the spot, blank expressions upon their faces; and each deep in their own dark thoughts.

'Come on. Let's get back to the nick and we'll open the incident room.' Dylan put his hand on Patrick Finch's shoulder. 'Can you ensure that we keep number fourteen as a crime scene. We'll need forensics out.'

Dylan texted Jen. *On my way back to the nick. Little Charlie's PM was bad. The bastard who killed him needs hanging and I'd willingly pull the noose. Shouldn't be too late tonight hopefully. Will give you a ring when I'm on my way x.*

Chapter Sixteen

'Hold on a minute before you update the team Dawn, I'd just like everyone to know that the arrest status of Susan Sharpe has been upgraded to suspicion of murder.' Dylan told the audience of team leaders in the incident room, who were eagerly soaking up the fresh information. He sat down and motioned Dawn to proceed with the briefing.

'Susan Sharpe, although twenty-one, only looks about fifteen,' Dawn said.' She's five-foot three, very thin and as you can see from her photograph, frail. She's got quite a few bruises on her body so I've arranged for her to be medically examined. Her best guess as to the father of Charlie is Jason Todd who is a relatively steady boyfriend, and, according to her, accepts the child as his own. He's on bail for a robbery and he appears to 'ave done a runner when she called the emergency services for Charlie. Jason Todd's previous, according to information we've got, is assault, burglary and robbery.'

The team hung on Dawn's every word. Some took notes. The room was silent and still.

'Susan tells me she doesn't cope well on her own and when Jason threatened to leave her recently, she allowed another lad to move in with them; a mate of Jason's, Alan. She says Alan's criminal record is not much better than Jason's, but she's too frightened to not do as they tell her.' Dawn coughed and reached for a drink of water from the glass on the desk in front of her. 'She said she called her little boy after a character in her favourite film, which happens to be, Willy Wonka and the Chocolate Factory.'

'What's Alan's second name? Do we know of him?' Dylan said sensing the sadness in the room.

'Alan ....err...Connor.'

'You're bloody joking.' Dylan stared heavenwards, as he rose from his chair and strode the few steps towards her.

'No, why?'

'He's the twat I stopped jumping to his death a while back...Chubby, Chubby Connor.' he said punching the desk.

'We don't know …'

'I wouldn't 'ave said he was hard enough to be a bully, he's a weak kneed little bastard,' he said with venom. 'And she must 'ave known. When you look at the house and the injuries... notoys, no photographs... no nothing.' Dylan's outburst brought a wave of agreement from the assembled few. It reminded him of a mob, ready to lynch someone.

'Does she 'ave any photos of Charlie? Did you ask her?'

'No, she doesn't, not one.' Dawn replied sadly.

'Dawn, I want her interviewed again. Get a description of Alan Connor and the date he moved in. It's important because some of the injuries can be dated as per the pathologist.'

'Okay. There was no food in his stomach. She says she believes he died from SID.'

'What? Sudden Infant Death syndrome? A cot death? ' Dylan shouted. 'Sorry,' he said, waving his hand. 'I'm pre judging people's abilities and education based on my own, and I shouldn't. Let's see what else she can tell us, eh? Then bed her down for the night and we'll pick it up again first thing.'

The team disbursed to get on with their actions.

'I'll get on with the next interview then, boss,' groaned Dawn, as she eased herself from behind the desk and stretched.

'Dawn?'

'Yeah?'

'You okay?'

'I'm fine,' she said, with a forced smile.

'Thanks.' He smiled weakly at her and headed for his computer to have a look at Jason Todd for himself.

'Pat,' Dylan shouted. 'Get direct enquiries carried out to find Jason Todd. Apparently there's a warrant out for him for robbery, 'non appearance at court' so that's easily enough for a lock up, and find Chubby Connor. It's more than likely this Alan Connor is going to be him.'

'Will do,' he shouted back from the far end of the office. 'Do you want everybody off at ten and back at eight?'

'Yeah.' Dylan replied.

Jen had run the bath when Dylan walked in. She pressed a finger to her lips to stop him from talking and took his briefcase from his cold hand. She pointed to the stairs. He kissed her briefly. The smell of roasting lamb wafted up to the bedroom and he undressed, taking in the luxury of his surroundings. He flicked on the big light in the bathroom, not wanting to be shrouded by the dim light of the candles Jen had lovingly placed around the bath; it reminded him of the darkness Charlie had had to endure.

He squeezed the bath foam through his fingers and the sponge as he absentmindedly patted the water whilst he soaked. Dylan closed his eyes. He heard Jen enter the room and he opened his eyes to find a cup of coffee placed on the side of the bath. She knelt down, stroked his brow and splashed water gently onto his chest.

'Remember I talked Chubby Connor out of committing suicide; the lad threatening to jump off Stan Bridge when we were going to the Isle of Wight?'

'Mmm ...' she replied, sleepily.

'Well maybe if I hadn't 'ave, little Charlie might still be alive,' Dylan said, as he stared up at the ceiling, through clouds of steam from the bath drifting up towards the light.

'Shhhhh,' said Jen.

'Am I losing it? Am I out of touch? Passed my best? Starting to make wrong decisions?' Jen foamed the soap on the sponge and gently rubbed the palm of Dylan's hand, holding it in her own as she listened to his self-torture. The thought of Charlie's injuries clung to him like a leach.

'I saved someone from taking their own life, perhaps only to have them torture and kill an innocent child. I won't be negotiating again for a while, that's for sure...if ever again,' he said. 'I thought I was doing the right thing and look what's happened now?'

Jen listened. She knew it had been a painful day. Getting up from her haunches and onto her knees, she kissed him, picked a plastic cup from the side and filled it with cold water from the tap.

'What the ...' Dylan stuttered as she threw it at him.

'Leg of lamb waiting downstairs in ten and you, will enjoy it, even if it's nearly midnight. I haven't been slaving over a hot stove all evening for nothing,' she said as she ran downstairs.

Dylan smiled; it was the first time he had that day Jen was his 'normal' and he knew how lucky he was.

Chapter Seventeen

'Sir, I hate to disturb you. I know you're up to your neck in Charlie Sharpe's murder, but...' John whispered tentatively the next morning, as he stuck his head around the SIO's office door.

'No, no, come on in, John. Just let me grab a cup of coffee and I'm all yours,' sighed Dylan. He looked at his watch: it was 7. 30 a.m.

Dylan sat quietly for John's update on the murder in St Peter's Park, as he sipped from the steaming mug.

'Like I said yesterday,' John went on eagerly, 'forensics' 'ave been able to get the chassis and engine number from the burnt out car, from which we've managed to get a registration number; personalised number plate LR 3. It's registered to a Liz Reynolds, The Grange, Harrowfield.'

Dylan lifted his eyebrows, 'God, that's a quick result. We need to speak to Mrs Reynolds' mother, Mrs Platt now as a matter of urgency, to update her on the development. She's the one that reported her daughter missing.'

'I can also tell you from our systems that Liz's husband is doing a five year stretch for receiving, and before you ask,' John said, holding up his hand as Dylan opened his mouth to speak, 'I've already checked to see; he's safely locked up in a secure prison and not been out on day release.'

'So what's next?' Dylan asked his deputy.

'Whatever you tell me, boss,' John said.

'Well, we've an opportunity to identify our burnt body, to confirm for sure that it's Liz Reynolds. We need access to her house, and house-to-house enquiries need to be made with her neighbours. She might've only been a missing person before, but now she may be our murder victim. Let's get into her house with a search team. Firstly a visual check around inside; we need to make sure there's no one else inside lying injured, and we need to check if there are any signs of a struggle-taking place. Find out who her friends are. Were there any previous incidents at the address?'

'I'll get straight onto it, boss,' said John, as he jumped up and left Dylan once again alone with his thoughts.

'I'll see you at the house in an hour. Give me a shout when you're about to go in. I just want to go to the briefing on Charlie's murder first.'

'Okay Boss,' John shouted.

Dylan went into automatic mode; writing his list for the immediate lines of enquiry for the Liz Reynolds murder:

- *Family Liaison Officers required*
- *Up to date photograph required from family*
- *DNA from Liz's home*
- *Prison visit to husband*
- *Forensics to the house – along with the search team*
- *Details of bank accounts, cash cards, mobile, house, telephone etc*

The list seemed endless.

Dylan needed anything that might tell him her movements prior to her death. It may also help him identify a motive for her murder. The intelligence gathering was ongoing and he knew he would just have to be patient.

The smell of bacon wafted into his office. He looked up to see Jen with a plate in her hand.

'Hello love. How nice to see you. Wow, what a delight.' Dylan's face broke out into a smile as Jen put a bacon bap on top of the paper he was writing upon.

'I thought if I didn't bring you something to eat you might forget today. Just bumped into John in the...'

'Canteen? He was supposed to be taking a team to go search a possible murder scene.'

'He has to eat too, Jack. What is it you're always saying, slowly, slowly?' Jen said, patting his hand. 'For goodness sake will you slow down and stop blaming yourself for everyone else's predicament. Life can be cruel, you know that,' she said soothingly. 'Oh, I nearly forgot. I've just had a call from traffic and they have located the car that hit me.'

'That's great.' Dylan's eyes lit up as he relished the taste of the bacon.

'Mmm...' the smile that crossed his face was as big as a Cheshire cat's.

'Yeah but wait for it, it's a hire car that's been stolen from the company it was loaned out to.'

'Oh, no. Nothing's ever straightforward is it? Thanks for this love,' Dylan said, waving the remainder of the bap in front of him before savouring the last morsel. 'Heaven,' he sighed as he smiled with contentment. 'I might not say it often enough but I do love you. Miss Jones.'

'Yes, well just pace yourself then, for me, eh?' Jen smiled.

'One day, lovely lady, we'll leave it all behind us. I promise.'

'And pigs might fly. I won't miss it, that's for sure, and remember you, there is always another day.' Jen walked to the door. Dylan got up and followed her. Turning her round to face him he cuddled her tight.

'You're gorgeous,' Dylan sighed into her hair.

Jen giggled. 'Behave yourself, or you won't have enough energy to last the day,' she said, prodding him playfully in the chest.

'Keep in touch eh? Let me know that you're okay.'

'I 'aven't much option, 'ave I?' Dylan groaned.

'Promise?'

'Promise.' He smiled.

Dylan arrived at 'The Grange' and from where he stood in the front garden he could do nothing but admire the splendour of the property before him. Uniformed officers guarded the doors. Standing quietly, soaking up the ambiance of his surroundings, he listened to the people moving about him. There was little talk. Like worker bees, his colleagues went about their duties, utilising their equipment and preparing their attire for the next stage of the enquiry. Before anything was disturbed, the house had to be videoed.

'John.' Dylan shouted, as he saw the figure of his deputy hurrying from behind the SOCO van in his protective clothing. John walked quickly, towards Dylan now instead of his intended destination, the gravel crunched beneath his feet.

'Sir.'

'You and I need to stroll round the house together to get a feel of the place. I want you to write up the policy book on this one.' Dylan slapped John on the back in a fatherly fashion, as they walked towards the front door.

'I've never done that before.'

'Policy books are something that you will need to become proficient in, so the more you do the quicker the format will become second nature.'

John's face fell.

'Don't look so worried, I'll monitor it. You'll 'ave to cover everything that goes on. Why we make a decision, why we don't; so I'll read it daily, with interest.' Dylan smiled as he spun around.' This whole circus is to help us build a fact file on Mrs Elizabeth Reynolds, and also,' he lowered his voice, 'to identify her visitors whilst hubby's been away.'

As they entered the hallway, Dylan stopped to look at a picture of Liz and Malcolm with their daughter Gemma, on the wall. 'Is Liz the burnt corpse John?' he asked, nodding towards the photograph.

'Who else could it be?' John looked puzzled.

'Now, that's a question and a half. Rule of thumb, never presume. It could be someone who stole Liz's car, perhaps?' Dylan said, as they walked on. 'Or someone might 'ave wanted us to think it was her, perhaps even Liz herself. Blinkers John, don't wear blinkers.' Dylan tutted as he walked ahead, up the stairs.

There was no sign of a struggle. The sheets on the bed in the main bedroom had been left in disarray, as were the ones in the back room. Wet bath sheets lay on the floor of the en-suite. Gemma's pink Disney princess bedroom, with a castle canopy over the bed, was neat and tidy. The sun shone brightly through the pink curtains of the child's bedroom, creating a rosy glow. It felt warm and cosy.

'Get the rooms fingerprinted and the sheets from both unmade beds seized, John.' Dylan went downstairs and John followed, making notes as he walked.

'Dishwasher's got unwashed glasses and plates inside,' Dylan noted, as he opened it with his gloved hands. He pointed to the overflowing dustbin. 'We might get DNA and fingerprints from the empty cans, and if we're lucky enough we might even get a saliva sample, if someone drank from them. Seize the wine bottles. Once we've collected everything that might 'ave some relevance or yield any evidence, then we'll meet up with the Scenes of Crime Officer, Exhibits and Forensics, to prioritise the exhibits, prior to their submission to the lab. Remember, there's a cost implication to the enquiry, even though it's murder.'

John nodded.

'Do you think she was entertaining someone the night before her murder?'

'Yeah, I do, and if she was, then closer examination of the bedding and the crockery will hopefully tell us who.' Dylan walked into the lounge. 'Telephone and address book needs seizing.' Dylan pointed to the book on the table. 'Anything that tells us her mobile number needs looking at, and keep your eyes peeled for a laptop. There is no obvious sign of a computer, but the murderer could be someone she's met on the net.'

'You remind me of an insurance assessor, looking at everything, ignoring nothing and evaluating what value it may have or reveal to the investigation.'

Dylan smiled. 'And so will you by the time you've finished working with me.'

Standing once again on the driveway next to his car, Dylan pulled off his rubber gloves and shed his protective suit, placing them both in his personal brown paper exhibits bag, marked clearly with his name. They'd already been in the house for over an hour.

'Liz's parents; Mr and Mrs Platt?'

John nodded.

'I think we should go and visit them now, don't you? We must tread carefully though. We aren't one hundred per cent sure that the skeletal remains are hers yet. We'll leave the rest of the team here.'

The search team were given their instructions and the two men set off in Dylan's car. Twenty minutes later, with John close behind him, Dylan took a deep breath and knocked on the door of the neat semi-detached town house owned by Ken and Connie Platt. He immediately recognised the lady who answered the door as Mrs Platt; the lady who had come to the front desk to report her daughter missing. Clinging around her waist was the little girl who'd been with her that day, Gemma.

'Detective Inspector Dylan, Mrs Platt,' Dylan said, showing her his warrant card. 'We've met before at the station if you remember.' She nodded. 'And this is Detective Sergeant, John Benjamin.'

'Hello, yes. Do come in.' Connie said, ushering them into the kitchen. She offered them a seat around the kitchen table and excused herself whilst she settled the little girl in the lounge and on her return, promptly shouted to her husband Ken in the garden.

'He loves sitting with a mug of tea, hands dirty, back aching, watching the fish in his pond.' Connie sighed as she filled the kettle at the kitchen sink. 'Can I offer anyone a drink?'

'Two coffees would be nice. Half a sugar for both of us, please.' Dylan smiled.

Ken ambled to the door and leaned on the frame, placing an empty mug on the unit as he mopped his brow with an old hanky. His face was red and puffy with over exertion.

'Bloody flies...as soon as the sun comes out,' he growled, brushing them away with his arm.

'It's the police love,' said Connie.

'Oh, sorry,' he said as he caught sight of the serious faces of the officers sat at his table. Shaking his head he stepped out of his gardening shoes and into the house. 'Not Malcolm again. Hasn't our Liz been through enough?' he sighed.

'No, we were wondering if either of you'd had any further ideas of where your daughter might've gone?' said Dylan.

'No. She just asked her mum if she'd 'ave Gemma,' he said, panting as he pulled a chair out from under the table. He sat down heavily, with a groan.

'She told me she'd got an appointment but she didn't say where or who with.' Connie interrupted.

'And she hasn't contacted you since?' said John.

'No, it's not unusual for her to ask us to babysit Gemma but when she's away she always stays in touch,' Connie spoke quietly. 'Gemma rang her at home the other night.'

'When was that?'

'The same day I picked her up from school and the first night it was planned for her to stayed over, which was why I came to report her missing, when she didn't return to pick

Gemma up the day after or the day after that. She always rings to speak to Gem you see, and we can always get her on her mobile but this time I've tried...we've tried to get her. Her mobiles' dead as a door nail.'

'She probably didn't take her charger with her; she's done that before now.' Ken said, gruffly.

'She's a one,' said Connie, shaking her head.

'What number have you got for her? Can I see please?' said John.

'Well course you can,' said Connie reaching out for her mobile phone.

'Come on, let's stop beating about the bush, eh? What's going on?' said Ken. 'Has something happened? Do you know where she is?'

Dylan saw panic flash across Connie's eyes, and he knew she hadn't told her husband she'd given his officer a key to Liz's house.

'The other day the police were called to a burning car at St Peter's Park,' Dylan said.

'Yes, I saw it on the news.' Ken covered his mouth with his hand.

Connie screamed. 'Tell me it's not...my baby.'

'Not Liz, please.' Ken said, reaching for Connie's hand.

Gemma burst in aroused by the raised voices and stopped abruptly when she saw her grandparent's tears.

'Why are you crying? Nana...Gramps? Are you sad?' she said grabbing the front of Connie's pinafore and staring wide eyed up into her face.

'Yes, darling, we're sad...we're very sad' Connie said, pulling Gemma to her and cuddling her tight. Gemma pushed her away and Connie bent down to her level. Dylan watched Gemma put her tiny hands to each side of her Nana's face before kissing her softly.

'Do you want a drink, love?' Connie said, gulping back the tears. She dabbed at her cheeks with a tissue from her apron pocket.

'And a biscuit please,' she whispered shyly, as she stroked her Nana's cheek. They all watched in silence as Connie guided Gemma to the door carrying her drink and biscuit precariously on a tray. Connie closed the door, behind them.

The kettle was whistling on the gas stove and John walked over to take it off. 'Shall I do the honours?' he asked.

'Yes, yes please,' Ken replied, in a daze as Connie once again took a seat next to her husband.

Dylan explained to them the circumstances of the body, the enquiries to date, the fact that the car had been proved to be Liz's and the activities at her home. John passed around the cups, placing one directly into Connie's hand, ensuring she gripped it properly as she shook uncontrollably.

'Here, have a sip,' he told her. 'Strong tea, it's good for you. It'll steady you,' he said holding his hand over hers whilst she took a sip. Connie shuddered and looked at Dylan her face aghast.

'Sorry, no sugar, it's not good for anyone in shock,' he said.

'It can't be her...I wouldn't let myself think she has been killed? I thought that things like that didn't happen to people like us...I thought you'd just find her . . .'

'Do I need to come with you to identify her?' said Ken.

'It's not that easy Mr Platt. You see, visual identification is impossible,' said Dylan.

'Oh, my God,' Ken cried, holding his head in his hands.

John had never witnessed such grief. 'I'll need the name of Liz's dentist if you have it please?' he said.

'Of course. You did say that at the station.' Connie rose to get the details that she had already written down for Dylan, in an envelope on the dresser. 'But I still don't understand,' she said. 'She was sat where you are just the other day.' Connie stumbled over her words, coughing frenziedly into her hanky. Ken rubbed her back and held the cup once again to her mouth. She gulped the hot liquid, gratefully. 'She would've told us if there was anything wrong. She was delighted Gemma had started school. She was so proud and coping well.' Connie continued.

'Do Malcolm and Janet know yet? Ken asked. 'ave they been told anything?'

'No, not yet. We know where Malcolm is obviously, but who's Janet?' asked Dylan.

'Janet's Malcolm's mum. She lives in Merton, Merton Village,' Connie got up and reached for her address book, from the worktop next to a bundle of cookery books, and handed it across the table to John.

'I promise we'll let you know as soon as we've got the test results. I'm sorry it's the most terrible news anyone could hear, but there is little doubt in my mind that it is your daughter. We know the car was hers and it's a female's body, and she's missing' Dylan only confirmed to them what they didn't want to hear; their worst nightmare. Connie let out a gasp, tears welled in her eyes once more, and she dabbed at her cheek as they fell.

'I assure you we'll do everything in our power to get the results to you as quickly as possible.' Dylan told Ken. 'There are two Family Liaison Officers on their way who'll be able to spend more time with you, answer your questions and try and explain the procedures we are going through at the moment. Of course, if there is anything else you think we should know or anything you think you can tell us about Liz, we would be extremely grateful.'

Ken nodded woodenly as he hung on Dylan's every word; desperately trying to take in the information that he was being given.

'They are PC Fran Hope and PC Clive Merton,' Dylan continued, 'experienced Family Liaison Officers. They'll stay with you as long as you need them. They're trained for this type of incident: they'll be able to help you.'

'Thank you, thank you.' Connie sniffled.

As if on command, a knock came at the door and John let the two officers into the house.

'John and I will head off now Ken...Connie,' Dylan said. Ken tried to stand and fell back on his chair. 'No, no don't stand. I can assure you both that everything that can be done is being done.'

'One question before we leave if I may, do you think Liz was seeing someone?' asked Dylan.

'You're joking she wouldn't dare; Malcolm would've killed her,' choked Connie. Ken shook his bowed head, crying softly.

'The address for Janet Reynolds is?' Dylan sighed heavily as he sat behind the wheel of his car next to John.

Chapter Eighteen

John knocked on the heavy, wooden cottage door. Wisteria hung plentifully around it. The garden was peaceful and the morning's dew glistened, still blanketing the grass in the shade. John's reflection shone back at him from the door's window, as he stood waiting for an answer.

'You won't find her in love,' called a bright and breezy lady's voice from behind the privet hedge that ran between the house and its neighbour. John craned his neck to find its owner, only to see the top of a mop of white hair.

'Do you know where Mrs Reynold's gone? I'm Detective Sergeant Benjamin from Harrowfield CID,' he said, straining his arm over the top of the hedge to flash his warrant card. 'And this is Detective Inspector Dylan.' His words seemed unnecessary, as the owner of the voice obviously couldn't see him let alone the man by his side.

'Oh...I hope nothing's wrong dear. I'm a bit deaf. If you want Janet she's on holiday.'

'You don't know where she's gone do you?'

'Why yes, she's gone to France, but I've no idea where.'

'When's she due back?' said John, grimacing at Dylan.

'Er...she's due back this Saturday. Leeds/Bradford Airport, she's being picked up at noon.'

'Oh, thank you, Mrs?'

'Duke, Thelma Duke' said the kindly, white haired old lady as she gathered her little dog from the lawn. 'Come on Sandy, into the house with you, my man,' she shrieked, in a high pitched voice.

John followed Dylan's suited frame down the path and stopped to shut the wrought iron gate behind him.

'Get someone to meet Janet Reynolds off the plane will you. We'll 'ave to break the news to her then. I don't want her seeing anything in the press or on the news until she's been told.'

'Yes boss, I'll do it myself,' said John, squeezing his large frame into the passenger seat of Dylan's car.

Dylan smiled. John was a man after his own heart.

The phone stopped ringing the moment they entered the SIO's office.

'Bloody typical,' said Dylan. It would probably only be more work, and there was a vast amount of information to digest and intelligence to go through already.

'We need to liaise with HMP Wakefield and ask for a special visit to see Malcolm to tell him of his wife's death,' Dylan said as he sat down. But he knew he needed confirmation it was her first, and quickly. John stood opposite, holding a pen and paper waiting for further instructions.

'Er...Liz's dentists get hold of them will you?' Dylan said, handing him the envelope with the details. 'Let's see if they've got her records and if so let's get them checked out. It's probably gonna be the quickest way.'

'Onto it already, boss ...' John said, as he went back to the CID office.

Dylan grabbed the ringing phone, quickly this time.

'Detective Inspector Dylan? Michelle at the press office. Have you any update for me yet on the police activity at 'The Grange', or the murder of Charlie Sharpe?'

'In a word, no. Look, give me an hour and I'll let you 'ave something to keep the wolves from the door.' Hopefully, he thought, as he crossed his fingers.

'Thankyou. They're only doing their job; chasing deadlines can't be fun, but some are a real pain,' she said.

'No problem.' Dylan said, biting his lip as he replaced the receiver. Immediately it rang again. 'Detective Inspector ...' Dylan started.

'Boss, Dawn.'

'Now that's a voice I'm always pleased to hear. How's it going? Managed to speak to Susan Sharpe yet?'

'Yeah, I'm just telephoning to update you on what she's been saying in interview.'

'Fire away.'

'Charlie had just been diagnosed with attention deficit hyperactivity disorder. Jason only came to live with her a couple of months ago, when he was released from prison. He's into drugs. She never had any money for food, as he took all her allowance money from her. He bought food when he wanted it, but more often than not he nicked it. Susan told us that he was going out robbing regularly but she doesn't know where. She daren't ask, but the job he was on bail for was an attack on a garage kiosk, when he threatened an attendant with an imitation firearm before attacking her. He was expecting to go down, which is why he didn't turn up in court.'

Dylan listened intently. 'The job Larry went to when I was away might've been him too?'

'Possibly, yes. Seemingly, Jason and Chubby shared a room in a 'young offenders' some years ago apparently, and when Chubby became homeless after the Stan Bridge episode, Jason invited him to come and live with them.'

'Interesting. So what about Charlie's injuries? How did they come about? Does she know?'

'She told me that Charlie was naughty, which made Jason mad and so he hit him, sometimes really hard.'

'What about her, Dawn? Did she admit to hitting him?'

'She admits to smacking him when he was naughty to stop Jason hitting him. When he didn't cry, Jason accused her of not hitting him hard enough. She told me Jason hit him once with a piece of wood, to show her how to make him cry, but she said she thought it hadn't hurt him because he didn't cry he just went to sleep.'

'Bloody hell.' Dylan sighed, feeling sick to his stomach.

'She says if she didn't hit Charlie when he was naughty, then she got a beating and Jason hit him harder still. So she started locking Charlie in his room to keep him out of Jason's way.'

'So, why didn't she tell anyone?'

'Petrified, boss, she was petrified of him.'

'So what happened when Chubby Connor moved in then?'

'She says she was chuffed when Jason asked Conner to move in, because she thought things would change and she didn't think Jason would want him to know that he hit Charlie. But it actually got worse because he showed off in front of Conner and played the hard man. He shouted at Charlie to make him do as he said, when he didn't, he hit him and dragged him around like a dog on a lead. She said she begged him to stop but Jason punched her in the face.'

'When did Jason disappear?'

'The morning she found Charlie. The night before he died, Jason and Chubby Conner had been throwing him to each other, having a competition to see who could catch him or who dropped him first. Susan says Charlie and she had been sat on the settee when the men injected, and Jason had started thrashing around with a pool cue. She remembers getting hit with it so she moved to the floor, but Charlie got hit.'

'And what did she do?'

'She doesn't remember, but she does remember Jason bragging to Chubby how hard his son was, because he could hit him and no matter how hard he hit him he didn't cry. She does have a bruise on her arm where she says Jason beat her, which is consistent with being hit with a stick of some kind.'

'Does she 'ave any idea where the men are now?'

'No, no idea. Jason's usual lays low at a mate's house in Blackpool if he's been up to no good, she tells me. Do you know, she can't recall the last time Charlie ate. She says she put food in front of him but he wouldn't eat it and Jason wouldn't let her feed him because he said Charlie wasn't a baby.'

'Oh God, he wouldn't 'ave been able to, his arms were broken. Did you ...?'

'We've videoed the interview but she ultimately pushes the blame onto Jason and Chubby, and doesn't think she has done anything wrong at all.'

'Why didn't she take Charlie to the doctors if he wouldn't eat and he had obvious injuries?' said Dylan.

'She knew asking for medical help would've created problems for them, she says, and Jason ruled the house. Chubby just did as Jason told him, like she did, because he was frightened of him too, she thought. Jason shaved Charlie's head when he was drugged up one night and thought it was funny. She thought the cuts would just heal by themselves. To be fair to her, she's not the brightest button, sir.'

Dylan tutted, 'Pathetic. How're you feeling Dawn?'

'I'm okay. We're doing fine,' she said, patting her stomach, 'but I'd like an hour with Jason and Chubby, I must admit.'

'You and me both, but you, my girl, are only going to watch from a distance. Otherwise, you'll be off home.'

'But Jack ...'

'No buts Dawn. You're my primary concern and I won't hear anymore on the subject, you hear?' Dylan barked. 'I'm thinking of charging her with wounding and child neglect at the moment, as a holding charge, but ultimately it's likely to be murder. We need to confirm who the father is. If she's not sure, DNA samples are going to be necessary and probably the best way of proving it.'

'I'll ask her again about the paternity of Charlie,' Dawn said. Dylan's mobile rang. 'Catch up with me later, will you? Finchy is on the other line.' He replaced one phone for his other one.

'Hello boss, just touching base. Jason and Chubby are both obviously on their toes. There's no sign of them, but we're still looking.'

'I've just spoken to Dawn. We need evidence to connect them both to the house; fingerprints and witnesses, or to a pool cue that she says was used on Charlie. Though, just her say so isn't enough. She told Dawn that Jason Todd likes Blackpool and usually lies low there. Can you circulate their photos over there, please? You never know, it's worth a shot.'

'Fingers crossed, I've put the pictures out across the force area too. Sooner or later their heads will pop up somewhere.'

'Thanks for that Pat. Hopefully Chubby hasn't gone over a bridge somewhere, or maybe that would be poetic justice.'

'I'd rather you call me Patrick, sir...' Patrick Finch said into the phone, before he noticed Dylan had rung off.

Dylan contemplated his next move. 'Hello love,' he texted Jen. 'No news as yet. Will speak to you later when I know what time I'll be home. 'His head was buzzing as he got out the policy book for both enquiries and updated them. The DSs had enough on their plate.

'Boss.' Half an hour later John stuck his head round Dylan's office door. Dylan looked up and saw his smiling face. 'Liz's dentist has been spoken to and officers are on their way to get her dental records.

'Fantastic. Get them to take them straight to the dental laboratory in Sheffield, to the odontologist. Hopefully we'll get an identification.'

'Already sorted boss. I haven't jumped the gun have I? I just thought the sooner ...?'

'Gosh no, you're right. Excellent. Fingers crossed.' Dylan beamed.

'The prison visit's arranged for tomorrow. We'll get some background from Malcolm Reynolds and let him know about his wife. Hopefully, before we go, we'll have confirmation that the body is Liz. Being the SIO, John, is all about being the bearer of bad news.'

'Yeah, well someone has to do it sir, don't they? I've told the team the debrief is at 6 pm if that's okay with you?'

'That's great. I'm doing little Charlie's debrief at five downstairs then I'll be with you.' Dylan realised at that moment he'd been referring to the job as 'little Charlie's' from the outset, not the Sharpe murder or the incident name; this one had touched him. Maybe he should have let Chubby jump that day.

'Susan Sharpe is charged,' Dawn informed the group at the debrief. 'She'll be up before the court tomorrow and hopefully remanded. I'll be there.'

'Priority enquiries are to visit anyone who's had the slightest connection with Alan 'Chubby' Connor and Jason Todd, tomorrow. You all have your targets,' Patrick told them. 'Search the homes, don't accept people's word. They should consent to you looking around, if not, let me know straight away.'

'I want you Pat, and the SOCO supervisor at the meeting I've arranged with forensics, to discuss their approach to the exhibits,' said Dylan.

'The Charlie Sharpe enquiry is ticking over nicely,' thought Dylan, as he walked up the staircase to the Reynolds' debrief. He dialled the press office to give them a brief update. 'Michelle can you put this out on the news line:

'A 21 year old woman will be appearing before Harrowfield Magistrates Court tomorrow, charged with wounding and neglect in connection with the death of a three, year old boy. Two men are also being sought in connection with the boy's murder.'

'Can we name the boy yet?' she said.

'Sorry, DS Finch and DS Farren are still trying to see if they can confirm paternity of the child at the moment, before the young lad can be named I'm afraid'.

Sitting with DS John Benjamin and the team from the Reynolds' enquiry, he soon realised that they would be in the debrief for some time. The information was coming in thick and fast. Luckily for them, in the Reynolds' morning post they had got details of Liz's bank account, showing that she had withdrawn five hundred thousand pounds the day before her murder. There was no sign of cash at the house, so it was an obvious priority enquiry. Her mobile phone was also the subject of one too. Fingerprints had been lifted off the wine glasses, and also such items as her hairbrush, make-up and jewellery boxes, and they were hoping to match up and identify Liz via the partial fingerprint lifted at the scene of the fire, the DNA from the hair root taken at the post-mortem and her dental records. Fingerprints had also been lifted from the beer cans. Early indications using ultra violet light suggested semen staining on bedding taken from her bed, and on clothing recovered from the laundry basket. It was a positive start; a lot to go on, to unravel the background. Was the motive money, sex or both? Only time would tell.

'Nice one team,' said Dylan as he thanked them for their hard work. Another long day, but progress is being made with positive lines of enquiry.' The meeting had lifted him. He took out his mobile as he strolled into the back yard of the police station and he could see his breath in the night air. The sky was clear and in the darkness the brighter stars were lost amongst the myriads visible. He leaned on his car as he called the press office. For once Dylan noticed that the stars twinkled, but the nearer planets didn't.

'Michelle,' Dylan turned to unlock his car door. 'Another update for you.'

'Go ahead, I've got my pen poised.'

'In respect of the burnt body at St Peter's Park; Police are making some positive progress and believe they may 'ave identified the woman who if confirmed, they'll be able to name in the next forty eight-hours, when relatives have been informed. Thanks. You on the graveyard shift?'

'Yeah, it's a bummer, I hate late shift,' she groaned. 'But this will keep me busy for a while,' she said.

'I hope it's a quiet one for you then. I'm off home to a nice meal and a warm bed.'

'Lucky you,' Michelle moaned. 'It'll be another six hours before I see my pit.'

'But at least once you're in it you won't be called out.'

'Too right I won't.' she said.

Chapter Nineteen

Jen walked out of the front door after Dylan. The glimpses of early morning sun were bright through the black clouds. Max barked around Dylan's feet.

'No boy, I'm off to work. Your mum's taking you walking on her own today mate,' he said, patting Max's golden coloured, silky head. 'Although I must admit, the last thing I want to do is go on a prison visit.'

'Never mind. One day, when you whisk me off to the Isle of Wight, we won't be going to the park but the beach for walkies,' Jen said, laughing. Max barked furiously. 'Come on you, before you wake the neighbours,' she said, lassoing Max with his lead. 'Bye love, have a nice day,' she called to Jack, as he put his brief case in the boot and slammed it shut.

'Will do. I'll keep in touch.' Dylan shouted. He watched Jen and Max walk up the road in his rear view mirror. What he'd give to be going with them. To be inconvenienced by Max's persistence to go out in the freezing cold this morning, would be a treat. The car felt chilly and he shivered as he turned the heater on full.

Dawn had left for court by the time Dylan arrived at the office. He wondered if today would be the day they'd positively identify the father of Charlie Sharpe or find Chubby Connor and Jason Todd.

Dylan was pleased with Patrick Finch so far; he could tell he was enjoying being in a detective role again on a high profile case too. He was a good replacement for Larry, precise to the point of annoying though sometimes. He had an eye for detail and was as keen as mustard. He wondered briefly what Larry was doing, and how Fred White was; but as no one had updated him, he presumed Fred was stable, and as for Larry...God only knew.

'Behave at court you. I hope you've remembered to switch your phone off, otherwise this will get you into bother,' read the text message he sent to Dawn. He smiled as his mobile bleeped send.

'I'll remember, don't worry, my names not Jack Dylan,' she texted back.

The morning meetings were over at last.

'I'll be ready to set off for the prison in five minutes, John,' Dylan shouted across the incident room.

'Okay.' he shouted back, from the computer station he was working at. Dylan saw him pick up the phone as it rang. He listened, put the phone down and walked over to stand at Dylan's door.

'It's Sheffield sir, confirming a positive ident on the dental records.'

'And?'

'It's Liz Reynolds.'

Dylan breathed in deeply. Malcolm Reynolds would be getting the worst news he could possibly hear today, and Dylan had to give it to him.

The prison car park was heaving.

'Spare one over there, boss.' John pointed to a parking space.

'You've got to 'ave eyes like a hawk. It's worst than bloody B&Q on pensioner's day,' Dylan muttered to himself, rummaging on the back seat for his suit jacket. John opened his door and stood outside. Rolling down his shirtsleeves, he checked his tie was straight before collecting his paperwork from his seat. Slamming the door, Dylan turned and looked at the austere Victorian architectural style building. Built with local quarried stone, it used to be a fortress; a castle where the brave used to fight to save the hamlet. Now criminals were sent there to protect the community.

'How bizarre,' he thought. Walking up to the stone flagged entrance they stopped between two turrets. John pointed up to holes in the wall.

'At one time they used to pour boiling oil down from them, to keep people out,' he said.

'Perhaps they should pour it on the people within now' Dylan replied.

'Did you know they still used to execute and hang prisoners here until 1961?'

'No, but I hear it has its own healthcare facility.'

'I suppose they need it with 550 cells full of prisoners; all Cat. B prisoners at that,' said John.

'Yeah, they need to make it difficult for this calibre of prisoner to escape and a trip to the hospital is all it takes for some. Not the friendliest of places to be eh?' Dylan laughed half-heartedly.

A uniformed guard came towards them, offering his hand. 'DI Dylan?'

'Yes and DS Benjamin. You've got our visiting orders here I understand?'

'You've just hit visiting time, unfortunately. It's a 'Special' if I'm right? Come straight through,' said the guard as he motioned them to follow him into the new gate complex. As they turned the corner, the queue of people lining the walls reminded Dylan of a shop at the start of a sale. Men, women, old, young, children and babes in arms; you name it, they were there. Dylan knew some would be putting themselves at risk, trying to smuggle things into the prison, and he also knew some would succeed. This prison was named as having the highest recorded drug use amongst prisoners and the second highest suicide rates of prisoners in England and Wales.

'We need to speak to the Duty Officer or the Wing Officer if that's at all possible,' John shouted above the noise.

They entered a vestibule and with the closing of the door, the noise suddenly cut dead.

'That's me. What's up?' The duty officer seemed genuinely concerned.

'We've just found out the burnt body in St Peter's Park, that's been in the papers recently, is Malcolm Reynolds' wife,' Dylan said.

'Blimey.'

The duty officer opened the door to the waiting room and they strode through with a purpose. There were so many young girls dressed in their posh dresses, wearing make-up. Mothers and fathers stood quietly; sombre, subdued. Why oh, why in God's name had the men inside risked getting themselves locked up, when they had people outside who clearly cared about them so much? Dylan would never understand.

'We believe it may be murder,' Dylan said, as he turned out his pockets into a shell like container to be checked.

'Poor bloke, he's a model prisoner,' said the guard, as he frisked him and moved on to John.

The meeting rooms were always cold and sparsely furnished painted with a pale grey gloss. They reminded Dylan of hospital waiting rooms. Windows at the ceiling were fitted with thick steel bars. Malcolm Reynolds was slouching in his chair, as they approached the table where he was sat with his feet up. His white t-shirt showed off his ample muscles, which no doubt had been toned in the prison gym. He chewed gum. The guard closed the door behind them and stood, centurion-like, indicating a seat for Dylan and John opposite the prisoner. John's eyes were fixed on Malcolm's trainers, his eyes dancing around the red snake like pattern that was carved into the soles, so he could avoid looking at Malcolm's face.

Dylan looked into Malcolm's eyes, 'DI Dylan and DS Benjamin.'

Malcolm took his feet off the table and leaned forward to greet them.

'Right, now you're here I'll tell you to your faces, I've nothing more to say to you. I'm keeping my head down and I'm doing my stretch. Now piss off and leave me alone.' He got up, walked to the door and nodded at the guard to let him out.

'Malcolm, sit down. We've some bad news for you and there is no easy way to tell you.' Malcolm's eyes fixed on Dylan and he sat down. Suddenly Dylan felt guilty; Malcolm wasn't the first to know about their investigation into the death of his wife.

'We were called to a burnt out car in St Peter's Park; a Renault. There was a body, burnt beyond recognition at the side of the car. We've now identified that body as your wife, Elizabeth Reynolds.'

'What?' Dylan watched Malcolm's hands clench and his brow furrow.

'Malcolm, I'm sorry to be the bearer of such bad news. We are doing everything possible to trace the killer. I promise.'

'Lizzie, my Lizzie? It can't be. 'Malcolm's eyes swelled with tears.

'Where's Gemma? Where's my daughter?'

'She's with Connie and Ken.'

'Hold on, I can't get my head round this. Why are you sure? If the body can't be identified? How? Why would she be in the park?' he shrieked.

'We're trying to find out why, Malcolm. But we're positive it's Liz; dental records 'ave confirmed it to us this morning. She had withdrawn half a million pounds from the bank the day before the incident. Do you know anything about that?'

'No, no. I've no idea...that's straight up. I wouldn't let her handle that sort of money, no way. Who the fuck would do that to Lizzie?'

'I've got to ask you. It's got nothing to do with you being in here has it?'

'I wouldn't leave anything...knowing I was coming in here and leaving her and Gemma alone. You need to find out what's gone on. I want to know; otherwise you'll have another murder on your hands when I get out. What the fuck's happening?' he said, running his hand through his hair.

'Then what does Gemma do without her mum or dad, eh? Come on Malcolm what else can you tell us?'

It took a moment for him to answer.

'Nothing, absolutely nothing.' Malcolm sat rubbing his head in his hands. 'I've had no hassle in here, you can ask them,' he nodded at the guard.

'We're trying to contact your mum but her neighbour tells us she's in France.'

'Let me tell her...I'll ring her from 'ere.'

'Okay. Whatever you want.'

Malcolm's head was down. He nodded, and then turned to Dylan, biting his lip. 'So what happens now? I'll put some feelers out see if anyone can tell me anything,' he said.

Dylan was satisfied that it had come as an absolute shock to him; either that or he was a very good actor.

'Can you get Janet to contact us to confirm you've broken the news to her, because at some point Liz's details will 'ave to go out to the media and her face will be all over the newspapers and on the TV. We need to appeal for witnesses as soon as we can.'

'Sure, but I want to know what's happening. I've a right. I want to know that Gemma's okay'.

'Look, we'll get a panic alarm fitted at Ken and Connie's house and keep you updated.'

'Was she killed in the park? Or somewhere else?'

'Burnt with the car. We're still doing tests, but for now that's all we know.'

'I need to get my head around this,' he said.

As they left the gloomy building, the sunlight burst through a cloud. Dylan put his hand up to his eyes so he could see John's face.

'He seemed genuinely shocked and upset, don't you think?'

'Mmm. Do you think he's owt to do with it, boss? Do you think she was paying someone off for him?'

'Who knows? The golden rule is, - never assume or presume, John. She'd got the money for something or someone. But who and why we'll 'ave to find out.'

There would be a lot more questions awaiting answers back at the office.

'I've had a call from Traffic. They've traced the person the hire car was loaned to on the day it hit me,' enthused Jen, as she bounded unexpectedly into Dylan's office.

'Great, who is it?' said Dylan, not lifting his eyes from his paperwork.

'Ah, well, they don't know exactly. It was hired out to a company, so it must be one of their employees who was driving it, and the traffic cop tells me that they should have driving records for him to check, which will then tell us who was driving it at the time,' she said, looking smug.

'You should get your wing mirror fixed properly.' Dylan looked up from his paperwork but his eyes concentrated on the computer screen as he typed. 'I thought they said it was stolen?'

'Yeah, they did, but I bet the employee who borrowed the car failed to return it because he'd had an accident in it.' Jen said, thoughtfully.

'Oh, quite the little detective aren't we?' Dylan laughed.

'Yeah,' said Jen, 'and how good is my memory then, remembering the car reg like that? You'll be wanting me on your team next.'

'Mmm not sure about that, I wouldn't get anything done.' Dylan smiled as he called up his messages on the computer. He looked studious whilst Jen stood quietly.

'Bye Jen is it then?' she said, teasing him.

'Oh, sorry. Make me a drink before you go will you love?' Dylan looked at her with puppy dog eyes.

'Oh, good enough for making coffee then, eh?' Jen said as she headed for the door.

'Let me tell you, Detectives, no matter how naturally talented they are, 'ave to start somewhere and making good coffee is a good start, ask Vicky.' Dylan smiled as he watched her leave.

Dylan read the email that told him Fred White was off the danger list and likely to make a full recovery; now that was good news. He rang Larry's home to let him know but there was no reply; he tried his mobile but it was dead. Dylan shrugged. Where the hell was he? Then he remembered looking at his calendar. Larry was due to appear in court. With everything else, Dylan had forgotten. Blast.

The next email told him Susan Sharpe's defence team wanted a second post-mortem on Charlie, and there would be a third when Todd and Connor were locked up.

'Bloody ridiculous,' Dylan said just as Jen walked back in the office with a steaming mug of coffee and a biscuit.

'What's ridiculous?'

'Little Charlie's body being messed about with, that's what. Very, very rarely do pathologists disagree. I can understand why they have to have two post-mortems when there is one injury, or an unusual cause of death, but with this case they've plenty of injuries to choose from. All this is, is folk making money out of others' grief. Prosecution costs are always transparent and monitored, but the defence team; who knows what, goes on? We certainly don't. So I guess it's either me or Pat that will have to relive the post-mortem of the poor little un twice more.' Dylan sighed.

'Sorry, love. I don't know what to say.'

'What can anyone say? Tell you what. I'm going to ''ave a word with the coroner and see if it's possible to get agreement between defence solicitors.'

'You can only try.'

'Hey, nice coffee Jen; there is hope for you yet in CID,' he said with a wink. 'And Fred White is on the mend.'

Jen smiled.' That is good news.'

Dylan walked with Jen to the main entrance.

'You'll be home on time?'

'Yeah, I won't be long now. I just want to call in on the incident rooms, then, I'll be coming home. What's for tea?'

'Chicken dinner, so don't be late otherwise Max might be eating it.'

'Will 'e hell as like. I'll be there,' Dylan said, as they smiled at each other.

Dylan wandered down the corridor and into the mailroom. The cupboard like room housed several pigeonholes marked with people's names, teams and rotas, all filled with internal and external mail. Pinned together but not in an envelope, there was a thick wedge of A5 size photographs, in Charlie Sharpe's incident room tray.

'Hell fire.' Dylan hollered, grabbing the photo's. 'Who the flaming hell sent these like this?' There was no one to hear his outburst. Dylan flounced into the incident room. ''Ave you seen these?' he said, throwing the photographs across Patrick Finch's desk. 'They've been sent through the internal mail just like that, for anyone to see. How bloody thoughtless can they get?'

'PM photos?' Patrick asked.

'Yeah, fancy how upsetting they'd be for anyone coming across them in the post. I'm not having this.' Dylan was spitting feathers as he picked up the phone.

'Could you put me through to the Imaging Unit please?' Dylan waited for the call to be answered.

'Imaging Unit Manager speaking,' rattled a distracted voice.

'This is DI Dylan. I've just received a full set of photographs of the murder of a young boy that display all his injuries, and the post-mortem photographs, through the internal mail.'

'Yes,' he said.

'But they're not in an envelope, anyone could see them,' Dylan said raging.

'It's policy. We've been told not to waste money on envelopes.'

'What? It won't be saving you money when someone collapses with the shock. What if a relative saw them? I want them sent to me under the cover of confidentially in future and in an envelope. Do I make myself clear?' demanded Dylan.

'Well yes you do, to me, but I'll have to take it back before the command team for their approval. Tell you what, put it in writing to me. If it's best practice ...'

'It's bloody common sense never mind it has to be approved by the command team as best practice. Oh, for Christ sake speak to whoever you 'ave to but I won't be so polite if it happens to me again,' Dylan yelled, slamming the phone down. He looked around him to tell someone about this outrage but realised he was alone in the office. Where the hell had everyone gone? Dylan sat down, put his head in his hands and sighed.

Dawn walked in some minutes later with a strong coffee. 'Here you are. I thought might need this before you blew a gasket,' she said chuckling.

'Can you believe, it's all about cost cutting and saving money? I'm sure some of 'em couldn't organise a set of fat Bobbies never mind run a police force,' Dylan said. 'Tell me what planet are they on?'

'Yeah...well, but hey look on the positive, who'd you be annoyed with if they made the right decisions in the first place,' she said.

'Probably you.'

'As if I'd listen?' she laughed, bringing a smile to his face.

Patrick swung open the door. 'Forensics is checking a bloodstained print from the doorframe of Charlie's room for DNA, and the print against Connor, Todd and Sharpe. It's too large for Charlie, so I'm just hoping it is Charlie's blood and one of their fingerprints.'

'Now that would be some justice, and great evidence wouldn't it?'

'They're also looking at marks and blood splashes on the walls, and are suggesting using 3D technology to show all the injuries on Charlie's body, for court purposes.'

'Wow, that's clever isn't it? Just think what an impact that would 'ave on a jury? Although if it's too damning, the defence will say it's unfair. I'm all up for it, Pat. Let's just hope the judge has some balls.'

Patrick sat across from Dylan at the desk. 'I wish you'd call me Patrick sir.'

'Yeah, whatever you like,' said Dylan. 'Any developments in the search for Chubby, and Jason Todd yet?'

'No, boss. We're still trying though.'

Dawn yawned. 'Hey lady, I hope you're not doing too much,' scolded Dylan.

She smiled, looking tired.

'Off home, now,' said Dylan, as he got up to leave for the Reynolds' incident room. He'd just check to see if there was any news in there before he went home too.

The HOLMES team were beavering away in front of their computers. He looked at the clock; 6pm and all of them still busy, it was never simply just another 'job' for the incident team members. Each and every person that was involved wanted the offenders caught as soon as possible, but most of all they wanted to be part of it. The HOLMES team members didn't just work on the computers Dylan had everyone involved in the briefings. Their collective knowledge was a catalyst and each person played an integral part.

A Post-it note was stuck to his in tray, 'Please ring CPS. Noel Cantrell X6110'. Dylan picked up the phone. Noel was a team leader and for him to call Dylan he knew it had to be serious.

As expected, the news was bad. He'd rung Dylan out of courtesy to tell him that DS Larry Banks hadn't answered his bail, nor had he appeared before the court on the charges against him. A warrant had been issued for his arrest. If he wasn't at home or in court today then where was he? Dylan put in a call to Force Welfare to suggest they made some urgent checks, but they'd gone home; no twenty four hour call-out there. He left a message on their answering machine.

He sat peeling a banana at his desk, and even though he was deep in thought he noticed some of the HOLMES team looking at him, over their computers. He pulled a face at them through the glass partition. Their tired faces broke out into smiles. Perhaps he was going totally mad, he thought. The fax at his side startled him, and he put the rest of the banana in his mouth, so he could pick up the paper. Intelligence from the prison backed up the claim that

Malcolm Reynolds was a model prisoner. There was nothing on record to suggest him and his wife had problems. He was a calming influence, the guards on the wing had reported; especially to Frankie Miller, his long term cellmate who had been released a few weeks ago. Frankie Miller, Dylan found out, was a career criminal who used violence at every opportunity; but there had been a bond forged between Malcolm Reynolds and him, which the prison authorities thought had been good for Frankie. He was a colourful, character no doubt. Dylan would generate an enquiry for him on the HOLMES system. An interesting read, Dylan thought, and a priority line of enquiry at that, if he was out and about.

Dylan stopped for petrol on the way home. Outside he noticed a bucket of flowers and grabbed a bunch for Jen. He picked up a dog chew for Max from the basket as he waited in the queue.

There was a police traffic car on the driveway of their home. The smell of roast chicken and stuffing wafted through the door as he walked in. Dylan didn't realise until then just how hungry he was.

'Time away from work is time wasted, officer,' Dylan shouted from the hallway. He could hear Max growling from the kitchen.

'Sir, PC Tom Dale,' said the traffic officer, as he stood up from his haunches where he'd been playing tug of war with Max and his toy. Hearing Dylan's voice Max ran from his newfound playmate and dropped at Dylan's feet, barking wildly.

'Hello there, mate. Nice to see you too,' he said, pulling the chew from his pocket. Max sniffed at it, took it into his mouth and carried it to his bed. Dylan handed Jen the flowers and kissed her cheek.

Jen smiled. 'Flowers, what you after?'

He grinned as he winked at PC Dale.

'Sit down won't you and drink your tea. Come with news about the accident?'

'Yeah, but not good news. The company records only show the stolen car being hired, but no one took it out legitimately that day.'

'Just my luck.' Jen said, as she moved to check the vegetables boiling in the steamer, then got a vase for her flowers from the cupboard.

'I'll get off then,' PC Dale said, 'and thanks for the brew, Jen. I'll see you later.' PC Dale shook Dylan's hand.

'I'll leave it with you then as they say,' Dylan said.

Yeah, sounds about right for CID.' he grinned, sheepishly.

Jen showed PC Dale to the door, as Dylan sat at the kitchen table. Max brought the chew back to him and laid it at his feet.

'Get away with that manky old thing.' Dylan said, throwing it back in Max's bed. Max jumped on top of it and whined.

'Thank you for the flowers, love. How're the enquiries going?' Jen said, kissing the top of his head as she came back into the kitchen.

'I found out Larry didn't turn up at court today,' he sighed.

'How daft is that?' she said, dishing out their dinner and putting his on the table in front of him.

'It makes you wonder, doesn't it, how much you really know about people you work with? Or about anyone, really,' she said, thoughtfully.

Jen got up and cleared the table and stood at the sink holding her back.

'You okay?'

'Yeah, just tired that's all and my back...argh it kills,' she said stretching her spine.

'Do you want me to make coffee?' asked Dylan.

'Not for me love, I've gone right off coffee. I'll make you one when I've finished this though, if you want to go up and get changed.'

Jen switched on the TV in the lounge for the late news. The room was warm and Dylan sat reading the Harrowfield Examiner.

'Breaking news,' the newsreader said. 'Manchester police have named a man shot whilst attempting to commit an armed robbery at Lloyds Bank at lunchtime today, as Frank Miller.'

Dylan looked up from his paper and turned to Jen.

'That's the name of the bloke celled up with Malcolm Reynolds.

'Frank Miller's not such an unusual name in the north.' Jen cuddled up close to Dylan, taking the paper off him as he turned his head for a kiss.

'No...you're right ...' he agreed, kissing her back. 'Let's go to bed eh? You look all in.'

'Yeah, I am,' she yawned.

Chapter Twenty

Dylan whistled as he walked into work the next morning. It wasn't quite daylight, because of the rain.

'Someone's in a good mood. Good night was it boss?' called Vicky from her workstation. Temporarily blinded by the glaring light in the incident room, he couldn't see anyone immediately, but Dylan felt himself go hot under the collar at her suggestive comment.

'I do believe you're going a lovely shade of red, sir,' said Vicky.

'Me? You must be joking. I don't think I've got a blush left in me,' he laughed. 'D'ya know something, Vicky, the last time I remember being embarrassed and I mean embarrassed, was when I was a young detective and went to a burglary with a very old detective sergeant,' he said, sitting on the corner of her desk. 'He seemed ancient to me; just like I probably do to you,' he said chuckling. 'As I took down the details of the break-in, he asked the old couple if he could use their toilet. The strange noises that came from upstairs were enough, but when he walked back into the lounge with his jacket over his arm, and still pulling up his braces, I tell thee I nearly died.' Dylan mockingly put on his best, deep, Yorkshire accent. 'By heck ba it makes tha wonder what thee heck tha puts in curries? Sithee later.'

Vicky fell about in a fit of giggles.

'Fortunately we were about to leave, as the smell started to filter down the stairs, it was gut-wrenching. Now that was what you call embarrassing,' he said, as he walked towards his office door.

'Urgh, you've put me right off my breakfast.'

'You don't 'ave to worry 'til I start wearing tha braces,' said Dylan, as he opened his office door. In the darkness it felt like his cell, and he turned on the florescent light that buzzed the place into life. Two bananas toppled from his briefcase when he opened it, and he picked them off the desktop and put them in his drawer. As he did so he noticed a note. Jen had drawn a smiley face and a kiss. He grinned from ear to ear as he placed it in his suit pocket, where he found another piece of paper that read, 'I love you. x.' Dylan was still smiling as he answered the telephone.

'Hello sir, it's Neil Thornton from the fingerprint department.'

'Morning Neil. And how can I help you?'

'Well Sir, it's more like how I can help you.'

'Ah, that sounds like good news.'

'Well, yes and no ...'

'We've identified some fingerprints on a wine glass and the beer cans at the Reynolds' house. It's a bit sensitive; DS Larry Banks needs to keep his hands in his pockets, or make sure he wears gloves next time.'

'Neil, Larry Banks isn't on the investigation and he hasn't been to the scene with us.' Dylan's smile faded quickly.

'Well sir, I have to tell you they're positive identification marks, and we've quite a few of his elsewhere in the house, too. The other significant marks are the marks of one person and they haven't been identified as yet, but I would think it's highly likely that they're going to be Liz Reynolds.'

'Thanks Neil. Will you keep this information close to your chest at the moment?'

'Sure. I'll send the report out to you in confidence.'

'What had Larry got himself into?' Dylan wondered, as he replaced the receiver. Dylan had never seen Larry Banks blind drunk, but he was beginning to think he might never have seen him completely sober either. He'd been drinking at Liz Reynolds'; now she was dead. But what was Larry doing at Liz Reynolds' house? It didn't make sense, any of it. This evidence put Larry forward as a suspect or the suspect for her murder. Was he capable of such a thing? What did Dylan actually know about Larry Banks? Not a lot, he conceded. He had knocked an old man over and left him for dead. So like Jen said, who knew what he was capable of?

John came in his office carrying a coffee, and both were a welcome sight. Dylan was saddened to think somebody who had worked alongside him closely for the last few years could be involved in something so bad. He shared all the new information with John, and ultimately they both knew they would have to share it with the team.

'Larry will be dealt with like any other suspect; it'll be no different for him because he's a police officer,' Dylan told John. 'I'll be given the task of tracing him and 'ave yet to confide in the force hierarchy, which I'm not looking forward to, I can tell you. The re arrest of a senior police officer is certainly going to be an embarrassment for them, but I'll do whatever I 'ave to, to find Liz's murderer.'

'If, Larry Banks was the last person to see her alive . . .' John said, looking as if he was finding it hard to take in.

'At this moment in time he is the prime suspect,' interrupted Dylan.

'Flaming hell.'

'Once I've informed HQ and the Command Team, then we'll tell the investigation team.' Dylan heaved a sigh. 'And at the moment I don't 'ave a clue where to start looking.'

'You can say that again.'

'Not only that, have you heard the news? A Frank Miller's been shot by the Greater Manchester police.'

'No,' replied John, startled by a further revelation.

'What I'm going to tell you this morning, will remain within the team. If I find anyone has been idly gossiping or speaking out of turn, they'll be off the enquiry and never again work on another major investigation. Do I make myself clear?' Dylan told the Liz Reynolds investigation team. There were one or two mumblings and then the room fell silent. The group knew from the look on his face that DI Dylan meant business. He explained to his team about the finding of the fingerprints, plus the positive identification of Detective Sergeant Larry Banks.

'Larry obviously knew Liz Reynolds. There may be some innocent explanation. If any of you know of one, or know where he is at this moment in time, then please share that information with me or DS Benjamin. It will be kept in the strictest of confidences, but until we talk to him and eliminate him, he's a suspect, he has to be,' Dylan told them. 'Priority enquiries will now commence, focusing on Larry. I will be prioritising actions for enquiries at his flat, his telephone;

anything that will locate him. He's the prime suspect in this investigation and will be treated as such.'

There was an unsettled atmosphere in the room, which was most unusual. Did someone know something, anything? Did everyone know something he and John didn't? Or was it just unease at the thought of one of their own being a murderer.

'Moving on. On last night's news there wa a bulletin about a Frank Miller being shot in Manchester.

'Is this the same Frankie Miller that was banged up with Malcolm Reynolds? Natalie, get onto it at once, will you?' Natalie, the researcher, nodded in the affirmative. 'I want you to liaise with Manchester police and start establishing if this is the case.'

Once again there was no movement and silence ensued. 'Is there anything anyone wants to share with the team, with us?' Dylan asked. There was a pause.

'No? Okay, forensics 'ave just informed me that they're positive they'll have further updates for us today, boss,' said Vicky.

'Thank you. If there is nothing else then pick up your actions and let's get the show on the road.'

Dylan sat back in his chair in the SIO's office, alone with his thoughts. He couldn't believe what was happening. If Larry was guilty, then why hadn't he attempted to clear up after himself? If Larry had murdered Liz, Dylan would have expected him to at least make an attempt to cover his tracks. His mind was being bombarded with all sorts of possibilities; one minute defending Larry, the next finding him guilty.

The day progressed with police liaison confirming that Malcolm Reynolds' mum Janet had been contacted by him. Now Dylan was satisfied that all of Liz's family had been made aware of her death, he could give her details and photographs to the press. He'd be asking for help from anyone who had seen or been in contact with her recently. The press release would be sent to all the media. Maybe - just maybe - someone would come forward with information that would move the investigation forward. Had anyone seen Liz with Larry? How did Larry know her? Maybe they had got to know each other when Malcolm Reynolds got himself locked up; Dylan knew Larry had been on the enquiry.

The morning had flown by.

He texted Jen. 'The day's gone into free fall. All sorts happening – catch up with you when I get a min x'

'Don't worry about me just don't overdo it. X.' was Jen's reply.

Vicky knocked at the door. 'An update already from forensics, boss. They've got a full DNA from the balaclava and it's going to be checked on the national DNA database. 'Dylan raised his eyebrows. 'And wait for it,' she said smiling. 'There are enough semen stains found on the bed sheets taken from 'The Grange' to get a profile from, and the burnt suitcase contained books; law textbooks.'

Dylan was so surprised by the revelation that he was lost for words.

'And there's more. Inside the burnt car, they've found the remnants of a mobile phone and are doing tests on the SIM card. They seem hopeful it's not totally destroyed. They're going to ring me back with their findings, ASAP. All good news, eh?'

'Brilliant Vicky,' Dylan said, forcing a smile.

The enquiry was buzzing but Dylan still couldn't help kicking himself. If he had done things differently over the past few weeks, could some of the incidents have been prevented? If he hadn't been so keen to help Chubby Connor, would Charlie still be alive? Boy, he thought, picking up the post-mortem photographs from their place upon his desk, had that little lad suffered. Why hadn't they managed to trace the twats yet? What if he'd spoken to Larry; tackled the addiction Dylan believed he had. Told him to go home and not come back till he had sorted out his problems, or even got him help? Would Fred White have been in hospital now? Would Liz still be alive? It niggled him like a thorn in his side. Was he off the boil?

'Shortbread, sir?' Lisa said, from the doorway. Dylan smiled weakly.

'Thank you; that would be lovely.' Dylan beckoned her into the office.

'We're worried about you. You're not usually so quiet,' she said as he picked a triangle from the box.

'I just don't like it when coppers are involved; it leaves a nasty taste.'

'Coppers and kids, boss, the worst to deal with, I remember you once told me. But we strive to get justice for the victims and their families, and we will never give up, you said.' She was right; he needed to think positive.

He stared out of his office window long after she'd gone, thinking about what she'd said. Leaning on his desk with both elbows he absentmindedly nibbled at his biscuit. He heard a tittering from the general office and looked over. The girls were mimicking him, and he laughed with them. He got up from his chair and stood at his door. 'Come on, let's get all this shit flushed away and get back to normal.' said Dylan. 'Quitters never win and winners never quit.' he said, dramatically slamming the door shut. His phone rang.

'Sir, PC Jordan. We're at the home address of Larry Banks, after a bad smell was reported by a neighbour. We've forced entry.'

'Oh, no,' Dylan whispered under his breath, as he put his hand to his forehead.

'We've found the body of a man. Face down on the bed. Paramedics were called and pronounced him dead, so we've come out of the scene to call you.'

Dylan sat down. 'Do you...Is it ...?'

'Sir... I didn't want to disturb anything until you're satisfied it's not suspicious. I can't see the person's face.'

'Yes, err...right...good. I'm on my way.' Dylan faltered. His stomach lurched, and fear crept through his veins. It couldn't be, could it?

Twenty minutes later, he had spoken to the uniformed officers outside, before stepping into Larry's apartment. Booted and suited he saw the body of the man was face down as PC Jordan had said. His face totally swallowed up in a feather pillow. Dylan's pulse quickened. He could only liken the atmosphere to that of a funeral of a personal friend or family member; quiet and penetrating. There was a note visible on the bedside table. The envelope read; 'To Whom It May Concern. 'Was it Larry's handwriting? He couldn't tell. It was printed in capital letters. 'Should he look at it first?' he thought. He took a deep breath and knelt at the side of the bed, so he could get a closer look at what could be seen of the front part of the man's head and sides of his face. He had to know.

Chapter Twenty-One

Dylan couldn't have been more than a foot away from the head. He rested his hand on the pillow and pushed, ever so slightly with his gloved hand, to reveal more of the man's face and let out a huge unsteady gasp. The relief he felt was enormous; it wasn't Larry, but who was he, and what was he doing in Larry's flat? He stood, and with shaking hands and a heart that would not be still, he picked up the envelope and carefully extracted the contents.

'Dear Mum & Dad

Sorry, I know you only wanted the best for me by sending me away to Uni. I really did try… but I'm so lonely and my life feels so hopeless. I know you won't understand, but maybe you will forgive me for being weak. I'm not as tough as you, Dad. I only wish I was. Now I've admitted it to you I can find peace.

Yours forever,

Gordon'

Dylan lifted his eyes from the letter and scanned the bedroom. A brief search found a rental agreement from Harrowfield Estate Agents, which revealed the body was that of Gordon Blake.

'Another sad one for the coroner's officer; how tragic. Bright enough to go to university but not wise enough to value his life,' he whispered. Although he was relieved it wasn't Larry, he felt saddened that anyone could take their own life over something that could have easily have been sorted. If only he'd talked to his parents and told them how he'd felt. He stared hopelessly at the small white tablets and plastic container near the body.

A lot of information was exchanged in the evening briefing and the team looked tired and hungry. It was late. Mr Ian Beckwith from Barclays Bank had come forward to say that Liz had withdrawn money; and a member of his staff had told him he had put it directly into a suitcase for her, the day before the murder.

'Vicky, go and see Mr Beckwith tomorrow will you. We need a statement from anyone who saw or spoke to Liz,' said Dylan.

'It's been confirmed that the Frank Miller shot in Manchester was the same Frankie Miller who'd been locked up with Malcolm Reynolds,' said Natalie. 'Seemingly, he walked into the bank with a shotgun and demanded cash. The panic alarm was activated and the shutters sprung up. He fired at the armed response team as he left the bank. They didn't hesitate. Frankie died instantly, from rapid fire from trained firearms officers who aimed at Frankie's philtrum, the point under his nose, which rendered Frankie incapable of pulling the trigger, or any other action, so they tell me.'

'And,' said John, 'I can now confirm, Larry had been involved in Malcolm Reynolds' arrest and conviction. Also, enquires at the Harrowfield Estate Agency revealed that Larry had commenced an agreement with Gordon Blake, via them, after he'd left the area.'

'So, where's the money? Did Larry 'ave it?' said Dylan.

'It's not in his flat.'

'There are still a lot of questions to be answered. Hopefully tomorrow we'll move things forward again. I'll be speaking with the chief constable and command team, letting them know, that on the evidence available at this time, we have no alternative but to arrest Larry Banks on suspicion of murder. And it seems likely that Interpol will 'ave to be involved. Thank you everyone for your efforts today. I'll see you here again tomorrow morning.' There was a knock at the door.

'Can I come in?' said Jen, hesitantly. 'I've brought jam doughnuts; they're still warm,' she grinned, as she handed them around to the team.

'Thank you,' Dylan mouthed to her, as he watched his team, licking the sugar off their fingers. They were smiling again; her gesture lifting their spirits.

Dylan's head ached; it was late. 'Time for home, my good woman,' he said, putting an arm around her shoulder and squeezing her tight, as everyone filed out, thanking Jen for her kind thought. She smiled, and looking up at Dylan thought how well he'd sleep tonight. He looked all in.

'I'll just finish up here and I'll be home shortly,' he said yawning.

'I'll see you in bed then,' she said, laughing. 'It's past ten now.'

Dylan had spent his entire working life thinking himself a good judge of character, but now he had to admit to himself, in Larry and Chubby's case, that tried and tested ability, had let him down badly. The only thing he could do now was make sure they were both caught and put before the courts.

The house was almost in darkness, apart from the light from the lamp in the hallway that Jen had left on for him. Max lay at the foot of the stairs. His tail flapped in acknowledgement of Dylan's arrival but he didn't bother raising his head.

'Good boy.' Dylan knelt down to pat him. 'ave you bin looking after your mam again for me mate?' he whispered.

Jen was fast asleep. Curled up under the duvet, she looked so content he didn't want to wake her, but he knew he would as soon as he put the light on. He touched her face and she stirred.

'Let's rewind the clock to last night, eh love?' he whispered.

'You want me to get up and make you a warm drink?' she murmured, sleepily without opening her eyes.

'Nah, I'll just crawl into bed next to you. I'm knackered,' he said before he went into the bathroom to undress.

Jen lay awake, waiting for him to get into bed, rolling to his side to warm it, best she could. Ah, it was freezing. She shivered. She wished he'd put in for a transfer to detective training; he'd work nine-to-five days, get every weekend off, never be on call. Jack had such a lot of experience to share with would-be detectives. The CID aides seemed to like him. He'd do a good job. She smiled to herself; a plan in the making she thought as she drifted off to sleep.

They were woken by the phone. Jen looked at the clock, it was four fifteen. Dylan's hand, robot-like, reached out to get it. He managed a grunt as he picked it up.

'Morning sir. I hope I haven't woken you?'

Why did people always say that? Did they truly expect you to be sat up twenty-for/seven?

'You did,' he said grumpily. He felt for Jen, as she wasn't on call, but she was always woken up too. Hang on a minute, he wasn't on call either.

'Night shift 'ave disturbed a burglar at the bakery on Greenhead Road. The officers chased him into the yard, and now he's threatening to jump from the rooftops. They've asked for a negotiator and I understand ...'

'But I'm not on call.'

'I know sir, but the on-call is halfway up the A1, en route to the Regional Crime Conference in Newcastle, and recommended you as the nearest, trained ...'

'Remind me to thank them. 'ave you started a log? It'll take me at least twenty minutes to get there.'

Jen was already pulling clothes out of his wardrobe for him. 'Not another body Jack, surely?' she groaned.

'Uniform's disturbed a burglar and he's threatening to jump off a building.'

She turned, hankie in hand. 'But ...'

'I know, I'm not on call,' he said, tying his shoelaces. 'I'll 'ave to sort it later.' He took the hankie off her and stuffed it in his trouser pocket. 'I was having such a lovely sleep,' he whispered, as he kissed her lips.

'Me - too. Look, there's some fruit, a cereal bar and water in that bag,' she said pointing to his briefcase. 'Please be careful and let me know what's happening when you can. Love you.'

Dylan reached out for a cuddle. 'That, you can be sure of, Miss Jones. I wish people would just leave us alone,' he moaned.

'You better go,' she said, biting her bottom lip. 'Don't forget to grab your scarf and gloves; it'll be cold out there at this time of the morning.'

'If they were going to do it, they'll 'ave done it by the time I get there, love. Hopefully they'll 'ave realised before then, that being smashed to pieces isn't as attractive as being locked up and I'll be back home soon.' Dylan had seen the bodies of jumpers that had landed feet first, ending up inches shorter than they once had been and he had also seen them land head first; leaving an absolute mess for some poor bugger to clean up.

Driving over the moorland to Greenhead Road, Dylan thought how prisons had changed over the past twenty-five years, not always for the better. A lot of the suicides he'd been called to, or threats of suicides, were people with long police records. The ones that really needed help didn't hesitate to kill themselves; it was done without a backward glance. How could anyone face such terror head on? He couldn't comprehend what must go through the mind of someone about to end their own life, and the different ways they'd resort to, to do it. He would always remember going to the body of a young woman who'd slit her wrists; the deep red blood bath that met him when he opened the bathroom door. Her pale grey lifeless body lay in a few inches of water in the moisture-filled room as if she had fallen asleep; her eyes closed as if at peace. A razor blade lay in her upturned hand, her arm draped over the side of the bath, and a pool of blood that had dripped from her wrist, lay on the cream tiled floor, seeping into the lines of grout. The memory of the smell made his nostrils swell and bile rise in his throat. He was making good time along the quiet streets now. Then there was a sudden bright pink flash of a speed camera...Oh God; that was all he needed. Endless reports to prove that he was indeed en route to an emergency. He looked at his Speedo 38 mph in a 30mph area.

A police car with flashing blue lights blocked the road ahead. Dylan drove towards it. An officer held up his hand indicating for Dylan to stop. Dylan took his foot off the accelerator and drove at a crawl. The officer drew his truncheon, seemingly threatening to put it through Dylan's windscreen. It had the desired effect. Dylan stopped.

The officer stormed over to the driver side and wrenched the door open.

'Can't you see the bloody road is closed ...' he started to say.

'Put that away,' Dylan said angrily, flashing his warrant card in his face.

'I'm your on-call flaming negotiator.'

'Sorry, sir,' he mumbled, 'I didn't recognise ...' he said, fumbling as he put the truncheon back in the pocket in his trousers. 'He's gone into the yard over there and up the old fire escape,' the officer said, pointing.

The building was semi-derelict. Sitting on the edge of its roof was the cause of all the commotion. One, two, three, four. Dylan counted the storeys and moaned. How the chuff was he going to get up there to speak to this twat? His legs went weak; shook at the thought. The male figure silhouetted against the dawn light looked ant sized from where Dylan stood. There was a loud crash making Dylan jump.

'A slate sir,' called a uniformed officer. 'He's keeping us awake by throwing them off.'

'You could 'ave bloody warned me.' Dylan yelled.

'Tell control I've arrived will you, and ask for an ambulance in case he does jump.'

'Or I faint,' Dylan thought.

'Ask for the fire brigade as well; we might need their turntable and ladders.' Dylan swallowed hard as he looked skyward. Should he try the megaphone first? He had it in the boot of his car with his scarf and gloves.

'What's he nicked?' asked Dylan.

'Bit of cash, some food, but we think he probably just wanted a place to get his head down for the night, and when he got disturbed he freaked out.'

Dylan inhaled deeply as he inspected the fire escape. He could smell Thomas's bakery. The staff were inside grafting away as usual at this time of day, getting their orders ready. Was there anything nicer than the smell of baking bread he wondered, and his stomach rumbled as if in response to his thoughts. Rusty metal crumbled in his hand as he fingered the ladder's rungs. He grimaced at the health and safety nightmare, but what choice did he have? Dylan could hear Jen's voice clearly as he began to climb. 'What the hell did you go up for? Are you stark raving mad?'

Two flights up and his head began to spin. The ground looked blurred beneath him and the noise of another slate hitting the ground echoed in his ears. Should he go up or back down? The fire brigade would be rescuing him at this rate. Dylan couldn't make out the facial features on the raised faces of the uniformed officers below. His throat was dry, his heart raced and he could hear his chest wheezing, as he climbed the next ladder. Dylan stood on the platform like a statue. His stomach clenched. His legs were like jelly. He leaned back to the wall. His fingers spanned the cool stone that he desperately tried to get a grip on. He closed his eyes. 'God help me,' he whispered. 'Why do I do this? I must be crazy...and for the love of the job,' he griped, breathing heavily.

'If you come any further,' a man's voice screamed, 'I'll...I'll jump... I mean it.'

Dylan stayed perfectly still. The air was blowing cool on his skin and the sky was black directly above him. Gasping for breath, he looked up. A dull pounding began at the top of his spine. He couldn't hold the position long. It was hard to see the Jumper's face in the little light the early morning was bringing. He glanced up again. It was as if someone below had read his mind, as they threw a switch on a lamp and directed the fierce light into his face. 'For fuck's sake.' he yelled, shielding his eyes with his arm.

The lamp moved in awkward jolts until it caught the Jumper's face.

'Chubby Connor,' Dylan said, under his breath. Was this deja vu? He could feel the blood running cold through his veins. This was one evil, murdering bastard who didn't deserve saving, and what made it even worse was Dylan was risking his own life for him. The sight of Charlie's little body on the mortuary table flashed through his mind. What the hell was he doing trying to save the bastard?

'Is that you Alan? Chubby?' he said calmly. His heart raced. There was no reply.

'It's not long since you were on the bridge. What's up now? Can't we try sort it like we did last time? It's Inspector Dylan.'

Was this his second chance with Alan 'Chubby' Connor? Fate was a funny thing. Be careful what you wish for son, his dad used to say.

Chubby had disappeared from Dylan's line of vision. Dylan's mind was fighting with his conscience; his head was saying one thing and his heart was screaming another. Dylan slid his back down the factory wall and sat on the landing of the fire escape. Chubby must have heard him. He came to the roof steps. The lamp now focused on them both, and 'Chubby' Connor was clearly lit, holding a roof slate.

'Were you starving son? Is that why you went into the bakery?' Dylan said. Chubby was silent.

'I bet you're bloody freezing, your bollocks will drop off up there. Come down,' Dylan shivered, but got his hankie out to mop his nose and his brow. Suddenly, debris flew past him and he heard a shout. Had Chubby fallen? Dylan's stomach flipped. He looked below. All was still.

'Bloody hell Chubby, why won't you come on down, or do you want to end up like that slate?'

There was no answer.

'Let's talk about it eh? Let's face it; you've nowhere to run to and nobody's going away.'

In the distance, sirens wailed, getting louder and louder as they got nearer. The blue lights whirred as the ambulance followed the fire engine that had raced into the yard. Oh my God, Dylan thought, what're they doing?

'What's going on?' Chubby shouted, as he noisily hopped from one foot to the other on the roof.

'Calm down......calm down. The ambulance is here because if you fall or jump you might not die; you'll be in tremendous pain and believe me you're gonna be glad of the paramedics. Someone in the control room will 'ave called them as a matter of course, so they can help you,' Dylan yelled over the engine noise below.

'I don't need help. Tell them to go away,' Chubby screamed.

'But you do need help. That's what this is all about isn't it? You need help now,' insisted Dylan.

The fire crews were tilting their turntable preparing it for use.

'What's happening? What's the ladder about?' Chubby asked.

'Fire brigade...they're used to rescuing people from rooftops of burning buildings; they won't mess about once they get set up.'

Chubby was silent, and Dylan caught him transfixed by the commotion below. The pain in Dylan's neck was intolerable as he watched Chubby, the man he had reluctantly taken into his care.

'They'll bring you down. My boss; can't do with the road closed at morning rush hour. He'll 'ave given them orders to bring you down as soon as possible. I don't think you're a match for them do you?'

'They can't do it...tell them...tell them...I'll batter the bastards with slates,' Chubby cried, holding a slate in the air.

'They want to help you. All them people down there are all there just for you.'

Chubby retreated out of Dylan's view and Dylan sat looking out on to the circus below. All those men and women wasting their time on a flaming murderer; it turned his stomach. He looked to the sky and felt the cold breeze on his face. Clouds skimmed what was left of the pale moon and he felt a light spray of rain brush his cheek. He waited. There was one thing for sure; if it was going to rain he was going to get wet. He stood up. His bum was numb from sitting on the cold platform, and a shiver ran through his body. This would teach him once and for all to bring gloves and a scarf with him, like Jen said.

'Chubby?'Dylan shouted, standing up.

'What?'

'Come on, otherwise you know what's going to happen. The fire brigade are coming up.' Dylan waited. The rain came in heavier drops and the operator swung the fire engines turntable in the yard towards the factory, awaiting his orders to move it upwards.

'Okay, Okay, tell them to fucking back off,' came the most unexpected of replies. Dylan held on tightly to the railings, feeling the encrusted, flaking paintwork crumble beneath his cold hands. Chubby started his descent down the ladder and within seconds stood facing Dylan on the small platform. He looked ill. His clothes were tattered, torn and stained and he stank of smoke and sweat. Dylan stared into the young man's haunted eyes. They were hollow and dark.

'Walk behind me when we get to the bottom. There's a police dog just outside the yard, so don't try and do a runner.' Dylan looked down. Seeing Chubby's movements, the people who'd been standing in the yard had retreated, and only vehicles remained.

Chubby Connor walked down the steps in front of Dylan and suddenly Dylan saw little Charlie Sharpe's body lying in front of him, all his injuries crystal clear. What the hell was he doing saving this piece of shit? He grabbed the collar of Chubby's t-shirt. Chubby turned, his eyes wide and pleading. Should Dylan push him? Who'd know he hadn't fallen or jumped?

'I shouldn't 'ave saved you last time you scum bag,' Dylan growled, gripping the back of his t-shirt tighter with a clenched fist.

'I got a donor card; it's in my back pocket,' Chubby said, calmly. The shock revelation halted Dylan's actions. He raised his eyebrows. Chubby Conner would never know how close he was to it being pushed.

'You're under arrest for the murder of Charlie Sharpe as well as burglary.' Dylan cautioned him as he handed Chubby to the uniformed officers. The latter charge, he knew, would pale into insignificance. His reply, for the sake of the arrest form, had been, 'Not me...not me...I didn't do it ...I swear.'

Chapter Twenty-Two

'Is the DI off today?' Tracy asked Vicky.

'No, not that I'm aware of...perhaps he was out on the town last night,' she said giggling.

'Oh, you're scandalous.' Tracy screeched.

Sitting opposite the pair, John Benjamin was studying the chief constable's log to see what had happened of note, around the force overnight.

'What's new Sarge?' said Vicky. 'Is the kettle on?'

'It says that Dylan was called to negotiate at a suicide attempt in the middle of the night.'

'Oh, no, hasn't he enough on his plate without that?' said Dawn, groaning.

Dawn was studying the Crime Information System, trying to locate possible associates of Jason Todd. According to Susan, no one else could be the father. The coroner would want to know who Charlie's father was and tests would have to be done to confirm it.

'The plot thickens,' John told Dawn, as he came off the phone to forensics. The DNA on the balaclava is that of...guess who?'

Dawn shook her head.

'One Frank Miller.'

'What was Miller doing in St Peter's Park?'

'I think I'd arrange another visit to the prison for Dylan, if I were you,' Dawn said to John. 'A-S-A-P.'

John lifted the phone; a voice was already on the line.

'Hello? Hello? DI Dylan?'

'No, DS John Benjamin, he's not here at the moment can I help?'

'Can you just tell him that DC Gary Warner rang from the Regional Crime Squad, and ask him to ring me back as soon as possible, please?'

John took his number and put the phone down. For a moment he stopped, and for the first time in his career he wondered if he really wanted to be an SIO. Thinking about Dylan's present workload, he didn't know if he could keep up with the constant demand the job presented or if it would be fair to his family. Even now he spent precious little time with his them, and he knew he'd have to think very hard if it was the career path he wanted to pursue. Yes, the job was undeniably interesting, exciting at times, but at what cost?

John kept a record of what information had come in to tell Dylan, and he updated the policy book. He decided to liaise with Greater Manchester police. He needed to find out more about Frankie Miller; had he a mobile phone on him? Where was his clothing? All the items would help their investigation, he had no doubt. In Dylan's absence there was plenty to do.

Dawn was on the phone, listening intently.

'Brilliant, that's really brilliant you can carry on giving us news like that,'

DS Patrick Finch stopped what he was doing and sat with his mouth open, eagerly waiting to find out what news was so good. She looked jaded, he thought, studying her face.

'The bloodstained fingerprint has been identified. Yeah, and it's that of Alan Connor alias Chubby, and the blood is Charlie Sharpe's.'

'That's a great result,' he said grinning. 'Dylan will have a good start to his day, when he surfaces.'

'Yes he will, and that forensically connects Connor for us too. I've done my bit now; all you 'ave to do is find and arrest Connor and quickly Pat,' she teased.

'I wish you'd call me Patrick.'

'Mmm, now what would Dylan say to you?' her finger touched her cheek in a thoughtful pose. 'You won't find him, sat on your arse in here.' she chortled. 'But before you set off, put the kettle on Pat, there's a love. Toast would be good too; remember I'm feeding two,' she said, patting her stomach.

Patrick gritted his teeth together and clenched his fists.

Dawn stuck her tongue out.

'Urgh, put that away. Goodness knows where it's been,' John laughed.

'I don't think that's appropriate, John,' Patrick scolded. John raised his eyebrows at Dawn and she smiled.

'I'll put the kettle on then shall I?' Patrick said.

'Maybe now, Dylan will give Connor's picture to the press and get his face plastered over the TV. That should make it hard for him to carrying on lying low,' Dawn said.

Dylan sat quietly for a moment, alone in his car. He felt numb, sick, tired and hardly daring to think just how close he'd been to pushing Chubby down the steps. Before his culpable feelings took over, he dialled the CID office and Patrick answered.

'Thought you'd be out looking for Chubby Connor and Jason Todd, Pat?' Dylan growled.

'Yes sir, I was just about to get on with it,' he said.

'Well, you won't bloody find him in the office drinking tea and eating toast now will you?' Dylan boomed.

Patrick looked around the room; how the hell did he know what they were doing, and how did Dawn know what he'd say?

'Second thoughts - don't bother going out looking for Connor, it'd be a waste of time because he's locked up.'

'Arrested? Chubby Connor? Where? When? How?' Patrick asked, and flicked the phone onto speaker, so the rest of the office could hear.

'He was the idiot on the roof of the bakery this morning, believe it or not.'

'Brilliant,' Dawn shouted, punching the air.

'Bet you were tempted to let him jump this time when you saw who it was, weren't you boss?' Vicky said.

Patrick scowled at her.

'He was never going to jump; he's pathetic,' Dylan said.

'You should've pushed the bastard,' Vicky shouted. If looks could kill, Patrick's would have deemed Vicky dead on the spot.

'I must admit I was tempted, very tempted,' Dylan said. If only they knew. He shivered an irrepressible convulsive shudder which brought on the goose bumps; and his old mum would have said it was caused by a person walking over the place where his grave would eventually be. His arms outstretched on the steering wheel were covered in pimples that made the hairs stand on end. 'Uniform are bringing him in now for you lot to sort out. I arrested him for murder and burglary. Put the kettle back on will you, if you can manage that,' Dylan said. 'I'll be with you shortly.'

'Yes, sir...' said Vicky, under her breath.

Patrick replaced the phone.

'If I know Jack Dylan, he won't let you forget that he had to get your prisoner for you. Be prepared,' Dawn said, chuckling at Patrick as she stood up and then sat down again quickly. The room spun.

'You okay?' asked John.

'Yeah fine, must be all the excitement.' she said, with a lopsided grin.

Dylan took a bottle of water out of his briefcase and sipped it slowly. He took a bite out of his apple, his mind devoid of any thought.

'Jumper safe. Chubby Connor won't be disturbing us again during the night.' Dylan texted Jen.

'Not him again. Pity he didn't jump and do everyone a favour x' Jen replied.

'I'm heading back to Harrowfield – catch up later x'

Everybody knows that no one likes murderers. Child murderers are disliked the most. Alan 'Chubby' Connor would find that out for himself, soon enough. Perhaps he would suffer in prison like Charlie had. If there was any justice in the world he would, thought Dylan.

Chapter Twenty Three

Dylan started to feel more alert after his second cup of strong coffee. Patrick, Dawn, Vicky and Tracy were in the CID office listening absorbedly to his news.

'I blame you Pat. If you'd got Chubby locked up I wouldn't 'ave had to risk life and limb on that bloody old fire escape in the early hours of this morning.' Dylan said, draining his cup. Dawn smirked smugly at Patrick in her 'told you so' way.

'I am trying,' he whined.

'Very,' laughed Dawn.

'One – nil to the boss. What he's really saying is you're fucking useless, Finchy,' chuckled Vicky.

'I don't think that is a correct way of addressing a senior officer,' reprimanded Patrick.'I take offence at that comment,' he said, as he got up and walked out of the room.

'Ooooo,' Vicky cooed.

'Vicky ...' Dylan growled. 'You'd better watch it, you're already on a Scarborough warning, young lady.'

'Well he'd rather hear that than be chuffing deaf wouldn't he?' Vicky said sulkily.

'You deserve a slap,' Dylan chuckled.

'Ooooo, yes please,' she giggled. Dylan shook his head.

'He'll 'ave the chance to prove himself when he picks up Jason Todd. It might put him in a better frame of mind,' said Dylan, studiously.

'Can't we give Todd's' picture to the press now boss? That would make it difficult for him to hide anywhere,' said Tracy.

'I'll think about it. Let's deal with the one we 'ave in the traps first. He's going to go not guilty I would've thought, by his reply after arrest.'

'I understand we've got him under constant supervision in the cells; open door because of his suicidal tendencies and all his clothing has been seized,' reported Tracy.

'Do you know, I'm pretty sure he's wearing the same clothes he had on when I talked him down from Stan Bridge. They might well give us some evidence,' Dylan said.

Dawn relayed the good news to Dylan about the fingerprint evidence.

'There is a God after all,' he said, clasping hands together. 'Let's get him a solicitor and see what he has to say in interview.'

'He might even tell all, if he knows he's going to be banged up. Now wouldn't that be a turn up for the books?'

'Sure would,' Dawn said.

'Right. Can I leave you lot to get on with it while I go and see John about the Reynolds' murder?'

'Sure thing, boss.' they shouted out in harmony.

'Morning Boss, I've loads to tell you.' John Benjamin pounced eagerly on Dylan as he walked through the door of his office.

'Let me get in first. Don't forget I've done a shift already,' Dylan said.

'Sorry Boss, bacon & egg buttie?'

'Now that sounds like a good plan.'

'Leave it with me whilst you get yourself sorted out here,' John said, offering Dylan his seat at the computer.

'What a good lad John is, Dylan thought. He'd go along way. Got his priorities right, John had; look after the boss. Dylan smiled.

Dylan set about updating the press office with information about Connor's arrest, but wouldn't give them his name for publication at this stage. However, he did tell them he would keep them updated.

'Mmm, an important part of policing, John a breakfast butty,' Dylan said, as he popped the last morsel in his mouth. He took his handkerchief out of this trouser pocket and rubbed his greasy hands on it. 'I'm all ears now, fire away,' he said licking his lips.

'Firstly, the DNA from the balaclava is that of Frankie Miller. I've taken the liberty of booking us a second visit with

Malcolm Reynolds and I've also put a call into GMP that I'm waiting to be returned by CID.'

'Why?'

'Regarding us having access to Frankie's clothing, phone and to glean from them any information they can about him.' John said. 'I've timed the call and recorded it boss, in the policy book.'

'I am impressed, well done. So we can place Frankie Miller in the park where Liz was found. Larry had been with her the night before, we believe. Frankie was celled up with Malcolm Reynolds and Larry was involved in putting Malcolm away. What are we missing, John? Do you think Malcolm got Frankie onto Liz because he knew she was having an affair? A contract on her even?' Dylan said, rubbing his stubbly chin.

'But if that was the case, why did she draw a large amount of money out of the bank the day before?'

'To pay him, neat job.' said Dylan.

'But why would she have a suitcase with her that contained law books?'

'Well, there's one thing; we know exactly where three of our players are, but where is Larry Banks and what's he up to? It's the last thing you expect from a DS, John, the very last thing, but I'm sure he could shed light on all this for us, if we could only locate him.'

Dylan and John sat mulling over the evidence; they could put Larry at Liz's house, but they had no evidence to put him in the car park at St Peter's Park. Yet, they could put Frankie in St Peter's Park, but not at her house or in the car park where she was killed. Why would Frank Miller be off his patch, with a balaclava, unless he was up to no good?

'Oh, boss, before I forget. Gary Warner from Crime Squad rang you this morning. Could you give him a ring? He didn't want to leave a message but I've written his number on a Post-it note for you and it's stuck to the corner of the computer.'

'I hope he hasn't got another job that's going to involve us. We're strapped for staff as it is, and before you know it, the review team will be wanting a meeting.'

Dylan peeled off the note and rang the number.

'We've been watching Miller's Haulage for a while,' Gary told Dylan.

'We had information that Frankie Miller was importing drugs on a large scale. I called into see you a while back and spoke to Larry Banks. I asked him if he'd update you with the information on Operation Whirlwind when you came back from leave.'

'He never did, Gary.' Dylan sighed.

'Nah, my fault. I should 'ave rang you myself. We understand Frankie Miller, one of the Miller brothers, needed money to pay an outstanding drug related debt after he got out of prison, but he got well and truly caught in the act at the bank robbery.'

'Surely he wouldn't 'ave gone to those lengths if he'd got Liz's money, would he?' Dylan said.

'There is no evidence to show he got any money and of course if he did maybe five hundred grand wasn't enough, who knows, but we've got one or two interesting bits of information that have come our way since he died. I can let you have his mobile data and you're welcome to share the intelligence we've collated.'

'Thank you. We can place Frankie in the park where Liz Reynolds was murdered, but that's all.'

'That was his cellmate's wife wasn't it?'

'Sure was. What we'd like to know is, did her hubby have anything to do with her murder? Why else would Malcolm Reynolds' wife be in the park where Frankie Miller his ex-cell mate can be put, when he's desperately in need of cash, and Liz Reynolds has drawn out a substantial amount the day beforehand from the bank?'

'I'll tell you what; I'll ask around to see if any of our lot can throw any light on any of it for you and I'll get together that information, I promised.'

'Cheers, Gary,' Dylan said, gratefully. 'I'll wait to hear from you.' And he hung up.

'Policeman, madman and husband – who dunnit, John?' Dylan asked, as walked out of the office to return to the Charlie Sharpe incident room. John shook his head.

'Got a full admission yet, you two?' Dylan called out to Patrick and Dawn, as he walked into the office.

'No boss,' they both replied.

'Found Jason Todd, yet Pat?'

'No sir.'

'So what new can you tell me then?' said Dylan sitting down opposite them both.

'Well Chubby Connor's clothes are all bagged up. Vicky's going over to forensics, so she'll drop them off at the lab for us today,' said Dawn

'The bloody trainers stink probably more than your old DS sir,' Vicky said, laughing.

Patrick frowned.

'Joke mate, joke,' said Vicky.

'You get your exams passed gal; you'd make a good sergeant.'

'What're you trying to say boss?'

'Well you'll never need braces to hold your pants up, will you?' said Dylan.

'What the hell are you two on about?' said Dawn. Vicky winked at Dylan as she gathered the exhibits in her arms.

'Who says I wear pants sir?' she said, as she strolled out of the office. Her raucous laugh could be heard from down the corridor.

'How does that girl manage to keep her sense of humour?' Dylan said, shaking his head.

Patrick lips pursed and turned to Dylan but remained silent.

'Right, who's Connor's brief gonna be, do we know?' Dylan said.

'Guess,' said Dawn.

'Seriously, don't tell me someone from Perfect & Best.' said Dylan.

Dawn nodded.

'No one else seems to be getting a look in these days. But to be fair to them, they don't hang about, do they? Mrs Yvonne Best is having a consultation with Chubby Connor right now,' said Dawn. 'And our first interview is scheduled for 5:30pm, so we might even get a second in tonight.'

'Then we'll need the superintendent's extension from the Divisional Commander early tomorrow, for a further twelve hours detention,' said Dylan.

'That doesn't give us long, sir,' Patrick said.

'It never does Pat, but somehow we always manage, don't we Dawn?'

'That's a picture of Jason Todd,' Dawn said, sliding the mug shot across the table to Dylan.

He picked it up and studied the young man's face; short hair, flat nose a star tattoo below his right eye; even a swastika on his left earlobe. 'Well, he's not going to melt into a crowd is he?' he laughed.

'Certainly not, and not only because of his tattoos; he's well over six foot. All his previous are for robbery, assault on police, resisting arrest; he shouldn't even be walking the streets,' Dawn mumbled.

'Well, hopefully we'll make sure he isn't again after we get him in custody. Who's in charge of the arrest team, and have we enough to restrain him if he kicks off?'

'Yeah, we should be okay; six of the best. 'Dennis the menace' is in charge. He won't 'ave chance to kick off,' Dawn said laughing.

'Dennis is the one who looks like 'Jaws' from the Bond films, and he's got a girly laugh hasn't he? Ah, remind me to let him interview Todd.'

'No, I want to interview with Pat. Please boss?

'We really don't need two sergeants interviewing Dawn,' said Dylan.

'Please...pretty please?' she begged looking over at him pleadingly.

'Okay,' he smiled weakly. 'But then we'll assess each interview as it comes. Agreed?'

'Thank you,' she said leaning across the desk. 'You must be tired; that was easy.' 'Oh,' Dawn held her chest dramatically, 'Oh, my, the palpitations.'

'Don't even joke about that, Dawn,' said Patrick.

'Take advantage of a tired old man would you?' said Dylan. 'Shame on you. Scary thing is, you know me too well. I am tired, very tired,' he said, yawning. 'And it's probably your condition that's giving you palpitations.'

'Oh, by the way, I forgot to tell you, the murderer of the two children might be putting in a guilty plea, but I'm hearing that off the record. If that happens he could be in court next month, according to my snout.'

'That would be great. When did you hear that?' Dylan asked.

'Five minutes ago from the cells. Custody staff 'ave been talking to Yvonne Best whilst she was waiting for Chubby Connor to be checked over by the doc.' Dawn looked like the cat that had got the cream.

'A good day all round.' Dylan yawned again, involuntarily. 'I'm knackered, so I'm off home. Will you give me a ring later to update me?'

'It's alright for some,' Dawn said playfully.

'I keep telling you, get your exams. Perks of the job; as a boss, you make the rules,' he joked. 'Hey, and don't you overdo it, neither.'

'I won't,' she groaned.

He headed for home, and all that he could think of was the comfort of Jen's arms.

'Patrick or Dawn will ring me later love, so if the phone goes, it doesn't necessarily mean I'm being called out,' he told Jen over dinner.

'Most people would've let Chubby jump. I don't know how you can deal with scum like that. It's not as if he's going to be a loss to society, after what he's done.'

'I know. If he'd jumped before, we'd have got to the Isle of Wight on time and Charlie would still be alive. Believe you me; I came very close to shoving him down those steps this morning. My thoughts scared me. All I could see was that little boy's body and his injuries.'

Jen slipped her hand into Dylan's and held it tight across the table. 'And?'

'And I still couldn't cross that line. That's the difference between criminals and us, don't you think? They do cross that line. I could never play God and live with myself.'

'But if you'd done nothing to stop him, and he'd jumped?'

'Come on Jen, if you 'ad the opportunity to save somebody's life you would, no matter who they were or what they'd done. It's instinctive,' Dylan said.

Jen was thoughtful. Would she?

'It's easy to say that they deserve to die; but in that instant would you honestly do nothing and be able to live with your conscience? I couldn't. Life's too precious to me.'

'It's very easy, Jack. I've never been in that situation, thank goodness. I think it's just a shame fate stepped in...that's all I'm saying.'

'So, convicted and executed before a trial, now that would save the country some money,' Dylan said.

'You always said you could pull the trigger.'

'I could, but that's when I'd had time to consider the facts first.'

'Let's not talk about it anymore, Coffee?' Jen said, getting up and switching the kettle on.

'Tea please. I'm awash with coffee today.'

'I'm sure you did the right thing. You always do,' Jen said, holding his face in her hands and dropping a kiss on the top of his head. He looked up at her and grabbed her around the waist, nuzzling into her stomach.

'Not only that; I'm the boss. If I'm wrong I'm still right.' He smiled up at her once more.

'Clever clogs,' she said, pulling away and playfully tapping his cheek. 'Go put your feet up I'll bring your cuppa in.'

Max followed Dylan into the lounge and when he sat down. Max dropped at his feet, placing his head strategically on Dylan's slipper, so he would know if he moved.

'Good boy,' said Dylan, closing his eyes as he patted the dog's head. Instantly both were asleep.

Dylan heard the phone ringing at his side. Pulling up from the depth of his dreams, he heard Jen answer his mobile.

'Hi Dawn, how are you?' Dylan heard her say. He was finding it hard to wake up and decided, in his semi-conscious state, not to bother opening his eyes for a moment or two whilst they chatted. He felt himself drifting back into oblivion.

'I'll just put him on,' he heard her say, as he felt her gently shake him.

Dylan groaned then yawned, smiling sheepishly at Jen as he held his hand out to take the phone from her.

'I'm off home now boss, I'll let Pat update you,' Dawn said. He could hear the tiredness in her voice and he said goodnight to her before she handed him over.

'To summarise, Sir,' Patrick said, 'Connor says he met up with Todd after the incident on Stan Bridge. He invited him to doss at his house with his bird and her kid. Admittedly he says he subsequently slept with Susan too.'

Dylan grunted. 'With regard to Charlie, he says that he hadn't had a lot to do with kids before, but the nipper was always misbehaving. Susan shouted at him, but it didn't make any difference. She asked Todd to make him 'do', so he did.'

'And how did they do that?'

'Well, when we pushed him on that point he said they took what toys he had away from him, and locked him in his room to punish him. In his words, Jason hit him just like any dad would.'

'Why didn't he stop him, them?'

'He says he was scared of Todd.'

'So he's 'Mr Innocent' is he?'

'Well, he appeared to be until the second interview, when we disclosed the evidence we had of the bloodstained fingerprint and asked him to explain how his and Charlie's blood was on the door frame.'

'And what did he say then?'

'I'll read out the bit I wrote down at the time:

'I did what they told me to do. Jason kept saying how hard the lad was. He told Susan to hit him and he didn't make a sound. Then he told me to throw him to him – I did and he didn't cry either. Jason said he wanted to toughen him up. He pulled him by his hair and whacked him across his wrists with a pool cue. I often saw him kick him and walk him around on a lead. The lad wasn't brought out of his room much.'

He describes Susan's attacks on the child as totally losing it.'

'So he admits being involved, and did he show any remorse?' said Dylan.

'No, not at all. In fact it doesn't seem to register with him that Charlie was a human being, to be honest. We've planned another interview for first thing tomorrow to go through specific injuries; see if he's more forthcoming then.'

'If he didn't think he'd done anything wrong, then why did he do a runner?'

'Says he doesn't like the police, and they'd blame him, even though he'd done nothing wrong because he's known to them.'

'How was the solicitor?'

'Fine, appalled at what had gone on. Off the record at Chubby Connors request she gave us an address in Blackpool where Jason Todd might be. She says she believes he's our main offender, not Chubby Connor. She asked Connor if he knew where Todd might be. He gave her a name of an associate in Blackpool so we've liaised with Blackpool police, and Dennis and the team will be going over there early tomorrow morning.'

'Thanks for that Pat. We'll see what he says tomorrow and meet up after the interview. I'm going with John to the prison to see Reynolds first thing so I'll come find you when I get back.'

'Come on tiger.' Dylan said, slapping Jen's thigh as she stretched out on the settee. Yawning, he put the phone down. 'Time for bed.' She reached out. He drew her up into his arms and she looked up into his face.

Dylan looked thoughtful.

'Stop thinking about work,' she said. 'As if he would,' she thought, as she got up and started plumping up the cushions. 'Do you know you live and breathe the bloody job when it's running? It takes over quicker than a Russian Vine in a garden.'

Dylan stumbled into the kitchen and Jen followed, clicking off the lights as she juggled with the cups and newspapers he'd left in his wake.

'Hello Jack, I'm Jen, remember me?' she called, as he stomped up the stairs zombie like, in silence. It made him smile. 'And don't you work Dawn too hard either,' she said catching up with him on the landing to the bedroom.

'No, boss,' he whispered in her ear as he cuddled her close.

Chapter Twenty-Four

It was very windy on the west coast. Six fifteen a.m was early enough for a dawn raid at the house the police had surrounded. 28 Tower Street was a rent paid, council semi, occupied by the Marsh family, who were well known to the Lancashire Constabulary as one of the boils on the backside of Blackpool.

The door ram's thunder vibrated through the nearby houses. Three attempts and they still hadn't gained access. A radio message from an officer at the back of the house told Detective Sergeant Dennis Dors from West Yorkshire Police that a man had come out with a knife and was holding officers at bay. Dennis's stocky, brutish body ran like a gazelle to help them, whilst his other officers carried on battering the front door.

'A knife?' yelled Dennis to his colleagues. His square, strong jaw under the frame of his jet black unruly hair and crooked nose gave him the appearance of a Boxer. It's a bloody machete,' he shouted.

The occupant of the house was swinging it round like a sword that he held firmly with both hands. There was no doubt in Dennis's mind that this was Jason Todd; he could clearly see the tattoo beneath his eye.

'Put it down mate. Don't be stupid; you're going nowhere,' Dennis shouted the instruction at him.

'If I'm going down I'm taking you fuckers with me.' Todd yelled.

Dennis looked around him, and placing his hands round a rotting fence post in the garden he pulled it out of the ground in one fell swoop. Stepping forward, he swung it head height with a roar reminiscent of an animal. Because of his build his clothing always looked tight, and the top button of his shirt never quite fastened; but he looked as though he was going to burst out of his uniform like 'the hulk' to those with a view of the fight.

'Put it down,' he warned

'Fucking make me, copper,' screamed Todd, as he lashed out in Dennis's direction. Dennis blocked the machete with the fence post, Todd's threats turning immediately into an action. Momentarily, the machete stuck in the wood. It gave Dennis sufficient time to land an almighty left hook that Henry Cooper would have been proud of, straight on Todd's nose; sending him reeling backwards to the floor. Dennis placed a foot on his arm. The officers moved forward, quickly pinning him to the ground. Dennis pulled the machete from Todd's hand turned him, over and forcefully pulled his arms behind his back. Handcuffed at last, he was under control and arrested.

'Thank God for the fence post,' thought Dennis, as they ungraciously dragged Todd up onto his feet. His nose had spread across his face, obviously broken. He shook his head in a daze, subdued but they knew that wouldn't last.

'Get him to hospital but make sure he remains cuffed to one of you at all times,' DS Dennis Dors instructed.

Dennis was sat panting, on his knees, as Todd was dragged away. 'I think I'll 'ave to go too,' he said, in a deep laboured tone, holding up his left hand that looked deformed, swollen and bruised.

'Looks like at least two broken fingers, argh.' he cried. 'Better than being caught with that bloody thing though,' he thought, as he collected the machete for evidence.

The rest of the team were now searching the house, having overcome the obstinacy of the front door. The Marsh family were surprisingly compliant when they were told the reason Todd was arrested. Clothing and other items were seized from the floor of a room where Jason had put his head down for the last few days.

It was 9. 40 a.m by the time DS Patrick Finch was informed of the full facts, and excitedly he went straight through to Dylan's office to pass them on.

'I've just heard from the team in Blackpool. Good and bad news.' Patrick was buzzing.

'Go on give me the good news,' Dylan said.

'Jason Todd's in custody.'

'Fantastic...and the bad news,' Dylan said, cringing.

'They won't be back with him until this evening.'

Dylan sat back in his chair and sighed. 'Tell them from me, we haven't got time to go to the Pleasure Beach. It's a bleeding murder enquiry,' he said.

'Yes sir.' Patrick said. 'But Todd's being treated for a broken nose and fractured cheekbone at the Blackpool Victoria Hospital.'

'And don't tell me Dennis?' asked Dylan.

'Yes sir and Dors possibly has some broken fingers. But in his defence, Todd did come out threatening them with a machete.'

'Bloody hell,' said Dylan. 'You don't argue with Dennis that's for sure. He's one you want on your side if there's trouble.'

Dylan was glad Jason Todd had come off worse. Dennis had done well and he'd tell him so when he returned.

'That gives you and Dawn all day to continue interviewing Chubby Connor. We'll get the superintendent's extension now with no problem.'

'Yeah,' Patrick sighed.

'Just to remind you, I've got to go to the prison with John to see Malcolm Reynolds. I should be back just after lunch.'

'By the way, Susan Sharpe was remanded on the wounding charge, sir.'

'She'll no doubt be charged with murder later, but I'll speak to CPS first. I'm looking at charging all three with joint enterprise. So you managed to level the score, one prisoner each, Pat.' Dylan smiled.

'I would prefer you to call me Patrick, sir.'

'Okay. Keep an eye on Dawn for me will you? I don't want her to get exhausted. No doubt I'll 'ave HQ on at me for letting her interview and they're probably right. Catch up with you later mate.'

Patrick shook his head as he left Dylan's office to prepare for the first interview of the day with Alan 'Chubby' Connor.

Chapter Twenty-Five

Malcolm Reynolds' previous facial stubble had grown into a silver beard since their last visit. His predominantly greying hair looked longer, greasy and bedraggled. The clothes he was wearing hung from his much slimmer frame, and his bloodshot eyes were overshadowed with red hooded eyelids and dark rings.

'I hope you've got some news for me,' he said. ''ave you any idea what it's like to be in 'ere and, not be able to do 'ought about your wife being murdered? Can you imagine just how fucking useless I feel? Sometimes I think I'm gonna go fucking mad.' Malcolm cried, as he leaned forward in his chair, in a submissive way this time; searching their faces for answers, clues as to what was happening, desperate for some information. Was he on the verge of a mental breakdown, Dylan feared?

'You heard the news about your old cellmate?' Dylan said, knowing full well that he would have heard about Frankie Miller's death.

'Yeah... well that's Frankie isn't it; that's how he'd want to go. There never was much evidence of much between his lug'oles, so it doesn't surprise me. He was daft as a brush. But, what's that to do with Lizzie's murder? Do you know who's done it yet?'

'How long were you and Frankie Miller celled up for?' asked John.

'Long enough.'

John took notes in his pocket book.

'Let's stop pissing about, eh? Have you come to tell me who murdered Lizzie, and if not, why not? What the fuck's going on?'

'We think Frankie might've had something to do with it,' said Dylan, matter-of-factly.

'Frankie? He's a fucking robber, a crackhead, he doesn't murder women. That's not his scene...no...no I can't believe that.' Malcolm said, shaking his head. 'That's nonsense. Nah, he wouldn't kill...a woman?'

'Approximately five hundred yards from Liz's body we found a balaclava.'

'And?'

'We 'ave positively identified it as belonging to Frankie Miller...One hundred per cent Malcolm.'

'But St Peter's Park is nowhere near...his patch. Manchester's his area.'

'Money? Malcolm, Liz had withdrawn money out of your joint account the day before she was murdered. Tell me, did he know Liz? Or where you lived?'

'You're doing my fucking head in,' he yelled, and the guard stepped forward.

'Did he know Liz?' pushed Dylan.

'No, no, they never met...he'll 'ave seen her picture. I've talked a lot about her, our lives, Gemma and that...what else can you do when you're locked up in this fucking hole; twenty-four hours a day, but talk? No...he wouldn't hurt my Lizzie...he wouldn't cross me. He wouldn't ...' Malcolm sat deep in thought. 'Hold on a minute. Why would he wear a balaclava if he was going to kill someone? There'd be no point, would there?'

'What about your house, your home address...would he know that?'

'I suppose he could have seen it on letters. There's not much privacy in a cell.'

'Telephone number?' said John.

'Maybe...but I still can't believe ...' Malcolm shook his head. 'No, never, I know he owed a lot of money on the outside, but he'd just go into a fucking bank like he did. He wouldn't kill Lizzie for it.'

'Malcolm, he was in St Peter's Park...we can prove that. He'd been with you. You're telling us you knew he owed money. Is there something else you want to tell us, Malcolm?' Malcolm shook his head again.

'Look, she drew half a million quid out of your joint bank account. Tell us, was she paying off a debt for you?'

'No fucking way. I would never put Lizzie or Gemma in danger. God, I worship the ground they walk on. I wouldn't do anything to risk their necks ...' He swallowed, determined not to show any weakness in front of the two men, although tears were close. 'I don't owe anyone...this is fucking stupid' Tears filled Malcolm's swollen eyes and he wiped them away with the back of his hand.

'Could she 'ave been an easy touch for him? Did he know you had money? The money's definitely disappeared. We know it wasn't burnt at the scene.'

'Not burnt? Then who's got it?'

Dylan stared into the pits of his haunted eyes.

'If Frankie had got his hands on the money, then why the fuck would he be robbing a bank? It doesn't make sense.'

'Are you sure there isn't something you're not telling me? For God's sake be straight with us.' said Dylan.

'I'm not keeping anything from you. I want her bloody killer more than you do, believe me. Is it right I can't even bury Liz yet? That's what the screws tell me.'

'Yes, that's true. There'll 'ave to be a second PM in a few weeks, or if we lock someone up for her murder, whichever comes first. The coroner will 'ave to open and close the inquest and then he'll release Liz's body to you for the funeral. Malcolm, think please, is there anything else you think we should know about, no matter how trivial?'

Malcolm slammed his hands flat on the table but the men didn't flinch. Once again the prison officer took a pace forward, but Dylan raised his hand to gesture to him that they were okay.

'I've told you everything I can think of. Do you think I've thought about anything else since you told me about the...fire?' More tears sprung into Malcolm's puffy already watery eyes and tumbled down his face. He let them flow. Was it sadness? Was it anger? Was it both?

'Malcolm, you're not going to like this, but I have to ask you, did you know Liz was seeing someone else?'

'What the fuck are you trying to do to me? Isn't it enough she's dead, without trying to mess with my fucking 'ead.' he screamed, as he stood and thumped the table with all his might. The prison officer came reaching out to hold Malcolm back by his shoulders. 'What are you trying to make out my lass is a tart?' he said, sitting down. The prison officer rested his hand on Malcolm Reynolds shoulder for an instant, before he resumed his position next to the door.

Dylan took a deep breath. 'Malcolm, evidence proves that someone shared your wife's bed the night before she was murdered.'

'What!' Malcolm screamed, jumping to his feet once more. His chair flew out from under him and landed on its side. He prowled around the room like a caged animal, grunting loudly.

'Sit down, Malcolm,' the prison officer shouted. 'Last warning,' he said.

Dylan turned his chair to face him. 'Look, Malcolm, I said we'd be honest with you and that's what we're trying to be,' he said. 'I'm telling you what we know; I think you deserve to know the truth.'

Malcolm picked up his chair and sat back down, his elbows resting on the table as he gripped his head in his hands. He whimpered as he stared at the floor.

'No...no...no,' he moaned, shaking his head to and fro. 'This is a fucking nightmare,' he wailed.

'Are you telling me you know who it was? Do you? Do you?' Malcolm said his voice growing louder and louder, as he struggled to compose himself.

'No, we don't, yet. Forensics are doing tests and we 'ave to wait for the results. If we get DNA though, and the person is recorded, we'll 'ave a name pretty quickly. You know how the system works Malcolm. Once we know we'll tell you.'

'And you think it's Frankie? This is just getting worse.' He looked to the ceiling. 'You think he slept with her, killed her and then took the money he needed to pay off his debt?'

'We don't know that yet. Like you, we're trying to piece together the information with the evidence,' Dylan hoped he sounded convincing. There was no way he was about to tell Malcolm Reynolds that at that moment in time he knew it was DS Larry Banks who had slept with her. He wanted more conclusive evidence to be able to give Malcolm the full facts when he gave him the devastating news.

'I keep going back to why would Frankie be robbing a bank if he'd got the money from Lizzie? Nah, I'm sorry, I'm not buying it. There's something seriously not right here. There's got to be someone else in this equation,' Malcolm looked Dylan straight in the eyes. 'What're you keeping from me? There's something you're not telling me.'

'Unfortunately we don't 'ave all the answers for you, but what I'm telling you is what we've got, Malcolm. I can only tell you what we know.'

'Tell you what,' Malcolm said, through clenched teeth, as he stood pointing his finger at them both. 'Don't bother coming back till you've got the answers for me, eh? You lot couldn't organise a piss up in a brewery. Someone is gonna fucking pay for this; I'll take their fucking head off.' Malcolm muttered, as he walked to the door. Not looking back, he punched the wall as he waited impatiently for the prison officer to let him out of the room.

Dylan was pleased that there had been no mention of Larry Banks. At some stage he knew he would have to tell Malcolm what he knew about him: he wouldn't be able to avoid it. After all it would come into the public domain through disclosure at the coroners' court and he was Liz's next of kin. It would be better coming from him than anyone else. But for now Dylan had a few more days to trace Larry, or find out what had gone on and why.

'Do you think Larry's capable of murder?' he asked John, as they walked to the car. A few heavy spots of rain dropped on his suit, and he looked up to the sky and frowned as he brushed them away.

'What do you think, boss? You know him better than most, I would 'ave thought.'

'Do we ever really know anyone, John?' Dylan sighed, as he opened the car door. Jumping in he slammed it quickly after him as rain suddenly pounded the windscreen, so heavily that when he started the engine and put the windscreen wipers on they couldn't cope with the deluge they tried to disperse. They sat and waited in silence for a few minutes.

'Once he knows a copper's been bedding his wife, that's going to be it, he's not going to speak to any of us again, and he'll accuse us of a cover up,' he shouted above the noise on the car roof, of the torrent of rain that the clouds had unleashed.

John agreed. 'We'd better ask for at least two prison officers in the room when we drop that bombshell on him.'

Dylan switched his thoughts to what Chubby Connor was saying in interview, as he eventually dropped John off at the main entrance to the station. Parking the car in his bay in the back yard, he contemplated waiting until the shower had passed but on second thoughts he decided against it. Knowing the weather in Harrowfield, once the rain clouds were stuck between the Pennines, it was unlikely that that would be anytime soon. Dylan ran into the station. He was drenched. Rain dripped from his hair and down the neck of his jacket as he fumbled to get his warrant card out of his wallet, to swipe at the door. He wriggled out of his wet jacket, shaking the raindrops off as best he could, as he walked down the corridor on his way to see Dawn and Patrick in the incident room. He opened the office door. They sat looking morose; both deep in thought, reading documents and clutching breadcakes in their hands.

'How're you doing?' Dylan gasped. 'Good news for me?' then he saw their faces. 'Bad?' he said.

'The night before Charlie died, Chubby admits throwing him about with Todd and he says Charlie hit his head on the wall, which caused it to bleed,' Dawn heaved a sigh as she attempted to straighten her aching back. She stretched shoulders back, lifted her chin high and cracked her neck to one side, before putting her sandwich down and pushing it away from her. She put her hand to her chest and burped.

Dylan sat down. 'You okay?' he asked.

'Yeah, thanks just indigestion,' she frowned, rubbed her chest then belching loudly.

'He says he carried him up to his room after they'd been playing around,' said Patrick, putting his sandwich back in its paper bag.

'Playing?'

'Well, to be exact Chubby called it larking around. He said, Charlie didn't get hurt. When asked how he knew that he said, 'because he didn't cry.' Dawn swallowed the bile that rose in her throat.

'So...he thought being flung against the wall hadn't hurt him, even though his head was bleeding...because he didn't cry?' Dylan asked. He listened attentively as he sat opposite the two sullen detective sergeants, deeply saddened by what he heard.

'Susan had her hands round his neck screaming at Charlie to cry, he said. Charlie wouldn't,' Dawn said.

'Charlie had refused to eat the food they were having, so Todd pushed his face in it and hit him round the head.'

'But the nipper's' arms were broken according to the pathologist, so how could he ...?' Dylan said. 'What did he 'ave to say, about there being no light in Charlie's room?' His jaw tightened as he waited for the reply.

'He said, Todd told him that the kid went to sleep better with no light. Susan tied the door so he couldn't come out, unless she wanted him to.'

'And the absence of food in the house?'

'He said, if Charlie was good he got food when they did, but if he wasn't ...' whispered Dawn. Dylan could see Dawn's eyes glistening with unshed tears.

'Any sign of remorse?'

'No tears, no emotion, he was more concerned that he'd be sent to prison if he was found guilty, and if that happened he wanted to die himself. We went through Charlie's injuries, and he told us the night before Charlie died Todd got a supply of dope. So he couldn't remember much, but he did remember that Todd was brandishing a pool cue and lashing out at him, Susan and Charlie. He told us Todd and 'he stayed up all night drinking smoking because they couldn't sleep.'

'Because, they were as high, as kites that's why.' Dylan said.

'Chubby said he took Charlie to bed because Todd and Susan were out of it and he'd fallen asleep on the floor, but he remembered Todd going upstairs and dragging Charlie out of his room later, when it was still dark. Charlie wasn't moving, so Todd held a cigarette to his foot saying that would wake him. When he didn't, Todd told Conner he was just acting about. Susan seeing Charlie in that state said she was calling for an ambulance and he says he legged it because he was frightened,' Patrick said.

'Connor's clothing?' Dylan asked.

'All bagged and tagged for the lab, sir.' Patrick's voice sounded stronger. 'His trainers look as if it might have dried blood on them. If that's Charlie's, and along with the blood stained fingerprint, he's well up the creek without a paddle. The evidence will tie him in nicely.'

'Let's get him charged with murder. I'll speak to the Crown Prosecution Service. We'll probably 'ave to produce Susan from prison and charge her as well before she's due to appear again. Better let the prison know about his suicidal tendencies too. Chubby Connor might after all his previous attempts, try to take his own life and succeed, and we don't want that before the trial. Will you let the press office know once you've charged him? Just brief details will do, and fore warn uniform of the court appearance,' Dylan said to Dawn. She looked decidedly pale, he thought, and was distractingly turning her wedding ring on her finger and staring into space.

'There are bound to be some angry locals, who'll try to take matters into their own hands,' she said, absentmindedly.

'Do we know for certain who Charlie's dad is yet?' said Dylan.

'We should have the results tomorrow, sir,' replied Patrick.

'Dawn, you okay?' Dylan looked at Dawn as she took out of her handbag a hankie and mopped her brow. She put her head on top of her folded arms on the desk. He could see she was breathing heavily and laboured.

'Yes, I'm fine...I'm just warm and tired,' she said, as she lifted her head for a moment and sipped water from a bottle. 'I'll be okay in a minute.'

'There'll be another post-mortem and an inquest, and then we can get the little lad buried,' said Dylan. 'Come on Dawn, it's about time you called it a day you're flagging.'

Dawn put her hands on the desk and pushed herself up. Dylan watched as her knees buckled from under her and she fell. Patrick caught her. Her forehead felt clammy to Dylan's touch, and she was shaking uncontrollably.

'Dawn, Dawn, come on Dawn you're okay? 'Have you any pain? Speak to us.' yelled Dylan. As Patrick laid her on to the floor in the recovery position, Dylan telephoned for an ambulance.

'Why oh, why did I let her interview?' Dylan mumbled under his breath. 'I should 'ave known better.'

Chapter Twenty-Six

Jen caught a glimpse of Dylan's face, as he walked down the path under the light of the security lamp. She could tell he was upset and went to see what was wrong.

'It's Dawn. She's collapsed and been taken to hospital,' he blurted out, as soon as she opened the door.

'Oh my God, the baby? What about the baby?' she cried.

'I shouldn't 'ave let her interview in her condition?'

'You can't blame yourself for everything, love.' Jen said hugging him tight as he buried his head in her shoulder. 'She hasn't lost it yet has she?'

'No, but she didn't look too good when they lifted her into the ambulance.'

'She's in the very best of hands. Come on, keep positive,' she said, as she led the way into the kitchen and poured him a brandy. Dylan stood at the worktop opposite her, sipping the warming, medicinal, aromatic liqueur.

'Urgh. I hate cognac,' he gasped.

'It'll do you good,' she reassured.

'If I hadn't been so bloody keen to save Chubby Connor,' he said, throwing the remainder of the drink down his throat. 'Argh...let's face it, in the end, the defence for Todd, Connor and Sharpe, is going to be that they blame each other ...' he spat. 'What's the point eh, Jen? What am I doing this bloody job for? There's no deterrent anymore.'

'For Charlie, Liz, Fred and anyone else who's a victim of crime, and their families, remember? That's why you're doing it. Come on, you've just had a shock and you're tired. If you'd 'ave let Chubby jump off the bridge that day, he might have landed on someone and killed another...It's fate love. You're just not thinking straight, that's all,' she said soothingly.

'They'd 'ave 'ad to be in a boat,' he managed a weak smile. 'Chubby Conner would've probably landed in the water from where he'd jumped.'

Jen punched him playfully. She smiled. 'You know what I meant.'

'You're right,' he reluctantly agreed.

'Come on, let's try and forget about everything for a while, walk Max and we'll ring the hospital when we get back to see how Dawn and the baby are, eh?' said Jen, as she reached out and touched his arm.

Jen went for her coat and Dylan picked up Max's lead. Excited Max jumped up at Dylan, with his ball in his mouth. Dylan took it from him and threw it down the hallway.

Max ran and fetched it back, barking enthusiastically. It made Dylan smile. Jen was glad.

'No, mate,' he laughed half-heartedly. 'We're not taking your ball tonight,' he said throwing it back in his basket. Max slumped to the floor with a loud groan.

'You're a flaming drama queen Maxie. Come on, walkies.' Jen shouted over her shoulder from the doorway.

The phone was ringing when they walked back in the house.

'Dawn and the baby are okay for the moment,' Ralph told Dylan. 'Apparently they think she might have pregnancy induced hypertension and they've established that she's also slightly anaemic, so they're keeping a careful eye on her blood pressure and iron levels from now on.'

'Thank God they're alright.' Dylan breathed a huge sigh of relief. 'I was sick with worry. I shouldn't 'ave let her interview Ralph, I'm sorry.'

'It's not your fault Jack. Think about it, you'd 'ave had a hell of a job stopping her. Neither of us blames you, or the job. Don't worry, we'll keep you updated, I promise.'

'Thanks Ralph...thank you for letting us know, I appreciate it. Give Dawn our best, won't you?'

The next morning, Dylan was sitting quietly opposite Patrick; both were deep in thought.

'Jason is Charlie's father. I've been to see Jason Todd and Susan Sharpe with their respective solicitors and an agreement has been reached regarding Charlie's funeral after the inquest,' Patrick said, breaking the silence.

'Thank you,' Dylan replied, gloomily.

'Once Todd knows that Chubby is in the system though, it won't be long before he gets to him for grassing him up, will it?'

'Not our problem, mate,' Dylan mumbled, as he studied the Chief's Log.

'I suppose Chubby Connor will remain in solitary for his own safety, in prison?'

'Mmm, probably,' Dylan replied, glancing up from his computer. 'We will have to have another two post-mortems now for the separate defence teams.' Dylan slammed the palm of his hand on the desk. Patrick jumped. 'No we won't. I'm going to get their agreement of the defence teams, to hold one post-mortem, if it's the last thing I do for Charlie. Perhaps if the solicitors had to endure the mortuary every time they defended a murderer, they'd at the very least, see firsthand, what their clients had done? Would they then be able to represent them as easily do you think?'

Patrick shook his head. 'I don't know, sir, I'm sure, but if it's the law?'

'Don't quote the law to me Pat, sometimes I think the law is an ass. Think about it: In a year's time there'll be a trial. The defence barristers will argue about how unfortunate Susan Sharpe, Chubby Connor and Jason Todd are; uneducated, unloved, no experience in looking after a child. Why on earth do we need a six week trial do you think? Don't tell me they didn't know the difference between right and wrong? They knew exactly what they were doing to Charlie. He was the unfortunate one. He didn't ask to be born. There, by the grace of God as they say. We can't choose our parents or where we are born. I wish I had a penny for every time a person said they were sorry after they'd been caught for committing a crime.' Dylan sighed. 'I need to concentrate on Liz Reynolds' murder this morning Pat, for a while. Can I leave this one with you?'

'Please sir, it's Patrick,' he said. Dylan nodded.

'Whatever.'

'I'll update you, sir.'

Dylan grunted.

'Will you be interviewing Todd with me, since Dawn's not here, sir?' Patrick said.

Dylan looked up. 'Why not?' he said. 'Why the hell not? I'm just in the mood for the likes of Jason Todd.'

Patrick smiled. He liked Dylan, he liked Dylan a lot. He might turn a blind eye to staff making unacceptable comments, but he'd challenge him about his concerns regarding the issues he had with political correctness on his team later. No, it wasn't the right place or time now.

'Where on earth was Larry Banks?' Dylan thought, as he ran up the steps two at a time. No matter where he was he must have seen a paper, the news, 'Sky', something to alert him of Liz Reynolds' murder, and the circumstances, or had he indeed been aware of it before any of them? Why hadn't he rung and talked to him, to profess his innocence, to explain what he knew? Dylan was beginning to think he was not only a thief, but a murderer too.

Larry had seen the Sun newspaper, and its coverage of the murder whilst basking in the sunshine on the French Riviera. His days were far different from policing Harrowfield. He strolled around Antibes between the azure sea and the snow-capped mountains during the day, and his nights were spent watching bats and fireflies as he drank at the bars. The food was great, the alleyways picturesque and the banking system absolutely bloody appalling he was told, but he could change his English notes to Euros, and that was all he needed a bank for. He told his newfound drinking friends that he was making a personal attempt to drink the vineyards dry, and he was even more determined to achieve that ambition since reading about Liz Reynolds' demise. One night, sitting in his favourite little laundrette near the campsite, he looked towards Fort Carre, where Napoleon was imprisoned, and contemplated his future.

He'd tried to write a letter to Dylan professing his innocence; or at least he thought he had. Yes, he had he remembered he'd given it to the nice barmaid at the campsite restaurant to post; it was the night he'd got home to find a hedgehog at his door.

Dylan and John were sitting in a meeting at the Greater Manchester Police HQ with officers dealing with the shooting of Frankie Miller. It was agreed that Frankie's clothing and footwear would be examined for any connection to Liz Reynolds and her vehicle. Dylan looked at the photos of the items, which had been seized. Gary Warner told the men that they were hoping soon for details of Frankie's mobile phone usage. The stolen vehicle he'd used was to be checked to see if its number plate had been recognised on the ANPR (Automatic Number Plate Recognition System), that the Vehicle Crime Unit in the West Yorkshire Police was trialling. Dylan and John would have to be patient, as Greater Manchester Police had a lot to do and those investigating the shooting of Frankie would be under the scrutiny of the Independent Police Complaints Commission, to show to the public that the police action had been lawful. It was frustrating. Dylan and John exchanged with GMP information and photos allowing them to raise lines of enquiry or actions, which hopefully would connect Frankie to Liz's murder.

A pint with the GMP officers, just to be sociable, was a welcome breather after the meeting. Knowing they were also interested in Frankie Miller brought new life; new sparks to their inquiry and for this Dylan was grateful. Also, meeting the officers gave Dylan and John contacts they didn't have before and it was nice to put names to people who'd only been voices on the phone before.

On the way back, over the dank moorland via the M62, Dylan and John discussed the arguments 'for and against' Larry or Frankie being the murderer.

'Well it could've been either,' said John. 'Both were definitely in the same predicament of needing cash, and money was missing.'

'Do you think they knew each other? They both knew Malcolm Reynolds. If you were a gambling man who would you bet your money on being the murderer, and is that the same person that's got the money?' Dylan said to John.

'That's a bit like asking me to predict the winner of the Grand National.'

'What you're telling me, John is that you wouldn't put your money on anyone yet, eh?' said Dylan. 'I don't blame you, but my gut instinct tells me it's Larry. Although I must admit saying that brings a bitter taste to my mouth. Frankie didn't need to do the robbery did he, if he had the money? I can tell by your face you don't agree.'

'No it's not that. I suppose anyone is capable of murder in difficult circumstances. Larry was always one for the ladies.

A bit of a 'jack the lad'. But he's not a murderer, surely, is he?'

'Who else would 'ave 'ad the law books; definitely not Frankie. Maybe they planned it together and Larry had intended to take Liz with him?' contemplated Dylan.

Back at the office, Dylan unpacked his briefcase and mulled over the meeting. He had finally got an agreement to circulate a description of Larry Banks to Interpol on suspicion of murder, so it got the attention it deserved, although he knew the evidence for murder was flimsy, to say the least. It had taken him ages to get the Command Team to consider and agree to it, and it had worn him down. Why did SIOs always have to fight with the hierarchy to get their approval for decisions they had ultimately made as the head of the enquiry? Because most of them were gutless, that's why, he conceded. He opened an envelope that had been left on his desk, and Larry's warrant card fell out. His mouth dropped open - As he picked up the ringing phone.

'Sir, a Mrs Day is here to see you.'

'What's it about?' Dylan said, as he picked up the card and stared at the picture of Larry.

'She's been notified that she may be called as a witness in a child murder case you dealt with that's up shortly and is wanting to speak with you about her attendance in court, sir.' 'She asked for me?'

'By name, sir.'

'Bring her through to my office will you please, but not through the incident room. I don't want her to be able to see the white board with all the information that's on it.'

A uniformed officer held Dylan's office door open for Mrs Day to enter. Dylan rose to greet her. Shaking her cold, bony hand, he noticed she was shaking.

'Now then Mrs Day, please take a seat. What can I do for you?' he said, with a smile.

'I'm sorry to bother you Mr Dylan. I know you're a very busy man,' Mrs Day's voice quivered.

'Not a problem,' he said. 'I'm sure you wouldn't 'ave come if it wasn't important. How can I help?'

'This is going to sound really silly to a man in your position,' she said, sniffling as she wiped her nose with a tissue. 'But I'm worried. You see I've been summonsed to give evidence in the Crown Court. I found the girl's body on the moorland, if you remember. I...I want to let you into a little secret. I've never been in a courtroom before and the man who murdered the two children is on trial.'

Dylan smiled at Mrs Day, sympathetically.

'I understand perfectly. If it'll help, I can arrange for you to go to the court beforehand and meet the ushers, even sit in on another trial. Now how does that sound?'

'Oh, Mr Dylan, I would be ever so grateful. It's causing me sleepless nights.'

'Mrs Day, you don't have to worry, my officers will be there to look after you and although you've been asked to attend, if the defence don't call you then you won't 'ave to take the stand. They might accept what you saw, from your statement that you gave to us at the time. If you wish you could still come and see him sentenced though, even if your evidence isn't required. If that's something that you feel you would like to do?'

'Oh, thank you Mr Dylan that makes me feel so much better. I can't thank you enough.' Mrs Day said, hesitantly. 'I hate this sort of thing. I'm just happy minding my own business, you know.'

'We are very grateful to you. Now that's settled, can I get you a cup of tea or something to calm your nerves?' Dylan smiled.

'Oh, goodness no. I've wasted enough of your time,' she pointed to the mountain of paperwork on his desk. 'Your wife isn't going to see you tonight if I sit here nattering to you, now is she?' She smiled gratefully.

Dylan reached out to shake her hand as she stood up to leave.

'Mr Dylan?'

'Yes?'

'I'm being nosey now, but I can't help but notice that man's photograph on your desk. Who is he if you don't mind me asking?' Mrs Day pointed to the warrant card.

'It's Detective Sergeant Larry Banks. Why?'

'Oh, nothing. I just saw him filling up one of those large mobile homes at the garage the other day. His face seemed familiar at the time. I think he came to take the statement from me, but you all look different out of your suits.'

'He was? He did? Sit down Mrs Day. Let me arrange that cup of tea for you, you might be able to help me.' Mrs Day seemed puzzled, but did as she was asked. Dylan got up opened his office door and shouted into the incident room. 'Tracy, could you get me a cup of tea for Mrs Day, please?' He sat back down behind his desk and looked at Mrs Day intently.

'Now where was I? This man.' Dylan held up Larry's warrant card. 'Did you speak to him? He didn't say where he was going by any chance did he?'

'No, but I did say a few words to him. Belle, my dog, wouldn't stop barking at him. Why?'

'We're trying to find out his whereabouts.'

'Is he in trouble?'

'We don't know that yet. Would you speak to one of my officers about the day you saw him at the garage? The information might be very helpful to us. I'll get them to do it straight away.'

'Well, if I can help in anyway... then I must get back to Belle. Do you have a dog?' she said as he walked her to the office door.

'Yes, a retriever called Max.'

'Much more agreeable than some people, don't you find, Mr Dylan?' she chuckled.

'I can't disagree with you there,' said Dylan, smiling. 'Tracy, can you take a statement for me from Mrs Day please whilst she's drinking her tea?'

Mrs Day shook Dylan's hand and Tracy led her down the corridor to an interview room.

It seemed a reasonable ID by Mrs Day for Larry, but Dylan knew only too well how sometimes witnesses although extremely emphatic – could get it wrong. It was certainly a positive line of enquiry though. Had anyone heard Larry talking about a mobile home? He didn't own one, Dylan was sure. He must have borrowed it from somewhere. Where was he heading? Dylan would hopefully know, by the time the statement was taken, what day Mrs Day saw him, at what time, and also at what garage. Was it before Liz's death or after he wondered? There may be CCTV at the garage. Could he even dare wish that that would give him a registration number? There can't be many mobile home hire companies locally. 'What are the chances of Mrs Day being a witness in two murder enquiries? Unbelievable, thought Dylan - a real life, although reluctant, Miss Marple.

Dylan had a spring in his step as he threw his suit jacket on to go home. Luck, he knew, was always important in solving a case, and maybe Mrs Day calling in to see him was just that.

Chapter Twenty-Seven

Whistling, he opened the front door and Max bounded towards him.

'Max, I've got my best suit on,' he said chuckling, 'I'm home,' Dylan shouted, as he ran straight up the stairs to change. Max bounded after him. Jen heard the bedroom door slam and Max's excited bark outside it.

'It's worse than having two flaming kids about the place,' she said, raising her eyebrows, as Max hurtled back down the stairs and along the hallway, skidding around the kitchen door, on the tiles.

'Steady, you silly boy, you'll hurt yourself,' Jen scolded, as his legs splayed so he came to rest on his belly, panting furiously.

Dylan walked in, carrying his shirt for the wash. His mobile vibrated in his tracksuit trousers pocket, just as he stood before her and held her face in his hands. ''What now?' He groaned, as he reached for it with one hand and held her hand in the other.

'DI Dylan?' asked the caller.

'Yes, speaking, whom am I speaking to?' he replied, pulling a face and hunching his shoulders at Jen.

'Boss, sorry it's a bad line. It's Gary Warner. Good news for you. Thought I'd ring you rather than wait till tomorrow.'

'Information from Frankie Miller's mobile,' said Gary. 'It appears he or somebody using his mobile called the Reynolds' home before and on the day Liz was murdered. The tech guys, using geographic mapping, can site the phone in St Peter's Park that morning, and on checking other incidents in the area it seems, there had been a slight accident on the main road above the park; him trying to get away quickly, perhaps?' The phone crackled. Dylan straining to hear all Gary was saying, let go of Jen's hand, and walking to the window put a finger in his ear.

'The driver in the offending car failed to stop, I'm told the accident report says,' Gary continued.

'Bloody hell, Gary, that gives us the connection with the park and with her home. Do you want my job?' Jen's hope-filled eyes looked up from chopping the cabbage. Dylan grinned at her.

'No thanks, sir, you can keep your job,' he said. The phone bleeped.'...Car was a hire...car...'

'Thanks Gary... you might be interested to know...' Dylan looked at his mobile phone's screen. The connection had been lost.

'Damn...You, my lady, are not going to believe this,' said Dylan.

'I'm all ears. Don't tell me ...' she closed her eyes, 'you're going to transfer to the Isle of Wight.' she said, flinging her arms around his neck and planting a kiss on his lips.

'Ah...it's not that good,' he said. 'You're going to be disappointed now no matter what I say,' he said, cuddling her tight.

'I'm not. I knew you weren't...I was kidding,' she said.

'Good. Well that was Gary Warner from the Crime Squad; it looks like it was Frankie Miller in St Peter's Park and who more than likely killed Liz. They think he used a hire car to get to the park. Could that 'ave been the hire car that hit you?'

'What? never. What does he look like, this Frankie? Because I'll never forget the look on that man's face when he stuck one finger up at me.'

'Of course. You saw him didn't you?'

'Yeah, and I'll have his face imprinted on my mind forever.' 'What did he look like? Dylan said sitting down.

'Ah, so you're interested in my minor bump now are you?' she said. 'I could have picked him out of an ID parade for you but...he's dead?' She frowned.

'VIPER.'

'Oh yes, of course, Video ID.'

'I'll arrange for you to visit the ID suite and see if we can get you to pick him out.'

'Does that mean I'll be able to make a claim on his insurance?'

'Stolen car. Dead driver...you might struggle with that one love.' Dylan said, with a wry smile.

'I'll make a detective yet, you'll see.' She grinned. 'A major witness in a murder enquiry, eh?' She whistled long and slow.

'A very important one, but only if you identify our man for us.'

She stopped what she was doing. 'I will. Well, I'll pick out the man that was driving the car that hit me.'

'We'll see, but the jigsaw puzzle is coming together. Who's got the money though, and why kill Liz?'

'That's for you to sort Jack. I've done my bit ...' She stood thinking, holding a knife and half a peeled potato in her hand. 'Am I a corner piece of your jigsaw, or a straight edge?'

'With those curves, definitely a corner piece, Miss Jones,' Dylan said readily. Now come here,' he said, grabbing her to him for a kiss. 'I need to say sorry.'

'What for?' she pouted.

'I pushed you aside when the accident happened, didn't I? I treated your accident as a minor occurrence, but if it was Frankie Miller who took your wing mirror off, after he had just killed one woman, then that's too close to my girl for comfort,' he sighed, squeezing her tight.

The next morning Dylan was in the office early, but John was there before him.

'You wet the bed, me old son?' Dylan said.

'No sir, I had one of them four o'clock thoughts and it niggled me so much I 'ad to get up.'

'Oh God...look...tip...write your thoughts down on a piece of paper and throw them on the floor till morning. I can do it without putting the light on now and believe it or not my writing is almost legible the next day,' he laughed. 'You'll learn...coffee?' Dylan shouted, as he walked back out of the office to make a brew. John followed him.

'Frankie didn't know Liz, right?' said John.

'Well he knew of her through Malcolm,' replied Dylan, as he spooned coffee into two cups.

'It's just Greater Manchester Police just rang. They've found a picture in Frankie's flat, of her outside her home.'

Dylan didn't stop what he was doing.

'And that's not all, John. Gary Warner called me last night. They can place Frankie's mobile in the park on the day of the murder. He'd also rung Liz's home several times in the days leading up to the murder. And remember Jen's accident the morning of the incident?' Dylan said.

John nodded.

'It might just 'ave been our Frankie in a rush to get away from the scene. I'm going to get a Video ID set up for her to see if she can identify the man driving the car that hit her.'

'Bloody hell,' John gasped.

Dylan laughed. Handing him his coffee. 'Perhaps that should be strong, tea John. You should see your bloody face, it's a picture.'

'What? Well nobody would believe that the boss's missus, on his enquiry, bumped into the culprit leaving the scene, now would they?'

'No, it's so unbelievable, it could be true. And, wait for this she says she got a good look at the driver too.'

'This morning couldn't get any better could it?' John grinned. 'Do you think she will ID him?'

'She says so, but you and I know from experience, how sure people are that they will never forget a face, and then when it comes to swearing beyond doubt...we'll see. We need to gather and secure all the evidence, in chronological order.'

'Do you want me to do Jen's Video ID?'

'I think it may be better to let the Video Unit do it. They'll be totally independent, and the last thing we want is for any suggestion from the defence of prompting, do we? We'll also have to put the relevant schedule in disclosure to highlighting the issue as it has potential to undermine our case or even assist the defence.'

John's eyebrows knitted together into a frown.

'Don't look so worried, this happens with lots of pieces of evidence and just has to be disclosed properly.

'I still can't fathom out why Frankie would kill Liz. Like Malcolm said, he wouldn't think twice about walking into banks and asking them to hand over the money. Yer know, like: *Handover the money or I'll blow your fucking head off.* So why bother with Liz and blackmail? It's not really his scene, is it?' said John.

'No, and I'm still not happy...Malcolm Reynolds and Larry Banks need a closer looking at. Nothing more come in on

Larry and his mobile home, or who's visited Malcolm Reynolds in prison, apart from his family?'

John shook his head and picked up the ringing telephone.

'It's for you sir, Finchy.'

John handed the phone over the desk into Dylan's outstretched hand.

'Yep.'

'Sir, Jason Todd will be with us at lunchtime. You still okay for interview around two o'clock, if I sort out his solicitor?'

'Yeah, count me in. I'd like to see what makes that bastard tick.'

Dylan replaced the receiver and he felt his pulse start to quicken. He couldn't wait to get stuck into Todd's ribs with the questioning. 'John, let's chase up the telephone connections with Liz and Larry and get them mapped. We'll plot all our player's movements on an Anacapa chart and see what it gives us. Who knows that may show something up we've missed.'

Dylan reached for the ringing phone this time. 'Jackie Stanley, Crown Prosecution Service. I'm just calling to let you know your double child murderer is to appear at Harrowfield Crown Court, a week on Monday, on the murder charge. His defence say he'll enter a guilty plea for Manslaughter ...'

'No, he won't.' Dylan interrupted. 'We'll run him for murder.' Dylan said, fuming.

'Good, I'm glad you've said that, they were my sentiments exactly. The defence are suggesting he was provoked.'

'Yeah, he will be when he's found guilty of two murders.'

'So, we'll go to trial, probably, in approximately nine months' time then. We'll have to wait for a date in the court calendar to be secured for it. I'll keep you posted.'

'Is the trial likely to be heard at a local Crown Court, or are the defence pushing for one out of the County just to make it awkward for witnesses or the fact that the public feelings are running high?' said Dylan.

'Not sure yet. The powers that be and the judge will decide that, but we'll know more once we have a request for witnesses, experts etcetera, so the duration of the trial can be planned.'

'Yeah, I know, but if it's possible I'd like it to be held locally for the families and witnesses sake let alone our officers. It would be nice if they could at least go back to their own homes after a day in court, instead of a hotel room where there's not enough room to swing a cat, in a strange city, miles away.'

'I totally agree, but you know and I know that we'll have to go where they send us.'

'Do yer best.'

'Don't worry DI Dylan; I'll do what I can. You'll be pleased to know, I'm hearing on the grapevine, that Judge Fryer-Black wants him in front of him. He's still known as the 'hanging judge' because he gives out such harsh sentences and if hanging were an available option to him, let me tell you, he'd use it.'

'Good. That would be a bonus. It's a shame the bastard can't be sent to the gallows...but as long as you can assure me there's no chance his manslaughter plea is going to be accepted I'm a happy man, for now. I'll make arrangements with the Family Liaison Officers to let the Hind and Spencer families know. Thanks for the phone call. I presume everyone else will be notified by you in due course?'

'Yeah, normal procedure will now commence,' the head of CPS said as she ended the call.

'John, I'm going into interview with Patrick Finch this afternoon. Will you ensure that all the evidence that we 'ave is gathered on the Reynolds' enquiry? Then we'll go and see Malcolm again.'

Lisa, the young office admin clerk walked in with an envelope for Dylan's personal attention.

'Some crank?' Dylan said opening it. Lisa shrugged her shoulders. The writing was spidery, spasmodically written and almost illegible. The paper was stained and so he strained to read it.

'Jack
I might be a lot of things but I'm no murderer.
Larry.'

'Got an exhibit bag in your drawer, John?' said Dylan, as he picked up the letter carefully by a corner, and placed it in the clear plastic bag John handed him.

'It's from Larry,' Dylan said. 'He doesn't say much. Take a look, then get it checked out for prints and identification marks to see if we can pick up any evidence from it or prove it is him that wrote it; post mark, DNA on the stamp etcetera.'

'The writing's...hardly...' John said, studying it closely.

'Yeah, but at least if it's his hand writing, we know he's alive somewhere. We just need to find him and soon.'

Dylan stood up to leave. 'Right, so if you'll ring the video unit for me and make sure everything is set up for Jen's visit? Let them know who she is seeing, will you? I get enough earache from police officers at work, without getting it from her at home about people's attitudes and unacceptable comments.'

'Yeah, will do, no problem. Let's see how good a witness she is.' John smiled.

'If she doesn't pick him out I'll never let her live it down,' Dylan joked.

'So, no pressure there then?' John laughed.

'Did I ever tell you about the case I once dealt with, involving my only witness, who saw the attacker just before he assaulted a woman?'

John looked inquisitive.

'The defence at the trial – in the middle of his evidence mind - asked him if he was born blind...and he said "yes." Nobody from the police or prosecution had any idea about his disability and he'd picked the fella out of a line-up. So you can imagine the panic, can't you?'

'So what happened?' John said.

'Our Queen's Council looked at me as much as to say, *Shit that's blown it*, but the defence continued questioning the witness about his sight and he confirmed that although he'd been born blind he'd had an operation as a kid which had enabled him to see, but not one hundred percent. You can imagine my heart was in my mouth by this time.'

'Christ Almighty. And this was your star witness?'

'Yeah, the one and only, and it was a really bad assault as well. The defence didn't leave it there. They wanted to show the jury that if the witness's sight was in question, then his evidence was too, so they decided to test him by asking him what he could see, in the courtroom. 'Can you see the judge?' The defence asked.

'Yeah,' he replied.

'Can you see the jury?'

'Yes, all twelve of them,' he said.

'The man in the dock?'

'Oh yes, he's definitely the man I saw.'

That obviously rattled the defence. 'Okay then, now can you see the clock at the very back of the courtroom?"

'Yes,' he replied obviously agitated.

'And that is about the distance you were away from the man you saw, would you say?' The defence asked, trying to smugly prove his point that he could only see the outline and not detail.

'Can you now tell the court what time it is, please? To which the man promptly lifted his arm, looked at his wrist watch and said 'Eleven thirty-two, sir.'

Dylan laughed out loud. John stood aghast.

'The court was in absolute uproar. The red-faced defence barrister didn't offer any further questions and quickly sat down, presumably because he was embarrassed. To my mind it showed the jury what an honest person the witness was and a credible one too. This of course wasn't the only evidence but what a bolt out of the blue that line of questioning was. The jury went on to find the perpetrator guilty and he got life imprisonment.'

'Don't tell me, Jen's got a problem with her eyesight?' said John.

'Well?' said Dylan thoughtfully. 'She's living me with isn't she?' Dylan sniggered.

'My point exactly,' John said.

'Careful John,' Dylan said, as he left the room.

The atmosphere in the incident room was more relaxed. They were making headway.

Dylan walked from John's office to his own, where he found a 'Kiss Me Quick' hat and a stick of rock on his desk.'

Out of the corner of his eye he saw Dennis Dors lurking in the corner of the general office. Because of his initials and surname Dennis's nickname was Diana Dors. In no way could a man with his stature be mistaken for a woman and he hated it with venom.

'Diana, My office now.' yelled Dylan.

Dennis was grinning broadly as he stood leaning on the door jamb to Dylan's office door. His left hand was heavily bandaged, and the size of a boxing glove; the only reminder of his altercation with Todd and the machete.

'What you got to smile about Diana?' said Dylan.

'Nothing, sir. There's only you could get away with calling me Diana ...' he chortled.

'Come in mate. Well done. Officers like you make me very proud. Would you like to join us in the office since you're going to be on restricted duties for a while?' Dylan said as he shook Dennis' good hand.

'That would be great Boss, thanks.'

'You can make coffee with one hand can't you?'

'Yeah, I'm sure I can.' Dennis grinned.

'Then you'll do for me kid,' Dylan said, winking at him.

Chapter Twenty-Eight

DI Jack Dylan walked into the interview room with DS Patrick Finch at his side. He was tempted to smile but resisted the urge as he saw Jason Todd sporting two very swollen black eyes. His nose was no longer central to his face, and had a large plaster across it.

His solicitor, Mr Hopkinson, introduced himself, explaining that he was representing Mr Todd; not Perfect & Best, whom Todd had requested, due to the conflict of interest the other arrests would have presented. After the formalities were over, they talked about his relationship with Susan Sharpe and her son Charlie.

Todd responded to the initial questions quite calmly and quickly, stating that he couldn't be certain he was Charlie's father.

Patrick Finch said that there was no doubt that the father of the child in question according to the paternity test, was him. He didn't flinch at the revelation.

When they started talking about the assaults on Charlie, his responses were a lot slower and to Dylan they appeared thought through. Todd didn't deny hitting him but he denied hurting him.

Then they put Charlie's injuries to him.

'I bet she's saying it's all me. I never wanted a kid in the first place. Susan said she was on't pill,' Todd said, raging.

The questioning continued to focus on each of Charlie's injuries.

'Yeah, I admit I wasn't the best dad in the world. I couldn't get him toys and that coz we had no money, and that's why I ad to go out robbing,' he said, trying to explain away his inadequacies.

'But Charlie didn't benefit from your robbing did he?' said Patrick.

'Why did you keep him locked away Jason? My dogs better looked after ...' he continued.

'That were her job, looking after the nipper, not mine,' Todd said.

The bleeping of the forty-minute tape brought the first interview to an end. Dylan was pleased that Jason Todd was talking to them. In the next interview he would get stuck into his ribs.

Patrick Finch started the second interview, and once again it began in the same vein. Then Dylan, no longer showing restraint, went straight for the jugular. 'Why did you hit Charlie with the pool cue?'

Todd looked shocked at Dylan's first question and stayed silent, glancing slyly across at his solicitor. There was something different about Todd that Dylan had noticed the moment he had sat down. He was short of breath, there were sweat beads on his forehead and he constantly wriggled in his seat.

'Why did you use a lead on him, break his bones and fracture his skull?' Dylan continued.

Again Todd didn't respond. His solicitor took notes but stayed silent.

'Do you use drugs?' Patrick asked.

'Yeah,' he answered.

'Why did you want the others to try to make him cry? They tell us they were frightened of you, and that you were the only reason they hit Charlie.'

'That's fucking lies. I didn't make them do anything. They're just trying to save their own necks.'

'Why don't you tell us your side of the story then, Jason?' said Patrick.

'We just want the truth.'

Todd glanced at Mr Hopkinson who nodded that he should proceed. Patrick looked at Dylan hopefully. Most solicitors would have asked for a break to advise their client.

'I didn't know the nipper was mine. She's been about a bit, but the council gave her the house because of him, so . . .'

'So you moved in for a free bed?'

'All he ever did was whine, he never stopped. He always wanted something. She shouted at him and slapped him, but it didn't make any difference, so I told her it was no use, she'd 'ave to bray him. If she'd 'ave just hit him once and it hurt, he wouldn't 'ave done it again would he? God she's as thick as a fucking plank.'

'So you just showed her how hard to hit him to make him cry.' Dylan said, trying to egg him on.

'Yeah, as he got tougher I had to use something other than me 'and to hurt him though. If I picked him up he bit me like an animal. He was crazy, like he was possessed or summat.'

'So, because he bit you, you used things like a pool cue to hit him with. Why?' Dylan probed.

'So he'd stop whining and he couldn't get near enough to bite me.'

'Did you take any drugs the night before Charlie died?'

'Don't remember, if I 'ad some I would 'ave.'

'Susan said you hit her.'

'Yeah, I did. She drove me fucking nuts sometimes.'

'Did Susan hit Charlie?'

'Yeah. She hit him and screamed at him like a nutter.'

'Alan Connor, Chubby told us you hit him and told him to hit Charlie.'

'No, I fucking never. What would he remember, he was well out of it. I didn't tell him to do 'owt. He's fucking mental.'

'Mental or not, Chubby Connor told us that Charlie wouldn't eat. Why do you think that was?'

'Because he was too bloody lazy.'

'Not because you had broken his arms, then?' Dylan said.

Jason Todd was silent and had the grace to hang his head.

'If you couldn't cope, why didn't you get help? You must 'ave known you'd hurt Charlie, when you saw his cuts and bruises.'

'No.'

'Does your nose hurt Jason?' said Dylan

'Yeah, it fucking does. I'm gonna sue that copper.'

'You're a big lad,' Dylan said. 'So if that hurts you, how do you think Charlie felt? He must 'ave been in horrendous pain, mustn't he? When you broke his arms and threw him into the wall?'

'He didn't cry.'

'Did you?'

Todd looked stunned. 'No.'

'You went wild at Charlie the night he died, and then ran away to Blackpool didn't you?'

'No.'

'You knew you'd killed him, didn't you?'

'No. He used to close his eyes when he didn't want to do what he was told. I didn't think he was dead.'

'Can you explain why Charlie deserved such continuous, violent beatings from you, Connor and Sharpe?'

Todd stayed silent, staring down at his hands on his lap.

'Well?' Dylan probed. 'Do you think you're a hard man Jason?'

He stayed still and quiet.

'Or just a bully? You attacked a poor, defenceless child; beat him with a pool cue, burnt him, broke his limbs. What on earth had he done to make you so angry with him? What?' Dylan shouted.

'It's what dads do.' Todd shouted back. 'Teach their kids to behave.'

'No. You battered him so hard you killed him for God's sake. You treat him like an animal...your own son, your own flesh and blood.'

'It wasn't just me,' he shouted.

'Where is the pool cue? Got rid of it because you knew it was the murder weapon?'

'No.'

'Where is it then?'

'I threw it.'

'Where?'

'Over a fence.'

'Oh, over a fence eh?'

'Yeah.'

'You mean you tried to get rid of the evidence. You knew exactly what you'd done. You tortured the lad daily, then beat him to death didn't you? Make you feel good did it?' Dylan was digging at him.

Todd got to his feet, fists clenched. 'That's bollocks it wasn't just me.'

'Sit down,' Dylan instructed him. 'Now.'

Jason Todd did as he was told.

Mr Hopkinson cleared his throat. 'Perhaps we could have a break at this time?'

Dylan nodded his head in agreement.

There was a chill in the interview room and the hairs on the back of Dylan's neck rose, as he stared long and hard across the table into the cold, dark eyes of a child killer, before he left the room.

In the next interview they would tidy up the other matters: resisting arrest, having an offensive weapon, robbery, but ultimately the main charge would be murder.

Dylan's problem would be identifying who caused which particular injury, so he knew he'd have to go for the charge of 'joint enterprise' and he hoped the prosecuting barrister, judge and jury would accept his decision that all three of them were collectively responsible.

'Patrick, will you charge him with murder, please,' said Dylan after the third interview. 'Whilst I ring Dawn and let her know what happened and see how she is?'

'I will, sir,' Patrick said. In Dylan's eyes, Patrick seemed to grow a foot taller as he watched him walk down the corridor to the detention cells. Patrick was pleased he'd called him by his name. Dylan was learning. 'That's job satisfaction for you,' Dylan whispered to Lisa, as she passed, and they smiled together. Lisa followed Patrick through the security gateway to the cells.

The Custody Sergeant brought Jason Todd to the charge desk. Patrick read out the charge of murder to him and the Custody Sergeant recorded the fact that he made no reply.

'How's my top DS and baby doing now?' asked Dylan.

'We're both fine. I feel so stupid; fancy. I'll never live it down will I?'

'You'll just 'ave to remember to take more water with it next time girl,' Dylan said, laughing. 'Now, are you sitting comfortably, because I don't want to cause any more traumas?'

'That sounds ominous,' she said, chuckling. 'But yes, I am.'

'Connor, Todd and Sharpe are charged.' Dylan said. A lump appeared in his throat as he heard her sob at the news.

'Oh, God I wish I could have been there Jack,' she cried. 'Hormones...'

'Well there'll be plenty of paperwork on the file, for you to do when you get back, so don't you think you're getting away lightly, girl. And some more news, our child murderer is at court a week on Monday for the murder of Daisy Charlotte Hind and Christopher Spencer. He wants to plead to manslaughter but ...' he heard her gasp. 'Don't worry, I've told CPS there is no way we're accepting the plea. His defence is provocation. So we'll 'ave a murder trial next year.'

'Thank you for that; it's got to be murder. It's so kind of you to ring me straight away after the interviews Jack; I was wondering how things were going, thank you. Oh, and I'll be at court with you a week on Monday. I've been for a check-up today and the doc says he's pleased with my latest bloods.'

'That's good news, now just you get yourself rested for then. We all miss you. Did you hear about Dennis Dors breaking his hand on Jason Todd's nose?'

'He never? Good for him. Give him a kiss from me.'

'I'd do a lot of things for you Dawn, but I draw a line at that,' he said with a chuckle. 'Now rest, there is nothing spoiling here, so don't rush back and that's an order.'

Before he put the phone down, he heard her sigh deeply, and he knew Dawn well enough to know tears would be running down her face, and she'd be wiping them with one of her pretty little hankies.

'Where's the prosecution's main witness,' Jack shouted as he went in the house.

'You tease,' Jen said, as she ran to meet him.

'I've just had a panic. What if I don't pick him out?' she said, as she reached up for a kiss.

'You can only do your best, love.'

'John Benjamin rang me, it's tomorrow; eek.' she screeched.

'Good. Get it over with,' Dylan said as he walked along the hallway to the kitchen. Jen started to serve tea.

'Do you want to borrow my specs?' Dylan asked, as he opened the evening paper and retrieved his glasses from their casing.

'Get lost, I want to identify him, not magnify him,' she giggled.

Jen woke up a few times in the night, anxiety gripping her. Jack had always talked about people making identifications; but now she was being asked to do one, she wondered if she would really remember that face as clearly as she thought she would in her mind's eye. Would Jack be disappointed with her if she couldn't identify the guy driving the car? She would be so embarrassed, after all the fuss she'd made.

The next day, they didn't keep her waiting long at the video unit. She was bombarded with questions:

When did she see the man? Where? How far away was he? How long did she have him in her view? Could she describe him? What did she remember about him? Did he have any distinguishing features? Had she seen him before that day? Had she seen him since that day? Had anyone shown her a photograph of him? The civilian officer's questions went on and on. She wanted to shout at him to stop. It wasn't easy, nor did she feel comfortable. A tap came at the door.

'Brew up?' said the nicely rounded, pinafore clad, tea lady, who entered the room.

'Oh, gosh a cup of tea would be lovely. We don't have a tea trolley anymore at Harrowfield: cutbacks,' Jen said, rolling her eyes.

'Well, it's nice that our boss still lets us 'ave one here,' said the kindly older lady. 'Keeps me out of trouble,' she laughed. 'I've been 'ere for thirty- eight years this year. Milk and sugar, love?'

'Milk, no sugar thanks,' Jen said, gratefully accepting the steaming cup from the old lady's arthritic grip. Jen realised her hands were shaking. How daft, she thought. Had the officer noticed she was trembling? His face was an unemotional mask as he continued.

'The man who you saw may, or may not be present on the video screen you are about to see. Look carefully at all the pictures of people you are shown and take your time, there's no rush. 'The computer sprang into action, and a screen of ten photographs, all with the same grey background, appeared. Naively she hadn't realised how similar the images would look. Her heart started beating faster. Her eyes flashed from one side to the other and back again. She couldn't see him.

'He's not there,' she blurted out.

'Okay, if you're sure, we'll move to the next page. Like I said, there is no rush. Just take as long as you need, there's no pressure,' he said soothingly.

'Tell that to my brain.' Jen laughed nervously.

Systematically she went through eight more pictures. No, no, no, she was about to dismiss them all too when she saw him.

'It's him. It's definitely him,' she shouted loudly, surprising even herself. 'That's him; the man that stuck one finger up at me.' She started to shake.

'Are you sure?'

'I'm certain that's him.' She touched the screen. 'That's him.'

'Thank -you,' the officer said calmly. 'Now all we need to do is get a short statement from you.'

As she left the building she rang Dylan.

'It's me. I did it. I picked him out. Tell me how proud you are? I picked him out.' she screeched.

'Who did you pick? What did they call him?' said Dylan.

'Oh, I don't know what they called him. I never asked, should I have done? But it was him. It doesn't matter what they call him does it? I'm positive it was the man in the car that hit me.'

'I'll ring and find out who you picked, and ring you back in a minute or two,' Dylan said, with a smile at her excitement.

Jen sat anxiously waiting in her car for Dylan's call. When the phone rang she pressed the button to receive the call. The phone went dead.

'Oh, bugger,' she said fumbling with her mobile as it dropped on her knee.

'Jen?' She heard Dylan's voice calling in the distance. She snatched the phone from her lap and put it to her ear. Her heart pumped wildly.

'Yeah, spot on girl. You picked out Frankie Miller. Well done. It was him after all.'

Jen took a deep breath and looked to the heavens. 'Good detective I'd make, eh Jack?' she sighed, her voice shaking.

'The best. Now be careful driving home. No more trying to apprehend criminals for me, I've got a team for that,' he said.

Dylan could now well and truly put Frankie in St Peter's Park at the time Liz was murdered. But he needed more. Nothing yet proved he'd done it. What the hell would make him go to such extremes?

Lisa tapped on his door, 'forensic on my phone for you sir. I'll put 'em through.'

'Thanks,' he mouthed as his hand hovered over the phone, waiting for it to ring.

'Hello? DI Dylan? It's Mike from the lab. You'll be pleased to know that we've retrieved the SIM card from Liz Reynolds' phone.'

'Miracles do happen,' Dylan said, leaning back in his chair as John smiled and left the office.

'But is the information retrievable?' Dylan felt his heart jump into his mouth. He didn't realise till he gasped that he had been holding his breath.

'The text may well be safe and sound. I'll send it over to you so your people can attempt to download the data as soon as possible.'

'No you won't. I'll send someone over to get it,' Dylan said, jumping up as he replaced the receiver before he had time to say goodbye.

Dylan needed to show continuity, and he wanted the data as quick as possible.

He looked to the ceiling. 'Thank you God, again,' he whispered under his breath. 'Just a few more pieces please.'

'Vicky, will you go to Telephone Section at HQ for me please, ASAP?' he shouted into the CID office.

Chapter Twenty-Nine

Mobile phone tracking, tracks the current position of a mobile phone even on the move. To locate the phone, it must emit at least the roaming signal, to contact the next nearby antenna tower, but the process does not require an active call. Recent advancement in this field had become a major asset in detecting crime, and Dylan was hopeful that the data would be retrievable. Then they'd be able to plot Liz Reynolds and Frankie Miller's movements, as well as hopefully link them to Larry Bank's phone number. That information would be priceless to the enquiry.

This would give an insight into where they met and the text message detail they had sent to each other. Dylan would get a crime analyst from the Intelligence Unit to chart it all, displaying all contacts. It might look like a map of the London underground by the time they'd finished, but the timeline and visual links would be clear on one page, for the investigators and courts to see, now and in the future.

Just when Dylan thought things couldn't get any better, forensics confirmed that they had a trace of petrol on the balaclava worn by Frankie Miller, minute, but sufficient.

Dylan discussed it with John. This proof was putting Frankie in the frame for Liz's murder, but why did he do it? It didn't make sense. Did Larry or Malcolm know why? The team didn't have a full picture yet, but Dylan was on a high and wouldn't let anything spoil the moment.

'Is that Mr Dylan?' said a light happy voice over the phone.

'This is your top detective.' He knew who it was in an instant.

'Hi Vicky, what's up?' Dylan smiled.

'It's me Jack.' Jen shrieked.

'I know it's you, ya fool.' he laughed.

'I was missing you and I just wanted to hear your voice.'

'Me too. Will catch up with you soon. Gotta go, I'm just in the middle of something,' he sighed as he replaced the phone on its hook.

Keeping in touch, however briefly, helped Jen cope. Just by the tone of his voice she knew he was okay and she was happy.

Dylan and John studied the information they had.

'Dead fish in the bin. Any significance do you think, boss?' said John.

'Don't know. Could 'ave been to frighten her. Did she tell Malcolm about the fish?'

'Malcolm's never said anything has he, so perhaps he doesn't know.'

'Interestingly, according to Malcolm's visiting schedule, Larry made a short visit to him in the nick three months ago,' John told Dylan.

'Did Larry submit an intelligence sheet in Malcolm Reynolds' file?' said Dylan.

'No, not a hint of his visit.'

'Let's 'ave a run out and see Liz's parents. Update them about Frankie Miller, and drop it on their toes that we think one of our detectives was friendly with the Reynolds', and see what reaction we get. Then we'll see if anything is fed back to Malcolm. It's time we gave Malcolm another visit too. We desperately need to find Larry,' he insisted. 'He won't be far from some bar, wherever he is.'

'Just a thought boss, do they 'ave a tracker on leased mobile homes?'

'Don't know, but what a stroke of luck that would be if they did. Write up an action. Let's make the enquiry a priority.'

Liz's mum Connie was a shadow of her former self. In fact, Dylan hardly recognised the woman who opened the door to them. Her hair hung lank around her face; her clothes clung to her stooped frame. Dragging her slippered feet into the kitchen and she offered the men a seat at the littered kitchen table.

'How are you?' said Dylan, although from her appearance it was obvious. Connie turned from the sink where she'd been filling the kettle. Her automatic response to a visitor in her home was to make a cup of tea.

'Honestly?' she asked. The men nodded. 'Some days, if it wasn't for Gemma, I wouldn't get out of bed,' she smiled feebly. 'But life has to go on I keep telling myself. I'm just having bad days and very bad days at the moment. They tell me it will pass.'

'And what help are you getting?'

'Frances, your FLO, suggested I go to the doctors, and he has referred me for counselling, which will hopefully help me deal with the thoughts when I'm awake, and the nightmares when I'm asleep.' She sighed as she brushed her fringe out of her eyes, and flopped down, with a deep sigh, onto a chair. 'But my daughter's dead, and at our age...what's there to unravel? Gemma's got to be looked after and that's my one and only focus. I don't need a shrink to tell me that, do I?'

'Maybe he'll be able to help you get some support. Connie, if there's anything that you think we can do...well you only 'ave to ask.'

'Thank you,' she said as she yawned. 'I forgot how demanding it is to look after a young 'un.'

The kettle whistled.

'Tea or coffee?'

'No, don't bother for us, we're fine. We just called to see how you were.'

Dylan and John got up to leave. 'You've enough on your plate at the moment. We'll come back another day for a chat and a cuppa, eh?' Dylan said resting a hand on her arm.

'Whatever.' She shrugged as she followed them down the hallway. 'You're always welcome.'

Dylan turned at the open door.

'Just while I think on, did you ever hear Liz or Malcolm talk of a man called Larry Banks?'

'No, sorry I don't think I did.'

'No sweat,' said Dylan.

Dylan and John got in the car.

'I think Jen's at home. We've got to pass. Shall we call in for a cuppa?'

'Good idea,' John replied.

Max was sleeping in the sun that shone warmly through the patio window, although it was still cool outside. 'Spring weather is surely just around the corner,' Dylan thought, but winter was not about to surrender without a fight this year.

'Well done with the ID Jen,' John said, as they entered the house.

'Crawler,' Dylan whispered out of the corner of his mouth.

'Thankyou. Glad some one appreciates my conscientiousness, John. Have a piece of home-made parkin, and how about a ginger biscuit? They've just come out of the oven.'

'Thank you, I think I will.' John smiled smugly. 'Do you know, I can't imagine why this man hasn't put a ring on your finger yet,' he said. 'And he thinks he's so darn clever.' John chuckled.

'I'm the eternal bachelor, that's why,' Dylan snivelled. 'And that's what you love about me isn't it Jen?' he said.

'That's right,' she smiled and turned away quickly, so he couldn't see the expression on her face.

'Come on, here boy,' whistled John. Max ran over and deposited a toy at his feet, and stood back barking.

'Don't you go giving him a biscuit; ginger gives him tremendous wind.' Jack said, grumpily.

'And we know who Jack blames for wind don't we Max?' Jen said, moodily, as she handed the men cups of tea, before reaching out to grab Max's collar. 'You'll cover them in hairs, come away,' she snapped.

Dylan frowned. 'Guess which hand the biscuit's in boy,' he asked Max, and Max dutifully pawed at his clenched fist and won his reward with ease.

'Do you think it would 'ave been easier to pick out a culprit in flesh in a line with twelve other men like they used to instead of looking at a video, Jen?' John said reaching out to grab another biscuit. 'These are absolutely gorgeous by the way.'

'Don't know.' Jen shrugged her shoulders. 'It would have probably been more intimidating, but I think I'd have picked him out the guy I saw, whatever. His face is truly imprinted on my mind.'

'What do they call it in psychology? Flash bulb? Flashback? A memory created in great detail, during a personally significant event. And if I remember rightly, those memories are perceived to have a photographic effect.'

Jen looked at Dylan. It was Dylan's turn to shrug his shoulders this time,

'Don't ask me?'

'Take no notice of him, I'm impressed and you're right that's true,' said Jen, as she cleared the pots off the table, to the sink.

'Don't be, I fancied my psychology teacher at school, hence I learnt things verbatim to impress her.' John laughed.

'Come on then, John, let's get going, there's no rest for the wicked, as they say,' Dylan said.

Jen stayed at the sink, her hand under the tap that was running for the washing up. She didn't turn to watch them leave.

'Bye Jen, thanks for the brew and the goodies,' John shouted, as he walked towards the front door.

'Bye love,' Dylan said, as he gave her a quick peck on her cheek and followed John close behind. 'See you later.'

'Bye,' she whispered, as the tears welled up in her eyes. Now Jack had said it out loud it was a stark reminder that she was destined to not only to be childless, but remain a spinster too. She sighed, and knew she should be happy. This was her lot and sooner or later she had to accept it. Why did it still upset her so?

'You okay mate?' Dylan asked as they drove back to the nick. John was unusually quiet.

'Yeah, just thinking what the odds are of the SIO's partner identifying a murder suspect in his case?'

'Millions to one probably,' Dylan chuckled.

'More than that, boss I should think.'

'Stop taking the piss, John. The defence barrister would 'ave loved that wouldn't he, if Frankie had been alive to stand trial.'

'Yeah, can you imagine? 'Did you show a photograph of Frankie Miller to your partner, DI Dylan? Do you take your work home, sir?' The press would've had a field day too. Just imagine the headline. Did Investigator showed culprits photo before she identified him: Sold some papers that would 'ave for them.'

The day had finally arrived. Dylan's double child murderer's case was before Judge Fryer-Black at Harrowfield Crown Court, for a plea and case management hearing. It was the only case on the list outside court number one. What a waste of time it was for Dylan and Dawn to be sitting outside in the foyer of the crown court all morning just to wait for a five minute hearing. Dylan always found it absurd that victims and/or their families, witnesses, suspects and their relatives, all waited in the same lobby to go into the court. It just seemed wrong that they were forced to sit with one another, but costs meant that this had to be so. The feeling of intimidation must be horrible, for some of the witnesses and victims about to give evidence.

The case was called by the usher, who, in her black gown, bustled into the busy corridor, from the courtroom. The court was packed when Dylan and Dawn finally entered. The media reminded Dylan of a pack of hungry wolves. 'There won't be many spare seats to such an event,' Dylan thought, as they filed into the public gallery with the other voyeurs. Dawn and Dylan stood in the aisle and scanned the sixteen seats, to see if any were free, or if they would have to stand. Dawn hoped not. Sometimes the judges wouldn't allow anyone to stand and they'd be asked to leave, which meant they'd miss everything; although amiable ushers, would often allow police officers to sit in the press seats.

'I'm disappointed with the not guilty plea to murder,' whispered Dylan, as they sat down.

'The bastard just wants to squeeze every last ounce of life out of the Hinds and Spencer's, I bet. You think he'd be satisfied wouldn't you: he'd got his revenge that he wanted by murdering their children, without rubbing salt in their wounds,' she replied. 'I feel so sorry for them, Jack,' she sighed as she shuffled on the rigid seat, trying to make herself comfortable. 'Gosh, it's warm in here,' she said, as she fanned her face with the previous conviction print outs and antecedents that she had brought with her, just in case there was a last minute change of plea; to guilty, and she was called to give antecedent history. It was her first day back at work, and Dylan noted that her bump was very noticeable now, but she was glowing.

'The inference is that he denies the murder on the grounds of provocation. The jury will sort him out in due course though, and the judge will slam him, I hope,' Dylan said. 'Are you feeling okay?'

'I'm fine Jack, thank you. Did you say they should hang him?' she said, wiping her mouth with her hankie. He hadn't seen her do that for a while and he knew from experience of her idiosyncrasy that she must be hungry.

'It won't bring back the kids, will it? But what a nice swing it would 'ave to it,' Dylan said chuckling.

Dawn rolled her eyes and groaned. 'You can buy me coffee and a bun after that attempt at a joke.' She laughed, realising how much she had missed the banter of her colleague. Debbie arrived with her hands full of paperwork, in a rush as usual, squeezing into a seat behind them. She always seemed so busy and yet, as an Investigative Support Officer, was able to answer all the questions asked of her, on all the different cases that she was putting case files together for. Debbie was a key cog in the wheel of the team; making sure deadlines were met with the CPS and defence, along with the rest of the team; but as a civilian, and because she just put her head down and got on with it, she was often overlooked.

'Sorry I'm late; couldn't find anywhere to park,' she said. Her little round face flushed. Debbie was young and pretty with thick, curly ginger hair and soft green eyes.

'You've not missed anything, only the news from our barrister that there's no change on the plea of not guilty.'

'Didn't expect there to be any change. I'm all ready with my diary to note down the relevant dates of the next hearing and trial date,' Debbie replied, as she searched busily for her pen, in her huge bag.

'All rise,' said the court clerk, as the judge walked from his chamber to address the court. Suddenly all cut to quiet in the room. Everyone in the courtroom rose. The High Court Judge Fryer-Black, in all his splendour, took his seat. He had agreed to hear the case, to set a date for the trial, in-between other court business that day. At least the hearing would be over in minutes; and they hadn't had to wait all day for the case to be heard.

The defence barrister, a Mr Leonard Passmore, stood up. He could be seen by everyone in the public gallery through a tinted plastic panel that separated it from the rest of the court. The hearing lasted minutes, as the not guilty plea was entered.

'What a waste of bloody time and money,' Dylan muttered to Dawn as they stood to leave.

Dylan was in the queue of the upstairs restaurant in the Crown Court, watching Dawn settling herself at a table in a quiet corner with Debbie. The room was packed and reminded him of any large department store's cafeteria. Witnesses, police and defendants with their families were thrown together. Once again he thought how frightening it must feel to be a witness here with an offender, instantly he thought of Mrs Day.

He recognised a well known young burglar, looking like he'd just walked out of Burton's window. Dylan wouldn't put it past him burgling a clothes shop especially to give a good impression for his court appearance. How well he scrubbed up for court. Some would do anything to give a good impression to a judge and jury; displaying a united front with their family, all fresh faced and angelic looking. How many times did he need to be put before the court before he was sent down? How many people and their homes did he have to plunder before he was safely put behind bars? And then there were the others; the ones who couldn't care less what anyone thought who were looking for a further spell inside prison. They didn't get nervous like normal people did. Being institutionalised was their way of life. Prison was a place they met up with their mates and learned new skills for when they were released. Court was a day out for them, a chance to catch up with family and friends.

'Coffee, tea, chocolate or Bovril?' asked the lady behind the counter, breaking his reverie.

'Sorry, I was miles away,' Dylan offered, by way of an explanation.

'Three coffees please, and the biggest cream bun you've got,' he smiled.

'Don't apologise. There's many in here that'd like to be miles away,' she chuckled as she placed the drinks on a tray. 'Any fink else?' she asked.

'No, thank you,' he smiled as he handed her a ten pound note.

Dylan pushed through the small crowd with his tray.

'Where's Debbie gone?' he asked.

'Oh, she got a call there's a trial starting on Monday, and she's still got some disclosure to finish, and exhibits to copy, and CPS want them 'yesterday' as usual, so she apologised and headed back to the office'.

'Hmm, more coffee for me then. Well Dawn, next year we'll be listening to the load of bollocks his defence team come up with. We can expect a drama from Perfect & Best. If nothing else they'll play up for the press,' he said, grinning as he placed the coffee and cream bun in front of her and put the tray on the spare seat.

'Where do you stand on sentencing then Jack? *Eye for an eye?*' Dawn asked, her eyes fixed firmly on the cake. 'That mine?' she said pulling the plate with the cake on in front of her.

'That feels like a promotion board question,' he said as he sat down.

'Come on it's me you're talking to. Do you really think that life imprisonment is really a deterrent?' she said, taking the largest of bites of cream cake.

'No I don't. People are living longer these days, so I think they should extend life to more than fifteen years, and no early release for good behaviour, if I'm honest. Or bring back the death penalty. That's my personal view.'

'Mmm,' she said, fighting not to lose a drop of the cream as she took another bite of the cake and quickly devoured the rest.'

'Let's face it, wouldn't you be good inside if you thought you were gonna get out a few years earlier? Someone who kills at twenty years old can be out when they are thirty,' he said, as he stirred sugar into the second mug of coffee.

'The pendulum of justice swings too much in the offenders' favour these days for my liking.' Dawn said, licking her lips.

'Mine too, especially when they go onto re-offend after being released. How can the sentence they served 'ave really been a punishment, otherwise they'd never dream of committing another crime.'

'If anyone takes someone's life, they should 'ave all their human rights taken away from them, never mind them having civil rights. At least that would be a start, and might stop the cheeky bastards trying to claim for stuff like clothing they say we've damaged when we apprehended them. Do you remember that murderer who wanted us to buy him a new leather jacket because he said we'd ruined it in the property stores? It had the victim's blood all down the front of it, goddamit.'

Dylan smiled at her. 'You're really on your soap box today Dawn.'

'Hormones. I blame everything on hormones these days, they're the most wonderful excuse,' she laughed.

'Yeah, well we don't make the laws, just uphold them, remember.'

Dawn rubbed her rounded stomach.

'You ever wanted kids, Jack?'

'I'd 'ave to find a woman who'd agree to marry me and this lifestyle first,' he said, as he stood up and looked around the room.

'Have you?' Dawn looked up into his smiling face.

'Had he?' He mused.

'May be but you're not in the need to know bracket,' he said, touching his nose. 'I thought we were sharing that cream bun,' he said looking at the empty plate.

Dawn ran her finger round it. 'And you know what thought did don't you?' she laughed licking clean the remaining morsels of the bun from it.

'Let's get back to the nick and get the Family Liaison Officer's to speak to the Hind and Spencer families. It's going to be upsetting for them, knowing he isn't pleading guilty, but nothing more than they would've expected from a serial killer I wouldn't 'ave thought,' said Dylan.

'I just hope that we get a local Crown Court. The baby should be here by then,' she said. 'But we'll just 'ave to wait and see where there's a place in the court calendar won't we?' Dawn sighed.

Chapter Thirty

Jen lay back and soaked in the luxury of a lavender scented bath. Max had been walked and fed, and if she knew Dylan, it would be a while before he got home because of the court appearance that day. Whatever happened, there would be work to be done back at the office, and depending how long he'd been at court, would dictate how much of his daily routine work he had to catch up on when he got back. She smiled, and then sighed; languishing in the bubbles she immersed her head under the water, loving the feeling that washed over her. The day had been long and her body was tense and aching. She was so tired she could have fallen asleep as the smell of the aromatherapy oil engulfed her senses.

Her mind drifted back to her day at work, and the awful news that the mother of one of her colleague's had been told she had breast cancer. It had been an emotional dinner-time, as the young woman had told Jen about the gruelling treatment her mum would have to endure, as well as coping with the fact that she might lose her hair. Absentmindedly her hand glided over her unusually tender breast. She cupped them in her hands and they felt heavy. Lifting her arms, she checked her armpits and then let her fingers probe deeper into her right breast and then her left.

Suddenly she stopped, feeling a large hard rubbery lump to the left of her nipple. A squirt of adrenalin shot into her stomach and she sat up. She'd always had 'lumpy' breasts, but this felt different. She felt a wave of nausea. Her hand wandered to her right breast to see if it felt the same. No it was definitely different. She stood up in the bath as a flush of panic ran through her body. She looked at herself in the mirror, over the washbasin. She turned from side to side. Her body was firm and well proportioned. Her breasts well rounded and her stomach was fairly flat she thought, as she grabbed hold of the excess fat on her hips and screwed up her face. Did one breast look larger than the other, she wondered? How was she supposed to know she didn't spend time feeling her breasts. Stepping out of the bath she grabbed a warm towel from the rail and started rubbing her body vigorously. She reached for the moisturiser and smoothing on the cream, her hand once more went involuntarily to her breast. No, it was still there, the hard unmovable mound hadn't gone. Did she honestly think it would? As she padded down the stairs in her pyjamas, she saw the security light come on outside, and was pleased that Jack was home.

'We won't tell Jack will we mate,' she said, as she hurriedly passed Max, who'd been waiting patiently for her at the foot of the stairs. Fleetingly, she cupped his face in her hands and kissed the top of his head. He stood and followed her into the kitchen. She switched on the kettle. Max sat watching her and her eyes filled with tears. 'What would I do without you baby,' she said. He crawled on the floor to her feet. A lone tear trickled down her cheek and she bent down to stroke him, her confidant, her friend.

Had it really been six years since she had chosen him? She had lavished her time on him and he had helped heal her heartache. He was her only companion when she'd moved from the Isle of Wight, unable to stay in the familiar surroundings after she had got the devastating news and her fiancé had left her. Max and she had been comfortable together since then, just the two of them, until Jack had come into their lives. She wiped her wet face with her sleeve and stood as she heard Dylan's key in the door. 'Jack's enough on his plate, hasn't he Max without our problems,' she muttered, as she reached in the cupboard for a mug to make Dylan a warm drink. Max being the eternal optimist, stood close behind her, assuming that he was going to get a treat and he wasn't disappointed.

'Now what shall I make to eat?' she sighed to herself, as Max bounded off to greet Dylan. Was it really nine o'clock?she thought, as she looked at the clock? Where had the evening gone?

The next day, the press office was hot on Dylan's tail.

'Ave you seen the bloody headlines? Families call for capital punishment to be brought back for child killers.' Vicky read out the front page of the Harrowfield Times.

'That's always gonna to be the case.' Dylan said.

'I'm surprised you didn't say 'owt to the press after the pre-trial hearing, boss'

'Ah, Vicky, an opportunity missed,' chuckled Dylan. 'That would 'ave caused ructions over at HQ wouldn't it if I'd put my two pen'orth in?' he laughed.

'You're too professional for that,' she said, causing her brow to furrow.

'So far,' he agreed as his mobile rang. She got up and left him to his call.

Dylan peered at the mobile screen over his glasses, 'unknown number.' It was probably some reporter trying to get him to comment on the not guilty plea. 'Dylan,' he roared, to scare off the caller. He heard beeps as if it the person was ringing him from a call box. He waited.

'Boss, it's Larry. Call off the wolves, will you? I want to talk to you. I'm not your murderer. I thought you knew me better than that.' Before Dylan could speak, he'd gone. His speech sounded slurred and his voice was tired and emotional.

'John.' shouted Dylan.

'Yes boss?' said John as he appeared at Dylan's door.

'Larry just rang. He wants to talk.'

'If he's still driving that mobile home in Yorkshire, he'll be lucky if he's not picked up by us before he gets to meet up with you.'

'Put a call out-to the force for officers to keep their eyes peeled for him, and get us an urgent visiting order for Malcolm Reynolds, will you? I think it's about time we see what happens when we tell him about Larry and Liz.'

The previous day's court appearance seemed a long time ago as Dylan launched himself into looking at the outstanding actions on his murder enquiries, but he couldn't get Larry, his letter, or the call - out of his mind. To Dylan's surprise, John told him Malcolm Reynolds had been moved to an open prison, and the level of security of that prison now concerned him.

'He's done well boss, getting that move so soon, hasn't he?' John said.

'Yeah, but to be fair to him, I suppose he's a non-violent prisoner who's done a good proportion of his time, with good behaviour. It's got to be expected at some point. I wonder if he'll be nipping out on day trips and to the local pub at night.' Dylan said.

'Most of 'em do, don't they? Then end up back on high security again because of the drink. They never learn.'

The surroundings of the open prison were pleasant in comparison with the high security incarceration. Dylan and John strolled into the almost empty visitor's centre at HM Prison Wealstun where food and drink could be purchased from the refreshment counter. Malcolm Reynolds was sitting at a table, two prison officers on hand. Dylan thought he looked a lot fitter, cleaner, and he hoped more amiable than the last time they'd seen him. He got up to greet them and shook them by the hand. The saying 'the calm before the storm' came to the forefront of Dylan's mind.

''Ave you got news?' Malcolm asked.

'Not a lot,' said Dylan. Malcolm's shoulders visibly dropped.

'We're still trying to piece together what happened. How well do you know a Detective Sergeant Banks, Malcolm?' Dylan asked. He noticed Malcolm's eyes flash with recognition.

'What the hell as that got to do with the murder of my wife?

'How well do you think Liz knew him, Malcolm?'

'What? Where are you going with this?' Malcolm's eyes glazed over.

'We know that the night before Liz was murdered he spent the night with her at your house,' said Dylan.

'No way. Why's he saying that?' he asked John. 'Where is Banks?'

'He isn't. We are. His DNA has been lifted from the bed sheets and his prints were found at the house,' Dylan said.

'The bitch. That bent bastard. Did he kill her? Was it him?' Malcolm raged.

'Calm down. I'm being straight with you, no matter how much I know the truth will hurt.'

'What? Why would I want to hear one of your guys was shagging my missus? If it's true, it's a good job she is dead...I'd 'ave killed her myself when I found out, and she knew it.'

'You still haven't answered me, do you know Larry Banks?' Dylan probed.

'Yeah, Larry was a bent copper. Didn't you know that?'

Dylan tried to hide his shock at hearing the revelation spoken out loud, or was it just that he didn't want to hear the truth.

'Why're you saying that? Because of what I've just told you about him and Liz?' Dylan said.

'Look, do you think I care a flying fuck whether you believe me or not? Think what the hell you like, but mark my words, he's a fucking dead man.'

'He's not here. We're trying to find him; he's wanted with Interpol. Do you know where he is?'

'Whoa. Why would I know where he is? I hope you catch the bastard. Bring him in here to see me when you do.' Malcolm roared.

Dylan ignored his outburst. 'So, how does he know Liz?'

'He did me a favour a few years ago...then...I was arrested.'

'Look, cards on the table apart from what we have said about Larry we can put Frankie Miller in St Peter's Park; around the time of Liz's death. He's been identified driving away from the scene of an accident in the area around the same time. A balaclava was recovered in St Peter's Park; that's where we've got his DNA from and we've found traces of petrol on it. We can show that he telephoned Liz at your home and he had her photo at his flat. Someone poisoned your koi carp. He knew your address.'

'The bastard...the absolute bastard. All the time he was celled up with me he was just gathering information. He knew I collected rare koi' Malcolm paused, shaking his head. 'Boy, did he groom me. How naïve was I? The stupid bloody crack head. Hang on though . Why would he kill her if he'd got the money off of her? He'd no need to murder her had he? She didn't know him, and if he was wearing a balaclava like you say.' Malcolm stopped to think. 'I knew once he got out of prison he 'ad to get his hand on cash. They'd given him time . . .'

'Who had?' asked John.

'Hey, I didn't ask any questions. Some drug cartel I reckon...but because of how prolific a robber he was, the boys gave him time to raise the money when he got out, that's all I know.'

'The boys?' asked Dylan.

'Don't even go there. So, where's the money? Where's the bloody half a million if Frankie didn't 'ave it?' Malcolm was sweating: his face was red and contorted in anger.

'The money wasn't in the case at the scene. It looks like remnants of books had been inside when it was set alight...forensics is trying to find out more for us.'

'Books? Liz doesn't do books. She does magazines with pictures. What are you telling me, you think she gave Larry the money?'

John looked at Dylan.

'That's what you're telling me isn't it? Larry caused her death didn't he? He's a dead man walking. I'm telling you now I'm gonna take his bloody head off.' Malcolm paced the visitor's centre's floor.

'Slow down Malcolm. We don't know that, but when we've got all the facts I promise we'll come and tell you in person, then you've got it from the man in charge and you can be sure it's right. Don't be making idle threats.'

'They're not idle threats mate, believe me...'

'I'm going to ask you one last time before we leave, 'ave you told us everything, Malcolm?' said Dylan.

'What else can I tell you?' Malcolm was overcome with helplessness, or so it seemed.

'We know Larry Banks came to see you in prison. What was that about?' asked John.

'I've 'eard enough,' Malcolm said, slamming his hands on his thighs. He stood up and walked to the door, where he waited in silence to be let back into his wing by the prison officers.

'Do you get the impression he is holding back?' John asked Dylan en route to the station.

'I don't warm to the man that's for sure, but then again, look at Larry Banks; a drinker, a womaniser who's had some close shaves over the years with angry husbands, but a thief? A murderer? Someone who did Reynolds a favour when he was on my team? Who knows? We'll just 'ave to see what the evidence tells us now. Only then will we get the truth, I suspect.'

Chapter Thirty One

Jen couldn't settle: the lump was still there, when she showered, when she lay down, when she stood up. On impulse she picked up the phone and rang the doctor's surgery.

'No, it's not urgent,' she told the receptionist. 'I found a lump in my breast, but I'm not ill,' she explained.

'I can get you an appointment today Miss Jones,' she said, without delay. 'Would half past four be okay?'

Back at the station, Tracy stopped Dylan as he walked into the CID office.

'Millgarth Police Station has just had a call from Screen Yorkshire. A mobile home hired by Larry Banks has been abandoned in front of their studios at 42, The Calls, Leeds, LS2 7EY,' she read from her pad.

'Leeds? Bloody hell, so he's back. Wonder where? Vicky, John, can you get over there and take Senior SOCO with you? The van will need searching and we'll need forensics to examine it. We might get CCTV from the surrounding area if we're lucky. Tracy, once Vicky and John get a statement from the hire company about the mileage that was on it when it left them and any further information they may 'ave that might help us with our enquiries. Can you also get Leeds police to watch for him...and get someone to watch his flat, Lisa. That cheeky bastard has enough gall to go back there. Keep me updated everybody. I'll get him circulated over the radio across the force area, again.'

Vicky looked crestfallen as she reached for her radio.

'What's up mate?' Dylan asked.

'I thought I was in for a trip to the South of France, not bloody Leeds.' She groaned. 'Story of my chuffing life; don't you know I need some sun,' she said.

Dylan grinned. 'Look on the positive side. You'll get some smashing pie and peas from the van in the car park next to Kirkgate Market for your tea; better than frog's legs any day.'

Dylan's phone rang.

'Hi love. How lovely to hear your voice,' he said.

'Do you know what time you'll be home tonight?' Jen asked.

'No, why?' Dylan's brows furrowed.

'Oh, I've just got a doctor's appointment that's all.'

'You didn't say. You okay?'

'Yeah, I'm sure I'll be home before you, but I was just letting you know in case by any stretch of the imagination, you got home before me,' she said sarcastically.

'Point taken. It's manic here. The mobile home Larry went off in has turned up,' he said. 'Looks as if he's back...so it may be a late one.'

'Oh, you better go then. I won't keep you. Love you.' Jen said as she replaced the receiver and started planning a nice supper for Jack, to try and take her mind off her doctor's appointment. 'Sirloin,' she said out loud. Max licked her hand and then paced in circles, before finally resting at her feet.

Feedback about Larry started to come in quick and fast, from all directions. The mobile home appeared to have been carefully cleaned before he dumped it. He was told there was a strong smell of bleach in the van, but there was nothing inside it to cause concern. This was more like it. Dylan would have expected Larry to clean up after himself.

Tracy rang Dylan, 'Sir, I've got the mileage for you from when it left. I've told them we need to examine it, so they wouldn't be able to have it back yet.'

'Thank you. Can you tell them we're searching it now, so we'll get it back to them ASAP.'

'Yes sir.'

Dylan ran his hands through his hair and checked his watch, waiting for news. A million thoughts raced around his head. Was Larry trying to make it easy for them? Or was he still scheming? Could he trust him when they caught up with him?

Dylan's mobile rang, 'unknown number.'

'I've got people hovering outside my flat. I'm near the electric sub- station in the car park of the Riverside apartments. Send two of your team over. They don't need to kick in my door. I'm ready to come in.' Larry hung up. Dylan quickly made calls to arrange for officers outside the flat to stay there. He diverted John and Vicky to Larry's flat to arrest him. Was he sober? He sounded like he was at least lucid.

Dylan texted Jen, 'Will be home much later than intended tonight love, sorry x'

An hour later, John and Vicky were back.

'Larry Banks is in the cells. Arrested on suspicion of murder. His brief, Mrs Linda Perfect, has been requested,' panted Vicky, her face red and glowing as she collapsed in a chair in Dylan's office.

'How is he?' asked Dylan.

'Quiet but he seems okay,' John told him. His eyes were bright and dancing.

'Sober?'

'Yeah, he is boss. His face is bloated from continual drinking and his eyelids are hooded over bloodshot eyes, but he doesn't seem unduly concerned about being locked up... His flat's being searched but as far as we can see there is no luggage. He was obviously anticipating his arrest.'

'Yeah, well he knows the system better than most and he's going to use handing himself in, to his advantage, isn't he?' said Dylan.

'Boss, I hate to ask, but it's my youngster's birthday today and although I'd love to get stuck into the interview, is there any chance I can get a flyer?'

'John, I'm glad you asked. If I'd 'ave found out you'd missed tucking your little 'un up on his birthday for the sake of a prisoner, I'd have been annoyed.'

'Thanks boss.'

'I'd love to interview him but if I don't make it home at some point before my son goes to bed, my missus will have my guts for garters,' he laughed.

'Vicky, what you doing tonight gal?'

'I'm all yours,' she said suggestively.

'Fancy interviewing a murder suspect with me, since you didn't get to go to France?'

'Don't I just,' she beamed.

'Just don't tell me Larry Banks intimidates you?'

'Me? You must be bloody joking. You know me better than that. No man intimidates me,' she said, grinning.

'I thought you might say that,' Dylan winked. 'Come on girl; let's get our interview strategy sorted. You wanna be the good guy or the bad?' he teased.

'Definitely the bad,' she said laughing, as John left them to it.

Right on time, Jen pushed the heavy fire door open into the light and sparse vestibule of the doctor's surgery. She peered into the vacant receptionist office and waited patiently. Time seemed to stand still. 'Why am I wasting the doctor's time when I'm fit and healthy,' she thought sitting down uncomfortably close to infected people, who were coughing and spluttering in the waiting area. Posters adorned every wall: informative and something to look at whilst you wait? 'More like overwhelming, hyper stimulation, confusion inducing overload,' she thought.

A bell rang, her name was called, and the doctor took no time at all to examine her.

'I don't think there is anything sinister there to worry about, but just to be on the safe side, I'll get my secretary to contact the hospital and we'll arrange for you to see a specialist. It'll give you peace of mind.'

Jen waited whilst the doctor's secretary rang the hospital.

'Tomorrow morning, okay?' she said, looking up at Jen.

Wide-eyed Jen nodded her approval.

'Thank you,' she said blindly, as she stumbled out of the surgery, an appointment for the Breast Clinic in her hand.

Chapter Thirty-Two

It was a strange feeling, sitting in the familiar interview room, opposite a man whom Dylan had interviewed with many times before. The atmosphere was electric as Larry's opaque eyes met his. Larry's solicitor spoke directly, after the introduction and caution for the purpose of the tape.

'My client denies emphatically the murder of anyone, or indeed any wrongdoing, other than a relationship with a married woman. That said, of course he will assist you all he can with your enquiries.'

'Mr Banks is very capable of speaking for himself, Mrs Perfect.' Dylan said, turning to Larry. 'You know why you've been arrested. Can you tell us what your relationship was with Mrs Reynolds?'

Larry cleared his throat. 'She came on to me; her husband was inside. I know I shouldn't 'ave, but you know me and women Jack: temptation got the better of me.' His lips curled in a half smile. 'With the breathalyser job pending, it was a bit of light hearted relief; a bit of fun, that's all it was.'

'So when did you last see her?'

'You obviously know, because you'll 'ave examined her house, it was the night before she was killed.'

'So tell me then, how you met and how the evening went,' continued Dylan.

'She gave me information about Malcolm Reynolds and his business dealings, which helped us put him away.' Larry sighed. 'I hadn't seen or heard from her since, until she texted me, right out of the blue, saying she'd just come across my phone number.'

'Just like that.' Dylan scoffed.

'Yeah, straight up. I met up with her at her house and before I knew it we were in bed,' he sniggered. 'Well, you know what I'm like.'

'Did she call you on the mobile you've got now?' Vicky asked.

'No, not this one,' he said, shuffling in his seat.

'Don't worry; we've got your old phone number, Larry. You're billing and cell site information, as you're aware, will show your contacts and where it's been used.' Dylan said, wishing he'd already got the data.

'I've nothing to hide, feel free.'

'Why did you clear off after you'd spent the night with her?' asked Vicky.

'I was going on my holidays, you can check. The van was planned and I'd a ferry to catch.' Larry shrugged his shoulders.

'So when did you and how did you find out about the death of Liz Reynolds?' Vicky continued.

'I saw the headlines in a newspaper while I was away.'

'Why didn't you come straight back?'

'I was on holiday, wasn't I? She was a one-night stand for God's sake. What would you have liked me to do? I sent a note to Dylan.'

'Drink's not affected your memory then?' Vicky commented.

'No.'

'So, a bit of light relief for you and then she was murdered the next day, just like that,' Vicky said.

He didn't reply.

'Was Liz being blackmailed?' Dylan pushed him.

'She didn't say.' Larry said, his voice rising.

'You're lying to me Larry,' he tutted, shaking his head. 'I'd expect better, but there again, why should I?'

'No...no, straight up I don't know...if she was, I wish she'd 'ave told me, then I might ''ave been able to do something to help her.'

Larry was gambling on his knowledge regarding the time it took for the team to get the telephone data back, and Dylan knew it.

'She'd all night to talk to me...but she didn't say ought.'

'So you're telling me you didn't see any money?'

'I never saw any money.'

'Your prints won't be on the suitcase that we found at the scene then?'

Dylan held his breath; he didn't have any evidence or information on the suitcase, but his gut instinct told him that if Larry was involved then his fingerprints would be on the suitcase.

'Inspector, I must interrupt...if you have my client's fingerprints why haven't you disclosed that to me?' asked Mrs Perfect.

Dylan ignored her comment.

'Well, Larry?'

'Well what? I touched all sorts of things in her home, which I'm sure you're well aware of. I never saw any money though. I left early the next morning as she didn't want any gossip getting back to Malcolm. I was well on my way before she ...' He gulped.

Was he upset? Dylan couldn't read him. Larry was sat on his hands. Dylan knew he was being shrewd. He was giving away as little body language as possible; controlling his reactions. He'd had plenty of time, knowing what he knew, to rehearse the interview in his mind, before giving himself up.

'So tell me, why did you wait so long to make contact with us, if everything was as innocent as you say? Or, for that matter, feel that you had to profess your innocence?' Dylan asked.

'With the old man...'

'Fred White's his name,' Vicky interrupted.

'Fred White, being on a life support machine...going to court for drink-driving...knowing I was going to lose my job and my pension, enough for you?'

'Do you know Malcolm Reynolds, Larry?'

'You know I do, coz I was part of the team that got him sent down.'

'He says he knows you.'

'And your point is?'

'Well, we had to go and tell him about his wife's last known movements and who she was with; and apart from being very angry he told us you were bent.'

'I'm sorry inspector: I have to object to your line of questioning. My client has been arrested on suspicion of murder.' Mrs Perfect said.

'You just did,' Dylan nodded to Mrs Perfect. 'Larry, is Malcolm telling the truth?'

'No, he isn't. Tell me what con wouldn't be angry if they'd just been told their wife had been found dead, and the night before, she'd slept with another man and that other man just happened to be a copper? He's just trying to get his own back, I can understand that. Like I said, I'm not your murderer.' Larry was keeping his cool.

The interview was going nowhere, and after forty minutes it was concluded.

Dylan walked quickly back up to the incident room, with Vicky running in the wake of his long strides. Their shift was far from over.

'Boy is he a slime ball. Urgh ...' Vicky griped as she caught up with Dylan.

'Let's try and get something that will rock him a bit, before round two, eh? The bastard's lying, I know he is.'

Jen went to bed early in the hope that tomorrow would come quickly. As much as she tried to sleep, Dylan's absence made it harder for her to nod off. What if she had cancer? She tossed and turned. Her stomach grumbled. She got up and took two paracetamols. The sight of the blood on the plate, that had ran from the Sirloin steak in the fridge, made her wretch as she took out the milk. It would have to wait for another night to be cooked, a night when her stomach allowed her to cook it, and Dylan was home to eat it.

It was pitch black outside the station, with not even a star visible in the sky but the incident room was a hive of activity and Dylan wanted a debrief before the next interview. The update from forensics gave them the information, that pages retrieved from amongst the ashes near the suitcase, were definitely law books. On arrest, Larry had had one hundred and thirty seven pounds on him, plus keys for his flat and two post office receipts. Unfortunately, getting evidence from the SIM card of Liz Reynolds' phone was not as easy as first thought. Carbon deposits had to be removed, which was a slow process, and it wouldn't be known for the next seventy-two hours if the process had worked or not.

Dylan was tense but focused, as they went into the next interview. He knew that Larry Banks, with all his experience of interviewing, wouldn't simply roll over. He opened up after the formalities.

'Was Liz Reynolds studying law, Larry?'

'No idea. Why?' he said, looking surprised.

'Because her suitcase the bank had filled with money the day before her murder, was found to contain nothing but law books.'

'I don't know what she was up to, I don't think we discussed it,' he said momentarily, looking up to the ceiling as if in thought. 'I once took her some of my old books round because she was arranging a book sale to raise money for Harrowfield Hospice. I've no idea why she would have kept 'em though, and why she would 'ave them in the suitcase, if they were the same ones that is.' He looked puzzled. 'Perhaps she was on the way to the charity shop with 'em.'

'So, you admit to having seen Liz recently, to give her the law books?' Vicky pushed him.

'Well no, not that recently,' he said quickly.

'When?' Vicky threw back her question sharply.

'Er...I don't know the exact date.'

'We're safe to assume that you kept in touch with her enough for her to ask and for you to give her the law books, since Malcolm's imprisonment?' Vicky continued.

'Well, yes......no...not as such,' he replied.

Dylan sighed; he was tired but spoke with great emphasis. 'We're fortunate that the SIM card from her mobile phone has been recovered, and it's only slightly damaged. That's being examined as we speak. In a short while we'll know who she was ringing and texting before her death. I'm giving you the opportunity to come clean, now Larry.'

'I've told you all I know. I don't know anything about her murder.' His repetitive answers were becoming annoying. Dylan stretched his shirt collar away from his sweating neck and undid his tie.

'You've two receipts in your property, for posting two articles earlier today. What were they?' Dylan asked.

'I posted the keys to the motor van hire company.' Larry said clearing his throat and shuffling in his seat again. Dylan could see by his body language that he was taken aback by that revelation. Why did that bother, him he wondered?

'Why didn't you drop the mobile home back at the garage?' Vicky asked, moving on.

'Too risky. I didn't want to spend any longer in the cells than I had. If I'd 'ave been running the operation, I'd 'ave had officers waiting for me to return it. I'm not bloody stupid.' He laughed confidently.

'Do you know Frankie Miller, Larry?' asked Dylan.

'No.'

''Ave you seen Malcolm Reynolds since he was sent to prison?' Dylan said.

'Once, briefly, to sign away some of his property we'd got in the property store.'

Larry seemed very positive, Dylan noted, as his replies once again became sharply answered. The interview plan systematically went through Larry's movements to Dover and France, and his return journey before Larry was taken back to the cell.

'Inspector Dylan,' said Mrs Perfect, 'Could I have a word, please?'

'Of course.'

'Mr Banks has been totally co-operative with you. Now, you haven't put any hard and fast evidence to him connecting him to the actual murder. It would appear he was elsewhere when the murder took place, unless you tell me otherwise of course?'

Dylan stood, hands in his pockets, looking down at the floor.

'He might be guilty of immoral behaviour with another man's wife, but on this arrest I'd expect him to be bailed, unless of course you've some startling evidence you've not yet disclosed?'

'Time will tell.' Dylan said, sighing tiredly.

'I know there'll be an adjournment on his drink-driving case. You know there is no evidence to keep him in custody. Be assured I'll be pursuing his release in court.'

Dylan squirmed; he knew she was right. They would have to give him bail wouldn't they; they had nothing on him. 'Smarmy git.' Dylan seethed, under his breath.

'She's right boss,' Vicky said thoughtfully, as they walked down the corridor, back to the office.

'Even so, he deserves to spend the night in the cells,' Dylan said. 'Get someone to make enquiries at the post office about them receipts he'd got in his pocket. They're bound to have someone at the sorting office overnight.'

'Will do boss, the cheeky twat must 'ave swapped the books for the money.'

'If we found the money, Vicky, we could hold him on the charge of theft, and then we could speak to the CPS with regard to the murder charge, although it'd probably 'ave to be dropped to manslaughter.

'Yeah, if he hadn't swapped it over she might still be alive, and we could at least charge him with summat.'

When he eventually crawled into bed in the early hours, Dylan's whole body ached. Jen looked so peaceful in her slumber, as he bent over to kiss her forehead. The white cotton duvet was wrapped tightly around her and he was afraid to pull it too hard in case he woke her, so he lay beside her. She usually woke when he arrived home no matter what time it was. She must be really tired, he decided. He was cold and his mind was buzzing. He switched on the television and muted it, so the soundless vision took his mind off trying to unravel Larry's thought process. He pulled a blanket over himself and listened to her shallow breathing. Within minutes he too was fast asleep.

Chapter Thirty-Three

The next morning, the sound of the telephone ringing woke them. The bedside clock showed it was 6 a.m.

'We've just been informed that Malcolm Reynolds is on the run from open prison, sir,' John shouted down the phone. 'I thought you'd want to know immediately.'

'Bloody hell.' Dylan groaned, as he threw his legs out of bed. He got dressed as quickly as he could, hopping into the bathroom to clean his teeth as he tried to put on his shoes. Jen opened her eyes and watched him scurry around the room, but she didn't move. He bent down to kiss her goodbye. His lips were warm and tasted of peppermint. Her stomach heaved.

'You okay, love?' he asked as he stroked her warm face. 'I've gotta go.'

'Yeah, just feel a bit sickly that's all.' She yawned.

'Maybe you're coming down with a virus or something. Take today off, I'm sure they can manage at work without you for a day,' he said, kissing her forehead before heading to the door.

'Yeah, I might,' she said, stretching her arms from under the covers. It was cold and she quickly put them back under the duvet and shivered. He turned off the light.

'See you when I see you,' he whispered before he gently closed the door. She heard him rush down the steps. 'Turn over and rest...I'll let them know in admin,' he shouted, and then she heard the door slam behind him. It was quiet and dark once more and she buried her head beneath the duvet and drifted back to sleep.

Jen felt a little dizzy when she arrived at the clinic later that morning, probably due to the fact she couldn't face breakfast. Dutifully as directed on the appointment card, she handed the nurse her urine sample with a shaking hand and then, not recognising her own quaking voice, she gave her the details of her medical history. She hadn't spoken of it for so long, why did it still upset her? She readily removed her upper clothing in compliance with the request from the nurse to perform a breast examination, and she sat alone waiting for the radiologist. The mammogram taken, she was asked to sit in her gown outside and wait once more. A lady already sat on one of the chairs that lined the wall of the corridor and she sat beside her. Like bookends neither of them looked at each other nor spoke, each absorbed in their own world. Jen wondered what thoughts were going through the woman's head, and if she'd been there before. The door adjacent to them opened and they both looked up expectantly, into the face of the radiologist who smiled as she walked past them, carrying a bundle of large brown envelopes. She knocked on the doctor's door. After a while she emerged from the room, told Jen she could get dressed and said that the consultant would see her shortly.

Leaving the changing room, she noticed someone in a Red Cross uniform sitting at a table massaging another patient's hand; they were chatting amiably. Jen picked up a *Cosmopolitan* magazine from the rack and opened it; but realised she wasn't absorbing any of the information in the article; she started to read over and over again. Glancing up periodically at the sound of doors opening, she caught the sight of Dawn talking to the receptionist. 'Oh, my God,' she thought. If Dawn saw her she'd tell Jack that she was at the clinic. Sliding the magazine onto the seat next to her, she headed for the ladies toilet and waited in a cubicle, praying that Dawn's enquiries would be brief. Luckily when she came out Dawn was gone.

The consultant, a tall man with greying hair, delicate hands, and an air of quiet authority, asked her to sit her down. He looked at her with kindly smiling eyes. 'I would like to do an ultra sound scan if that's okay with you Miss Jones,' he said. Jen took her blouse and bra off once more and lay on his examination table, shrouded by curtains. She watched as the consultant squeezed clear gel from a tube. He passed a microphone back and forth over each breast, whilst he watched a computer that was converting sound waves into a picture for him to see. She watched intensely for a glimmer that all was well in his expert eyes. There was none. He wiped the gel from her breast and left her to dress.

Sitting opposite him at his desk whilst he made notes, she tried to read his facial expression, again there was none. Eventually, he looked over his reading glasses at her and put his pen down.

'There was something palpable when we examined the breast, so a mammogram was done which proved negative, but these don't always pick up cysts very well, which is why I did an ultrasound scan. However, that is also clear,' he announced.

Jen let out a huge sigh and the doctor smiled.

'There's often an oestrogen surge, and breasts become very reactive to that in your condition, Miss Jones and I think...' he said.

Jen started to cry. Tension poured out of every pore of her body. She took a tissue from her handbag and attempted to stem the tears, apologizing profusely.

'And that's all it is,' he said, reassuringly. 'Use warm, wet compresses, have a warm shower or massage your breasts. They tell me wearing a cotton support bra in bed will help with the pain as the breasts enlarge.'

The specialist stared at her. 'Are you okay, Miss Jones, you look decidedly pale.'

Jen's eyebrows drew together. She stopped for a moment. 'Enlarge...condition?' she asked.

'Miss Jones, you did know you were pregnant didn't you?'

'But, I can't be. The surgeon, when he took away my ovary...Oh, I'm sorry I'm not making any sense am I?' Jen stopped once more, and took a deep breath before she continued. 'You see a few years ago, I discovered I had polycystic ovaries and had to have one taken away, when it became twisted and caused me internal bleeding. The other ovary was damaged. I was very ill. They told me that it would be highly unlikely that I'd ever get pregnant,' she signed and blew her nose. 'My fiancé at the time couldn't deal with the fact that he would never have children, and well, I eventually moved away to start again. It has never been an issue with my present partner because he doesn't...he's never...we've never...he's so career minded,' she sniffed.

Dylan had released Larry on bail, for the murder, but knew he was still going before magistrates for his driving offences, and he thought Larry would elect to take his chance to have his day in court. It also gave the team a bit more time for further evidence to come to light. Mrs Perfect was sure he would get bail. Larry hoped and prayed that was so, as he had posted a package containing a large amount of money to himself at his home address. How quickly they checked with the post office about the receipts found on him when he was arrested, determined if he would get away with it or not. As far as he was concerned he wasn't giving any of it up, and neither was he going to prison. He knew all he had to do now was keep calm and bluff his way through.

The magistrates granted him bail on the understanding that he surrendered his passport and that he signed on daily at the police station before twelve noon, and he readily agreed to do just that. Larry was leaving the court building when he saw Dylan sitting waiting for him on the steps.

His heart sank. Had he been rumbled? Dylan knew him well.

'You'd be better off inside Larry,' he said, as Dylan walked towards him. 'I've just come to warn you that Malcolm Reynolds is on the run from prison, and he's one angry man.'

'Appreciate the warning Jack,' he replied, walking straight past him. But his heart sank. He held his breath not daring to turn around. He listened to see if Dylan followed. His head was buzzing; he couldn't hang about for the post now. He couldn't risk going back to the flat. He knew he was working against the clock and he had to get out of Harrowfield immediately. Would he be under surveillance? No matter, he had no choice but to risk legging it, if Malcolm Reynolds was out.

There was no early information about Malcolm Reynolds' whereabouts. Liz's parents received a letter from him with a London postmark, asking them to look after Gemma and giving them the authority to sell 'The Grange'. He said in his letter he'd sent a copy to his solicitor. Due to the timing he must have written them prior to absconding from prison and posted them in the capital, Dylan presumed. But where the hell was he now?

Jen stood in the silence of the kitchen, a hot cup of sweet tea in her hand, still wondering what she was going to tell Jack. Her mind was in a fog.

She studied her diary, long and hard. Was there an event that would spark off a memory of her last period? But that wouldn't help as her periods were so irregular. Granted, she'd felt emotional lately, but no more than usual, had she? 'Oh, my God...how do I...how am I...what am I going to tell him?' she whispered, raising her eyes to the heavens for divine inspiration. She waved her arms to the universe as if it might yield an answer. Where would she begin? They'd never talked about children. For God sake, she didn't even know if he liked kids. She'd have to choose her time wisely, but first and foremost she had to come to terms with the knowledge herself. After all, he'd said himself he was a confirmed bachelor, and for all she knew he might not stay around. How ironic would that be?

'I'm pregnant,' she said calmly, rehearsing her speech as she sat at her dressing table. Max looked up at her. To her ears it sounded surreal and Jen put a hand to her mouth to halt her words. She watched her other hand in the mirror rest at the small bump of her stomach. Should she feel different? Excitement took over despite her predicament, and she laughed out loud. Max jumped up, bemused. Were they going for a walk? Jen smiled, whatever happened, she loved this baby. It was Jack's baby, and, whatever happens, I've still got you mate, haven't I?' she said, rubbing Max's head.

Only twenty-four hours had passed. 'Surprise, surprise, Larry Banks hasn't signed on at the nick, boss,' Vicky yelled, as she flounced into Dylan's office. 'And, they've found a package; eventually. It was waiting to be picked up by him from his local post office.'

'He's in breach of his bail conditions. Put out the message to arrest on sight,' Dylan ordered. 'Get a warrant for breach of bail from the court; looks like he's failed at the first hurdle.'

'Call for you boss.' shouted Tracy from the CID office. 'I'll put him through.' Dylan picked up.

'Detective Inspector Dylan?' the man said, in a thick London accent.

'Speaking.'

'Ello mate. DI Giles Hendon, CID. We've just dragged a body out the Thames. It's not bin in there long otherwise there'd be nothing left of' im.' he chuckled. 'As luck would 'ave it we've bin able to piece together documents that we found in is pocket. It appears this bloke might be your Larry Banks you've got circulated'.

Dylan froze as he sat at his desk, like a rabbit in a vehicle's headlights.

'You still there? Bit of a shock for yer eh? But wait, that's not all; he's got a bleedin great bullet hole in the front of is skull. Seems someone tried to take is heed off. No doubt we've got us a homicide. Thing is, we don't know where he went in the water. The PM won't 'appen 'til after the weekend...Your chap's DNA will be on the system, won't it?'

'Er yeah...sorry...it's a bit of a shock,' Dylan stuttered. 'He got himself into a spot of bother, sleeping with a con's wife. Malcolm Reynolds. I think you should know he's on the run too, from open prison. In fact, Mr Reynolds sent a letter from London to his wife's parents. I'll fax you down the intelligence and the background to his wife's murder. I think I'd better arrange for a couple of my officers to come down and see you.' Dylan replaced the phone and sat back in his chair. Had Larry met up with Malcolm Reynolds by agreement? By chance? It seemed to have happened so quickly, or had Malcolm been having Larry watched?

The long awaited data from Liz Reynolds' phone SIM card showed Dylan she'd asked for Larry's help.

They now knew why Larry wasn't at his flat when the officers checked up on him after he didn't turn up for his bail, but there was a note from the post office hanging out of his letterbox. 'Parcel to collect – attempt to deliver failed.' Dylan had it collected and his worst fears were confirmed. The parcel contained near on five hundred thousand pounds. Dylan was like a bear with a sore head. He should have known. He knew Larry's claim to fame was locking up a bank robber who'd done the same. He could have had him nailed if he'd only thought before he bailed him. Why the hell hadn't he remembered? Larry had slipped the noose, but ended up killed. Did he go on his own or was he taken to London? Maybe they'd never find out.

Dylan hated loose ends; unfinished business. Oh, he was sure he knew what had happened. He was satisfied that Frankie Miller had killed Liz in a fit of rage and Larry Banks had put her head on the proverbial chopping block by switching the money for his books. It was so frustrating though, not to get that confession from him.

Malcolm Reynolds was the main suspect for Larry Banks murder. Where was he?

'Jen take me to the Isle of Wight' he texted. 'I need to get away x'

An hour later their trip was booked. A couple of days off were what he needed. Time to clear his head.

In the tranquillity of the island hotel, Jen told a snoring Jack, 'Things could be worse; a lot, lot worse, love. You did everything you could.' She stroked his brow, watching him sleep. Sitting on the edge of the bed she took a deep breath and looked out to sea.

Listen to the wind
The sound of the sea on the shore
Listen to your heart
And never ask for more

She read the words from an old framed cross-stitch on the wall. 'It's now or never,' she whispered to Max. He cocked his head as if pressing her on.

'Jack?'

'Mmm ...' he said, stirring.

'Hold out your hand and close your eyes I've got a present for you.'

He looked up at her with a, just awoken, puzzled, expression on his face. Jen's heart fluttered incredibly fast in her chest. Her eyes blurred with tears.

'What is it?'

'I said close your eyes,' she giggled. 'It's something that's already yours but you haven't worked out that I've got it yet.' She smiled.

Jack obediently closed his eyes again, and gave her his hand. Shaking, she turned it over and placed his palm on her tummy and held it there. Jack opened his eyes and stared at her. 'Is this for real,' she read in his eyes, and she nodded. He began to gently stroke her stomach, as he lifted himself up to hold her face in his hands, so that he could kiss her lips, her cheeks and her eyelids. She put her hand to his cheek and brushed it with her fingers.

'I never thought...When's this amazing event gonna happen?' he finally asked, with tears in his eyes.

'I don't know yet,' she grinned. 'In about seven months.'

He flopped back on the bed and pulled her with him, holding her tightly in his arms. Neither of them wanted to break their moment in time.

Dylan felt like he was walking on air, on his return to the CID office. His first meeting was with Patrick Finch, seeking confirmation that the paperwork in respect of the murder file for Charlie Sharpe was on schedule, and the three murderers were still on remand.

'Well, congratulations, that's your first murder case as a deputy SIO well on its way, Pat. It wasn't too bad was it? We were lucky to 'ave a good team on it, weren't we?' he said enthusiastically.

'I wanted to have a word with you about . . .'

Dylan frowned. 'Go on.'

'I've some concerns about unacceptable comments made by some of the detectives during the enquiry, sir,' said Patrick.

'What're you on about?' Dylan said.

'Some of the remarks they came out with at times were not at all appropriate. We could have had a major problem if someone took offence and took us to a tribunal.'

'What?' Dylan said.

'Well, like Vicky talking about her breasts and swearing. In fact, I've compiled a report with examples for your attention and further action,' he said, holding a document out for Dylan to take. 'And I really would be liked to be called Patrick not Pat in the future by everyone because that's my name.'

Dylan was raging.

'You've done what? I'll tell you something now Pat, if it wasn't for the banter and sense of humour in our team, on a murder enquiry, or any enquiry come to that, we'd never cope with the things we 'ave to. None of the comments made in my earshot were offensive, so don't you go and make something out of nothing. Do you hear?' Dylan said, snatching the paperwork Patrick offered him and throwing it directly in his bin.

'I was just trying …' Patrick Finch quickly tried to explain.

Dylan pushed past him, slamming the office door behind him. The force of the impact seemed to rattle the whole incident room. He strode purposefully to the Reynolds' incident room.

'The DNA's confirmed the body was that of Larry Banks,' Dylan was told as he reached John's desk, where his determined stomp came to a sudden halt.

'And that's not all.' John continued, as he handed him an envelope. 'A letter has been handed to me by Mrs Perfect, Larry's solicitor, specifically for your attention.'

Dylan took it from him and sat down to read the contents.

Dear Jack,

I crossed the line and knowing the kind of person you are, I can't expect you to understand.

I'm writing this because if I know Malcolm Reynolds, he'll be intent on revenge and won't be satisfied until he knows I have taken my last breath. Who can blame him? The drink was my downfall. I don't need to tell you that but I do want you to know the truth.

Liz was being blackmailed and needed my help. I let her down by taking the money but believe me I honestly never thought the blackmailer would kill her.

I also let you and the team down Jack. Forgive me.

Larry

*P.S You work too hard. Don't let the job ruin your life. You should **Work to live, not live to work.***

Larry's words went round and round in his head and with tears in his eyes. He pushed his chair back and stood up.

'Put it on file after you've shared the contents with Hendon CID, will you,' he told John, offering him the letter.

John nodded, but didn't speak.

With determination in each step, Dylan walked down to his own office, picked up his suit jacket from the back of his chair, locked his desk drawer, stood his briefcase by his filing cabinet and walked out of his door, shutting it behind him.

'Would you like a coffee, sir?' Tracy asked stretching as she yawned loudly.

'No thanks, I'm heading off; I've a mission to accomplish,' he said, winking at her and Vicky. Dramatically, as he walked past, he slung his jacket over his shoulder and threw his head back. He flung open the fire exit door and stood for a moment to inhale the fresh, cold, morning air that blew in. He turned his face up to the sun and felt its warming rays. The girls stared after him, then at each other.

'Oooh, what's got into him?' Vicky shrieked with laughter. A shrug of Tracy's shoulders met her gaze but she smiled.

Dylan patted his trouser pocket. The diamond ring he had chosen was safe. Hopefully, Jen wouldn't see it until the time was right. He hummed to the CD he'd put on before he'd sprinkled peppercorn over the steak, and putting a knob of butter carefully on the top of each piece, he placed it under the hot grill. Jen couldn't contain her surprise at the beautifully decorated dining table, with the candles and the flowers, which she saw from the hallway when she walked in the door. The lights were dimmed.

'Miss Jones?' called Dylan.

'Yes what's that wonderful smell?' She giggled, coming up behind him and putting her arms around his waist, as he took the plates out of the oven where they'd been warming.

'Your slippers are by the fire, and when you've put them on you can sit down. Dinner, my love, will be served in a few minutes,' he said, as he turned to hand her a drink. As she took the glass from him, he reached out to hold her face in his hands and smothered it with tiny kisses.

'Mmm...I feel really special,' she sighed with contentment, as she sat at the table and put her feet up, raising her glass of fruit juice to him. He raised his glass of wine and took a big gulp. Max circled once or twice at Jen's feet and lay down.

'Mmm ...' she sighed, taking in the moment. Jack caught her gaze, and not taking his eyes off hers, he walked the few steps to stand before her. The moment felt dreamlike, as she watched him put his hand in his pocket and bring out a blue silk box. For a few seconds time stood still, before he dropped on one knee in front of her and opening the box,

asked with tears in his eyes and his voice filled with emotion,
'Please say you'll marry me, I love you so much.'